Robin

in the Hood

by

Diane J. Reed

"This is my heart —
This is my heart on CRACK."
— Robin when she first
meets Creek

— Diane J. Reed

ISBN: 978-0-9849129-3-3

- R -

Bandits Ranch Books, LLC
www.banditsranch.com

Dedication

This novel is dedicated to all those who have
the courage to dream big dreams and to be
themselves, no matter what anyone else thinks.

Chapter 1

Bank robbery wasn't exactly what I had in mind when I filled out my career development profile in class this year. Sophomore girls at my school are expected to check off lofty goals, like "doctor," "lawyer," or my personal favorite, "entrepreneur." According to our mission statement, we're the movers and shakers of our generation, destined for Ivy League colleges like Harvard or Yale. But one thing you learn quickly at The Pinnacle Boarding School for Girls—everyone is lying through their teeth.

The truth is, we're modern Geishas. Oh sure, we know all about their clever ways from the Asian culture classes we've been force fed to give us a global edge. And we can be whatever you want us to be and say whatever you'd like to hear—for a hefty price. Silk kimonos and bound feet have given way to designer labels and perky nose jobs, of course. But nowadays, we also require the latest handbags, unlimited spray tanning, and V.I.P. seats to see the hottest pop stars to smash the charts. Nothing is off limits for us Pinnacle girls, because we view soaking our parents as pennies on the dollar for staying out of their hair. Oh, you *don't* want my stepmom to know you're cheating on her again? That'll be free passes to King's Island and Disney World for, let's say, *life*. And that little email you accidentally forwarded to me about dumping stocks on an insider tip? I'm thinking a sporty Miata convertible for my 16th birthday, preferably in sunshine yellow. After all, fair is fair—I don't rat on my dad as long as the money keeps flowing. Because let's face it, everyone in Cincinnati knows, despite the slick brochures and recruitment DVDs, that Pinnacle is nowhere near the best-rated high school in the Midwest. It's simply the priciest. Quick translation: it's the swankiest prison for teenage girls that money can buy.

So my entire high school career so far was spent trying to survive in that gilded cage, funded by people like my screwed-up dad and stepmom who have no intention of ever being part of my life. I guess it might seem like I was abandoned in a way, but don't think that means I have no values! On the contrary, girls at Pinnacle are famous for being religious fanatics. And the God we learn to worship, in all its glorious forms—from the American Express platinum card to a line of credit at Tiffany's in Fountain Square—is the almighty dollar. For me, it's the only higher power that's ever come close to balancing out my folks' messes—their hopeless addictions and sloppy affairs, and especially that train wreck they call a marriage. Yes, nearer to my heart than Jesus is my most loyal BFF: cold, hard *cash*.

Is it any wonder that I became a bank robber?

It all started back in March when my dad, Royle McArthur—a partner at *the* prestigious law firm of Tweedle, Beckman & McArthur—suffered a stroke in his office with half a line of coke on his desk, an unfinished high ball on the filing cabinet, and a burning cigarette still glowing in his ashtray. Yep, Dad pretty much hit the trifecta for crummy health habits, so even though his stroke wasn't entirely unpredictable, his timing couldn't have been worse! There I was, suddenly yanked from decorating the dance hall for our spring mixer with the boys at Breton—the only time we ever got *near* anyone of the opposite sex—when I was thrust into the hyper-sanitized world of Our Lady of Redemption Hospital's rehabilitation ward.

"Your father is partially paralyzed on his right side," a doctor took me aside to explain. "And unfortunately, he's been left with only a quarter of his former brain power. I doubt he'll ever recognize you again." If that weren't bad enough, after three weeks of being allowed to skip school to watch my dad drool through meals and listlessly pantomime a physical therapist, I learned an even more brutal truth.

We were broke.

Um, not just a little broke.

I mean, really broke-broke. Super-nova broke. As in, time-to-slit-your-wrists broke.

Broke to the tune of $300,000 in hospital bills, 2 million in back mortgage payments for our posh Indian Hill home, and a law firm that had gone belly up after years of mismanagement and embezzlement.

I only learned this stuff because everyone from bank managers to bookies had lined up to talk to me in the hospital as my dad's last remaining "next of kin."

What?

What the hell happened to my stepmom?

Apparently, she'd already taken off for a monastery somewhere in the Himalayas to eat, pray, and love her way to international immunity, cashing out what little remained in my dad's accounts. Oh, and my dad's fierce gambling habit that I didn't know about, along with his fondness for raiding the company till, had put us in the red for about the next, say, million years.

Oh God, it doesn't get worse than this!

In one fell swoop, all the money I'd ever known and cherished was gone. I didn't even have a roof over my head, because there was no way in hell that goddawful Pinnacle would take me back if we couldn't pay tuition. I stood there in the hospital, utterly stunned and staring at the eager crowd of collectors who were huddled in front of me.

"Uh, w-would it be all right if I took a walk?" I sputtered to a nurse.

I had to get out, to breathe some fresh air. And to be totally honest, my mind was on a whole lot more than walking—I had an overwhelming urge to change my name and hitch a ride to the next state.

But then something happened that I'll never forget. My dad, from in his wheelchair, reached over and grasped my hand, clenching my fingers so tightly it felt like a death grip. Surprised, I winced and glanced down, when I caught a peculiar look in his eyes.

He was begging.

I swear, the expression on his anguished face seemed to be saying, *Please Robin, for the love of God, please don't leave me here.*

Shit. So much for not recognizing anybody.

Knowing Dad, he was probably faking it all this time to fool his creditors. But just to make sure I wasn't imagining things, I squinted and stared once more into his eyes.

There it was—that same desperate look, along with tears welling up in the corners, like he actually expected *me* to be his salvation or something.

Well I'll be damned.

Could he possibly be serious?

How freaking dare he!

All my life I'd wanted to forge a real connection with my dad. To just for once see his face in the audience when I was petrified at a ballet recital, or to get a hug after the only time I'd ever scored a run in cricket, or even to lay on the grass in our yard on a warm, spring day and pick out silly shapes in the clouds. But no—instead, my childhood was filled with cold and moldy nannies and chauffeurs who never ceased to remind me, with their firm lips and sideways glances, that affection wasn't exactly written into their contracts.

And now my dad expects me to save his butt?

I couldn't help myself—I yanked back my hand like I'd been bitten, vigorously rubbing my fingers to remove any lingering hospital stink. Then I leaned down beside him.

"Do you have any idea," I whispered angrily, motioning to the cluster of men and women in suits, "how fun it would be for me to watch you *fry?*"

I thought surely my dad's eyes would widen in horror. Or at the very least, that he might bury his head into his hands and moan at the perfect, cosmic justice of it all.

But he didn't.

My dad simply gazed at the floor. He took a long, deep breath, as if summoning all of his strength, and opened his mouth at an awkward angle. For a while he released a steady stream of drool that pooled into the lap of his hospital gown. Then he struggled to lift his chin to my ear.

"Ayyyy . . . yuvvv . . . yooo . . . enny wey," he mumbled with extraordinary effort.

At once my heart climbed into my throat.

Did I hear him right? My very own father saying *I—love—you—ANYWAY?*

Of all the lowdown, dirty, rotten tricks.

I shook my head. For a man whose brain was supposed to be reduced to the IQ of a rabbit, he sure as hell knew how to get to me. Instantly, I felt my heart waffle.

Okay, so the guy's a known crook.

And he did exile me to girl-prison and oh-so-happily threw away the key.

But he's still my dad.

So if ever I wanted to check off that whole, goopy "father-daughter-loving-bond" box in life, this was probably my last shot. Besides, I could always dump his body in the Ohio River if he's flat-out lying to me.

But what really cinched my decision was the prying case worker who'd just slipped into the room and lip-synched the word "foster home" to a nurse when she thought I wasn't looking.

Holy crap. Even I could do the math:

Dad—

Or foster home—

Dad—

Or foster home—

Suddenly, a vision flashed into my mind of bunking down with a dozen skanky kids at night in a crackhouse while our so-called foster mom smokes a joint and performs phone sex in the next room. Like a bolt of lightning, the path to my future had become excruciatingly clear.

Make a run for it. Now—

With that, I seized the handles of my dad's wheelchair and gave him a bold shove toward the door.

"Excuse us for a second," I said abruptly to the nurse, "we're just going to mosey down the hall for a minute."

Immediately, I made a hard right and picked up speed down the hallway. "Hang on, Dad, we're gonna play by my rules now!" I declared as his wheels squeaked against the linoleum floor, my legs stretching into long strides beneath me. Gaining momentum, and feeling a little cocky, I made another hard right and swerved past an orderly, barely missing a patient on a gurney, when all of a sudden I was confronted by a large figure in black whose shoulders nearly filled the entire hallway.

Heaven help me!

It was none other than Darth Vader.

The Lady in Black.

The most feared entity ever to set foot on the grounds at Pinnacle. Our dreaded Mother Superior—all six feet of her—in a heavy black habit with only her crooked nose and beady eyes peeking out to silently condemn me.

I'd only seen her a couple of times since I'd started high school, on those rare occasions when she descended from her stone office tower beside the chapel to make an appearance on campus. But I knew her reputation for being "The Enforcer", the one who squeezed every last dime from our parents when tuition came due, or the school needed new computers, or she wanted to fund a new wing to show off her Medieval artifacts collection, which was rumored to contain instruments of torture. With a few whacks of her gnarled mahogany cane, Mother Superior could put the fear of God into any Pinnacle girl who dared to even think about boys, or tattoos, or drugs, or—heaven forbid—altering our hideous blue and white uniforms in the slightest way. Many a Pinnacle girl had been sent to her office for a seemingly minor infraction, never to be heard from on campus—or Cincinnati, for that matter—again. And now, here she was, towering over me with a creepy smile on her face like the Grim Reaper, more than thrilled to have cornered a new victim.

"Miss McArthur," she trilled in a strange tone, as melodic as a lute despite the deep grooves in her ashy, sagging face, "it has come to my attention that your tuition payments are looong overdue. That means you are perilously close to expulsion, my dear. I must have a word with your father—"

"Oh my gosh, really?" I interrupted, pretending surprise. My Geisha skills always came in handy at moments like this. "Um, you want to speak to my dad? Well you're in luck. Because, uh, here he is!"

Wham—

Just like that.

A well-aimed kick to the back of my dad's wheelchair, and he rolled into her like a battering ram, toppling the witch over in seconds flat.

Sometimes, it's that easy.

And I'll probably spend a millennium in Purgatory for that little maneuver!

Of course, she was left sputtering and flailing her arms like an overturned turtle. And if I wasn't mistaken, I thought for sure I heard my dad giggling. You know, in that cotton-mouthed, stroke-victim kind of way. He turned to look back at me with a mischievous half-grin.

"Attah gurrrl," he slurred.

He even clutched his belly and let out a full-blown chortle. Followed by a snort.

And by this time, I'd started giggling, too.

In fact, I doubled over and laughed so hard, I thought the hospital had begun to shake.

Oh my God.

Near as I could tell, this was the first "happy family moment" I'd ever experienced in my whole life.

All right, so maybe my dad and I didn't bond over normal father-daughter things. Like eating hot dogs while watching the Cincinnati Reds, or polishing off black-raspberry chip ice cream at Graeter's. We're McArthurs, after all, so there's got to be some bad behavior to keep us going. But I have to say, in that instant, nothing could've stopped me from running over to my dad and giving him the biggest squeeze ever.

Don't get me wrong.

It didn't last long —

"CODE BLACK," the hospital P.A. system broadcast so loudly it hurt my ears. "All security personnel to the exits immediately. CODE BLACK. Prepare for extreme measures —"

What the hell?

My dad looked up, wide-eyed, like he'd heard a trumpet from on high.

Even Darth Vader stopped thrashing for a second and sat up on her elbows, her mouth hung open.

I shot a glance at my dad, dumbfounded, when I saw two burly men appear at the end of the hallway in gray uniforms. Attached to their belts were holsters—Holy Moses—as in, real guns.

"Daddy!" I gasped.

"Wuun Wobbbbinnnn," he lisped.

"What?" I panicked.

"Wun!"

Oh, run! Yep, that would be the smart thing to do. I grabbed my dad's wheelchair handles and whipped him around, heading for the green glow of the elevator this time. Thank God I could see the doors sliding open in front of us. So I put my dad on coast, riding the back of his wheelchair until we were inside, where I slammed on the brake. My dad jostled a bit—but miracle-beyond-miracles—the poor guy didn't fall out. And I could hear him laughing! When I turned him around and looked into his face, his eyes and cheeks were crinkled with pride. I felt so happy I wanted to cry.

"Guuud gurrlll," he smiled as the doors sealed shut. He pointed at the elevator controls.

"Floor two?" I offered. But then I saw the words *Maternity* printed next to it. Floor three was *Neurosurgery*, floor four was *Dialysis*—and every other floor had another specialty in bold letters. Impulsively, I hit the "B" button for the basement, and gave my dad a shrug. Surely there'd be a convenient exit there, right? The elevator dropped to the bottom of the hospital like a stone, and when the doors opened, I spun my dad around. All we could see was black.

Maybe an underground tunnel?

Okay by me, as long as we could get the hell out. But all of a sudden, the air felt cold and clammy, and there was that terrible smell . . .

Hesitantly, I wheeled my dad into the darkness, taking a couple of strides, when I heard a metal crash.

"Fwuuuck!" my dad yelped.

Wrong move. Guess the tunnel wasn't empty after all.

"Sorry," I whispered, patting my dad's head. I reached out and ran my fingers against a wall, fumbling until I found a light switch, and flicked it on.

Ow . . .

The fluorescent lights were so bright, I felt like they'd seared my eyeballs. I blinked at the shiny metal drawers that lined the room, resting my gaze on a steel table in front of us. It held a body.

Um, a particularly gray body.

Sweet Mother of God—

A *corpse*.

"Blood-curdling" doesn't even begin to describe the scream that left my lungs.

My dad started hollering something in gibberish, while I instinctively made a sign of the cross. It really didn't help matters that my cell phone went off at the exact same time, nearly making me jump out of my skin.

Wow, there's nothing like getting a text for fifty-percent-off at Macy's in Fountain Square when you really should be running for your life—

"Dumpf itt!" my dad barked.

"Yeah, dammit!" I agreed. "I could be getting spring sandals right now for a song—"

Before I could finish, my dad grabbed my cell with his only good hand and dumped it into a beaker of fluid. Tears slipped down my cheeks as I watched my pink, diamond-studded cell phone give off sparks and bubble slowly into what must've been formaldehyde.

"Daaad, that's Sparkle!" I hyperventilated—the pet name I'd given my only friend in high school who didn't get all clicky and turn nasty on me, even if she did bill me for the service.

"No won kan trathse uths," my dad said defiantly.

No one can trace us—

Oh my gosh, he was right. Swallowing hard, I nodded at his logic and blew my sweet Sparkle a kiss goodbye, still sniffling. My dad pointed to a bag on the floor.

"Thstreet kloaths."

"Street clothes? You gotta be kidding me. You want to put on stuff from a dead guy?"

Just then, the hospital P.A. system crackled and began bleating like a goat.

"All security personnel. Check building extremities. Now."

"Good God—okay, Dad, let me help you up." I hurried to lift him from his wheelchair and onto his feet. Since he hadn't consumed much more than cigarettes and stimulants lately, he was remarkably light. Nevertheless, my heart drummed as I bent down to open the plastic bag he'd pointed out, only to find a truly unfortunate wad of polyester.

"Oh Daddy, I'm sooo sorry." I shook my head, pulling out a bright orange suit and a purple paisley shirt. "There's no two ways about it. You're gonna look like a pimp."

Stifling a giggle, I swung the shirt over his hospital gown and stuffed his arms inside, doing the same thing with the jacket and buttoning him up. Then I picked up his feet one by one and guided them into the obnoxious pants. For the life of me, he looked like a neon tangerine nightmare—by a junky on acid. And he was still barefoot, the way the Beatles appeared on that freaky *Abbey Road* album.

"Royle . . . is . . . dead," I moaned like that Satanic 1960s recording I'd heard played backwards on a dare on YouTube, watching my dad smirk at the joke. Creepy, yes, but this twisted outfit was the best we could do.

A lucky thing, it turned out, since I could hear people scuffling beyond the door.

"Hold on, Dad." I dashed to lock the door of the morgue. "You ready?"

My dad took a deep breath and nodded. Wrapping my arm around his waist, I helped him limp slowly to the exit at the opposite end of the room, and swung the door open wide.

There she was, like a vision stretched before us. My dream come true . . .

A shiny Miata convertible with the top down, her bright cherry finish sparkling in the afternoon sun.

No driver, no passengers—

Just the gentle purr of her idling engine, like she'd been *waiting* for me.

Forget all those religious education classes. Now I know that heaven really does exist!

"Angel," I whispered.

Okay, so she was a screaming red instead of a sunshine yellow. And she had to belong to some doctor who'd sprinted into the hospital for a second to pick up notes. But who were we to be picky? As far as I was concerned, this heavenly beauty was *mine*.

"Coming, darling!" I called out. My dad looked at me like I was crazy, but he didn't argue when I led him to the passenger's side and settled him into the soft, buttery leather seat, then trotted around and plopped myself behind the steering wheel.

She was an automatic, thank God. Considering I still hadn't gotten my learner's permit yet and only had a few lessons from our chauffeur, it was no small miracle.

"This is it, Dad," I said, shifting awkwardly into drive. "All we need now is some cash. Got any tips for knocking over a bank?"

My dad stared at me as if I'd mutated into a sociopath.

"Hey, like father, like daughter!" I reminded him.

Gritting my teeth, I stepped on the gas. My poor dad's head snapped back as though we'd rocketed to the moon.

Fortunately, I only turned over one garbage can and plowed through a small sign and two flower beds on our way out. But for all intents and purposes, we were as free as birds.

And that was how I began my career in crime.

Chapter 2

I barely made my way through the tangled bird's nest of streets in Cincinnati to find Route 125 and headed southeast, hugging the center line of the highway like a drunk driver. I didn't dare look at my dad anymore, because the last time I'd checked, he had a white-knuckled grip on the dashboard with his good hand, and his face was as pale as a sheet.

Gee, Dad, if you'd sacrificed a little of your precious time to help me learn how to handle a car before this, I might be a better driver! At least I didn't hurt anybody.

But no biggie. As long as I ignored the twigs that were still stuck to the windshield from the shrubs I'd barreled through on Liberty Street, we were set. And I actually began to enjoy myself a little. I mean, here I am, in a siren-red convertible with the top down on a warm, spring day. It doesn't get any better than this! Too bad there were only mullet-haired truckers and local yokels to flirt with. Just for the hell of it, I gave each one a wink and a toss of my long, chestnut hair. Hey, practice makes perfect. But by the time we'd passed our hundredth farm on this rolling stretch of highway outside the city and I still hadn't spotted a single hot guy, I decided to use the downtime to focus on my main goal:

Bender Lake, Ohio.

Yep, it's the kind of hick place that people head to when they're, well, craving a bender. Just a remote, "hush-hush" neck of the woods, ideal for lost weekends of drinking, drugs and rock and roll, with minimal city ordinances against disturbing the peace, lewd behavior, or fraternizing with vampires.

Whatever you want, Bender Lake's got it. And best of all, *nobody talks*.

Perfect.

But don't think Bender Lake has anything like the bright lights of Las Vegas.

No, what we're talking about here is a cross between the boondocks in that creepy *Deliverance* movie you sometimes see on Saturdays and a Bermuda Triangle, of sorts, for losers.

According to the rumor mill in Cincinnati, especially crazy partiers like CeeCee Stone, who everyone at Pinnacle called a "drug-slut" long before she got kicked out, people have a way of "disappearing" into the miles of thick hardwoods and brush surrounding Bender Lake and never getting caught. Deep caves, camouflaged camp sites, mysteriously concealed trailer parks—hell, I've even heard talk of UFO abductions that helped people avoid arrest! If you're running from the law, or you simply don't want mommy and daddy to hear about the crap you've been jamming up your nose or into your veins, Bender Lake is *the* place in Ohio to go.

But there was only one problem.

We were running out of gas.

And since all of my dad's accounts were frozen, making my credit cards utterly worthless, we didn't have a dime. So before I hit Bender Lake to find us a little "out-of-the-way vacation cottage" to anonymously rent, I was in desperate need of cash.

And what better place to go than a bank?

Okay, so maybe my idea of robbing banks was originally a joke. My dad had checked off a startling number of criminal boxes lately, so I thought it would be fun to add a little "glamour" to his list.

But not anymore. This was serious stuff, and as the Miata's low fuel signal flashed orange on the dash and rang at a furious pitch, I realized I needed to get down to business—quick.

Luckily, I'd spotted a blue-gingham sign for *Home & Hearth Savings & Loan* near the highway, with a convenient exit up ahead.

Home & Hearth? I'd never heard of it before, but it sounded like the kind of place that handed out free crock pots to folks who opened savings accounts. As long as they filled mine with hundred-dollar bills, I could forgive the country-kitsch logo.

So I pulled off the exit ramp and onto a humble little road that held a white clapboard church, a seedy coin-op laundry, a boarded-up diner—and a small bank. I couldn't even tell what the town's name was as I steered towards the Home & Hearth building and jostled over their curb, cranking my front tires off the sidewalk and back onto the street with a jolt. Glancing around the empty town, I smiled sweetly at my dad.

"This'll just take a minute!" I promised.

My dad clutched my forearm like a vise, squeezing the life out of me.

"Ouch!" I cried, trying my best to pull away. Jesus, for a man who was partially paralyzed, his left hand could still pack a punch.

"No, Wobbin," my dad insisted, glaring at me. All of a sudden, his expression resembled a wounded animal's. "Day-enj," he struggled, the words turning into marbles on his tongue. "Day-enj! DAYN-JER-OOS!"

I nodded, getting his drift. Funny how a guy who'd hardly had anything to do with me until now suddenly thought he could play warden.

"Listen, Dad," I sighed, "this isn't exactly my first choice. But short of becoming a streetwalker, I don't know how else to take care of us. Not even Graeter's hires fifteen-year-olds! And in case you forgot, we're probably wanted by the law, so I might as well give them a run for their money. Oops, pardon the pun—"

I planted a quick peck on his forehead. "Now I'm off, before I lose my nerve."

Wrenching myself free from his grip, I bolted from the Miata and refused to look back, slipping the keys into my pocket. I could hear my dad's slurred protests as I scurried up the sidewalk, but that wasn't what really bothered me.

No, what really got under my skin was this strange, haunting feeling . . .

Like I was being watched.

And not just by my dad.

I froze in place for a second, mere steps from the bank door.

There it was again . . .

That odd sensation that someone's eyes were on my back.

Could the bank have hired security to watch over the building?

I swiftly scanned the roof and did a little spin to check the street on either side.

Give me a break, I thought, this is Podunkville! It's not like they're gonna have snipers in the bushes.

Sucking up my courage, I pointed my finger beneath my school cardigan like a concealed weapon and prepared to head inside. My heart started to do backflips, and I felt like any second it was going to spring from my chest.

"You can do this," I barked under my breath, "you've got to! Just walk in there like you own the place, head to the nearest teller, and make your demand."

Aside from the full-blown terror that popped and sizzled through my brain, another sound began to filter into my ears.

Laughter.

I slid my hand to my chest, just to check if it was me. After all, people do weird things in a panic, but I soon discovered that I wasn't the source of the sound.

Glancing up, I spotted a shadow.

Straight ahead, beside a large sycamore tree. And it *moved*.

I squinted and inched to the left, peering into a particularly dark patch beside the wide tree trunk.

And that's when I saw him.

Or I guess I should say, he *chose* to reveal himself.

A tall guy, maybe a year or two older than me, in a black t-shirt and torn, faded jeans. His tangled, sun-bleached hair looked like it had never seen scissors, yet it framed his tan skin and piercing blue eyes like a rugged surfer's. To my surprise, he flashed a half-smile, making the jagged scar across his cheek press into a dark, thin line, like a dagger. For a second, I wondered if it was a warning—

"You gotta be kidding me," he shook his head, folding his tattooed arms. "You honestly think you can take on this place?"

He leaned his tall frame against the tree, appearing amused. Instantly, I could tell from his ripped clothes, sinewy body, and nearly feral gaze that he was pretty much *everything* Pinnacle had been paid so handsomely to keep out of my reach.

Beautiful.

Deadly.

And *well* within kissing distance—

Without warning, his intense eyes locked on mine as if we were the only two people who'd ever mattered on planet earth.

And all at once, I felt a weight dislodge and explode into a gazillion pieces inside my chest.

This is my heart—

This is my heart on CRACK.

I hyperventilated for a moment, fully acknowledging that I *am* the most undersexed teen this side of Mississippi. As long as no one counts kissing Laura Ritter, but that was only because she sobbed and got all needy on me and promised to write my "Female Power in Japanese Culture" essay.

Get a grip, I snapped at myself. Focus!

Okay, so I know most girls like me are diamond-wise and boy-foolish. Except for CeeCee Stone, of course, whose conquests rival alley cats. So surely the only reason the hottest thing in the known universe is standing in front of me right now is because . . .

Well, um, because . . .

He wants to rob the same bank.

"Dammit!"

The guy laughed like I'd said that out loud.

"Shit!"

Yep, I'm pretty sure he heard that one, too.

I shuffled my feet, heaving a big sigh.

All right Mr. Rugged & Beautiful, I thought, folding my arms across my supremely-dorky school sweater. Think you can psyche me out? Well I've just completed a year and a half in mean-girl lockdown, where they make you check in your soul at the door in exchange for verbal switchblades, so don't even *think* I'm gonna cave any time soon.

No fear.

I lifted my chin and gave him my iciest stare.

"First one inside hits the jackpot!" I said, darting into the bank's front door before he could blink.

At least, I'd thought I'd made it before him. But in the time it took me to absorb Home & Hearth's truly horrendous country-blue lobby with white geese & little red hearts on the perky gingham wallpaper borders, I could feel the guy's warm breath against my neck.

"Okay, Silver Spoon," he whispered from behind me with a laugh, "let's see what you got."

I whipped around, but he was already half-way out the door.

Holy crap.

It's *showtime*.

Without wasting another second, I marched up to the only teller—a round woman with a doughy face and gray, curly hair—and shot her my very fiercest look.

"Give me the money," I stated, spying the name tag on her blouse, "Darlene."

No finger in the cardigan, or note, or even a hint of violence.

In the heat of moment, I'd forgotten all about that stuff, but there was no retreating now.

The woman's face broke into the sweetest smile I'd ever seen.

"Thank you, Jesus!" She clapped her hands together loudly, her eyes tearing up. "Honey, I been prayin' for you!"

She waved her hands in the air to some unseen troop of angels and nodded at me as if I were her walking dream-come-true. Then she turned to grab a basket full of muffins.

"Here, sweetie. We usually hand these out to customers who open up new checking accounts. But I thought it might be a nice touch to give it to you, too."

Before I could speak, she'd plopped the basket into my arms. Then she pulled out a quilted fabric purse and opened it wide, removing a thick wad of bills held together by a rubber band. Eyes sparkling, she dropped the bills into the basket like it was Easter candy.

"There you go—three-hundred and fifty whole dollars! I won it at bingo last Wednesday, and I been askin' the Lord *all* week to show me a sign for who to give it to. And here you came in like sunshine and made it clear as day!"

Her gaze narrowed for a moment as she carefully looked me up and down. "What's your trouble, honey? You pregnant?"

"Huh? N-No!" I replied, utterly confused. "I mean, what? This isn't the bank's money—it's *your* money?"

I couldn't help it. I started to cry. I'd never seen anyone do anything so . . . selfless . . . in my whole life.

"Th-thank you," I sputtered, hugging the basket to my chest. The blueberry muffins smelled like pure heaven. "I-I hardly know what to say—I—"

"Go on!" she smiled. "An' spread your blessings out there like seeds, child. The way the good Lord showed us. Now hurry up, before the day gets away!"

Thoroughly stunned, I turned and walked in a total daze to the door. But as I opened it, I began to wonder: What if that guy tries to snag the basket from me?

Clutching the basket tighter, I quickly stuffed the bills into my pocket and steeled my back, taking confident, measured strides out the bank door to our car.

Jesus or no Jesus—I resolved, clenching my fists—if anyone so much as looks at these muffins, they're going to eat a basket sandwich today for lunch.

Chapter 3

My mind was still reeling from my first "bank job"—a.k.a. charity case?—and run-in with the hottest guy in the free world as I pulled the Miata onto a road near Bender Lake. Sure, I guess I was lucky he'd been nowhere in sight after I'd bolted from that sweet bingo lady at the bank. But deep inside, I'd hoped to catch just *one* more glimpse. I mean, guys that dangerously good-looking almost never cross into my world, unless they were stealing plasma TVs or Porsches. Without even trying, he'd suddenly made the boys at Breton look like sissies with their pin-striped uniforms, designer sneakers, and glow-in-the-dark smiles. Oh, how I wondered what it would be like to run my fingers through his wild, sun-kissed hair . . .

A pothole shook me from my reverie as the Miata nearly stalled in a stretch of mud. The road we were on was unmarked. Hell, everything around here was unmarked! But that's what the owner of a nearby filling station had warned me to expect. When I'd asked him about rentals in the area, he took one look at my dad, snoozing in our now hopelessly-dented Miata with leaves and muffin crumbs plastered all over his face, and heaved a sigh. Shaking his head like we were certifiable losers, he muttered under his breath.

"Well, I reckon the last dirt road west of Bender Lake might have something for you. *If* they let you in."

Let me in what? I'd wondered later as I cautiously steered the Miata towards a dark stand of woods, scanning the old tires and rusty appliances that littered the overgrown road. I turned to my dad, who'd finally woken up and was devouring the last of the blueberry muffins, and patted his arm.

"So, you sure you're ready for the high life?"

My dad shrugged, so I proceeded slowly over a rocky patch until I saw a broken, homemade sign on the ground.

Turtle Shores Trailer Park.

A smiling turtle by a lake was painted on one side with an exploding cannon on the other.

Kind of a mixed message, if you asked me. I didn't think much of it till I saw my dad glance up and shift uncomfortably in his seat.

"B-B-Bunther? Bunther LAYK?"

"Yeah, Dad, we finally made it to Bender Lake. And don't get all fussy on me. It's the only place where no one's gonna pry into our business. See what I mean?"

I pointed to a coffee can in the mud with the words *Leave Rent* scrawled on it.

"Wow, something tells me you don't have to fill out an application to live here. Must be a pretty trusting crowd, if that's where they leave their cash—"

"No!" My dad shook his head. All at once, his eyes looked strangely alarmed. "Ammo, Wobbin. They goth ammo— DUCK!"

Before I could ask questions, a screeching sound soared over our heads, followed by a fiery blast. Screaming, I dove to cover my dad, coughing at billows of smoke.

"JUSTIN! JASPER!" I heard a woman holler. "You knock that off, ya hear?"

Too frightened to budge, I kept my face buried in my dad's orange polyester blazer, my forehead sweating up a storm.

"Oh my Lord, she's just a baby!" I heard a woman cry. "And you gone and scared her half to death. Come here, sweetheart."

A pair of unwelcome arms pulled me upright in the seat and nearly squeezed the stuffing out of me. When I was finally released, I found myself staring at a very large . . . skunk?

Black, bouffant hair with platinum streaks filled my vision, until I leaned back and took in the fluorescent purple eyeshadow and blood-red lips with a strategically-placed beauty mark on one cheek. For a sophomore who wasn't even allowed to wear makeup at Pinnacle, the effect was downright . . . frightening.

I screamed again.

"Aw, it's all right, honey," the woman purred with another bear hug. "How do! I'm Brandi with an I," she winked, "not a Y. Welcome to Turtle Shores."

She waved aside a cloud of smoke. I couldn't help noticing that her frame was squeezed into a skin-tight black velvet jumpsuit with rhinestone swirls in embarrassing places. Like maybe she was a pole dancer channeling Elvis?

"Sorry about the TNT Twins." Brandi rolled her eyes at the two large boulders that had begun to wiggle. To my surprise, the boulders actually stood up, and a helmeted head and set of limbs poked out of each one. They cautiously inched closer until I could see their get-ups were made of stone-colored paper mâché.

"Those two will blow up anything that don't have sense enough to run for cover," Brandi sighed. "And they're a bit touchy about newcomers."

"You the law?" One of them growled.

I glanced down at my nerdy uniform and mud-splattered sportscar.

"In a convertible?" I replied. Funny how no one seemed to be bothered by the fact that a nearby bush was on fire.

"Could be undercover. They got all kinds of tricks," his boulder buddy snarled, holding up a smoking PVC pipe. From the odd, french-fry-crossed-with-gasoline smell, something told me they'd just shot a potato out of it.

"Who you runnin' from?" His partner persisted.

Everybody! I wanted to say.

"Well, uh we," I began to explain, "Ouch! Sweet Mother of God—"

Gasping, I grabbed my arm, realizing my dad had actually *hit* me.

"No innnfo, no naymzzz," he hissed into my ear, spraying spittle while he was at it.

Gotcha—no info, no names. Nodding, I rubbed dad's slobber from my ear. Just for kicks, I decided to play this one straight.

"Listen, people. And boulders," I said boldly, "we're just looking for a place to stay. You got something or not?"

"Why, you don't need to say another word, child!" Brandi cut in, giving me yet another hug.

Swear to God, if that woman so much as touched me one more time, I was gonna slap her silly. Luckily, she lifted her chin instead to Tweedle-Dee and Tweedle-Dum and set her hands on her hips.

"You boys know the rules," Brandi chastised with a shake of her finger. "T'ain't a soul here that's got to explain nothin' if they're willin' to be neighborly and pay rent."

"We can pay rent!" I promised excitedly, feeling the bingo lady's money burn a hole in my pocket. Seeing this as our only chance, I unbuckled my seat belt and popped out of the Miata.

"Here, how much for the first month?" I pulled out some cash and took an enthusiastic step forward. "Do you have a roomy double-wide, or—ahhhhhh!"

Quick as a flash, I found myself in total darkness, like I'd fallen into a hole in the ground. Yet every time I tried to move, my limbs were hindered by something gooey and gelatinous and horribly disgusting, like . . . like . . . jello?

"Ahhh!" I cried again. Struggling to reach up, I pushed over the grassy trap door that had slammed over my head. But my relief at seeing daylight was shattered by the sudden arrival of a dozen orange and honking . . . beaks? All at once, they nipped at my forehead, cheeks and nose until I was practically in tears.

"Ow! Ow, stop it! Get back, you rotten—"

"Attack Geese! Attention!"

A sharp whistle drilled my ears. Instantly, the birds backed off and fell eerily silent.

Petrified, I swallowed gulps of air to try and calm down. Then I dared to peek my nose out of the hole. Before me stood a grizzled, one-armed man with a gray ponytail and an army-green patch over one eye. A line of white geese were parked in front of him like a row of soldiers. With another shrill blow of his whistle, the birds obediently waddled off into the woods in single file.

Laughing, the boulder boys high-fived each other and did an awkward, mid-air tummy bump, landing in the mud. They rolled over and grinned like happy pigs. I glanced over at my dad, who was shaking his head like he'd expected as much.

What?

Why did my dad seem so casual with all of this?

"You can call me Colonel," the old man announced, interrupting my thoughts. He stepped forward and held out his only hand to give me a lift. "You already met my special forces. Finest avian defense squad within a hundred-mile radius."

With surprising strength, he jerked me out of the hole and onto my feet in seconds flat. Just as I suspected, I was covered from head to toe with oozing, red gelatin. Curious, I swept a little off my lips with my tongue.

Strawberry-banana. God, if it wasn't so damn creepy, I'd actually say it tasted good! But what if I attracted ants?

"Figure you'll be wanting a trailer," the Colonel stroked the stubble on his chin, "for what we like to call an indefinite period of time?"

Trembling, I nodded, feeling unbearably itchy.

"Well the only one I got left is back there, in them trees."

He motioned to a shadowy and foreboding stretch of woods, the kind Hansel & Gretel and Little Red Riding Hood definitely should not be wandering into. Squinting, I couldn't make out anything at all, like the trailers had somehow been . . . camouflaged?

"No guns, no drugs. Period. You got that."

It wasn't a question but a command. The Colonel glared at me with his flinty eyes until I agreed.

"We got our own style of protecting each other here, as you can see. Anybody who brings in guns or drugs will be hoisted by the TNT Twins' trebuchet and sent flying till they drop into the middle of Bender Lake. Rent's due the first of every month, which happens to be next week. I don't think I gots to explain what will happen if ya don't pony up your share."

I shook my head vigorously.

"Excellent. Now Justin 'n Jasper, you man the tree stands with your spud cannons in case anybody's on the prowl for this little lady or the fella she's with. And Brandi will show you your new digs and help you settle in. Oh, and she'll give you a map so you don't fall into any more holes."

I breathed a shallow sigh of relief.

But the old man just glared at me and waited.

Nervous, I shuffled my feet, feeling gelatin squish between my toes. The silence got really awkward, but his stone gaze wouldn't let up.

Honestly, I didn't have a clue what this guy wanted, or what the rules were in this nightmare fairy tale from hell. All I knew was that the slimy jello inside my bra was starting to make my skin crawl. Finally, it hit me—

"Oh, th-thank you!" I stuttered, feeling so icky I thought my skin was about to peel off. With a quick downward glance, I was quite certain it was time to kiss my red-stained uniform goodbye.

The Colonel gave me a little wink before he turned to leave. "My pleasure. By the way, darlin'," he added, "that pretty car o' yours sure as hell better not have a tracer."

A what? I fretted as he walked away, wringing my hands. He soon disappeared into the woods without looking back.

Holy cow, was any of this for real?? I stared at my dad, who was leaning his chin on his hand like he'd already resigned himself to our fate. Before I could grill him about his peculiar familiarity with this place, Brandi sidled up to me again. I quickly held out my palm so she wouldn't even think about giving me another hug.

"Watch your step, honey," Brandi smiled brightly, plopping herself down on the hood of the Miata for a lift, "and you'll avoid all the traps. Too bad you didn't get the one filled with coconut custard. It's really good!"

"All I can say is,' I huffed, slipping behind the steering wheel of our car and feeling the jello slosh in my underwear, "our new trailer had better have a hot shower."

"You know, plumbing can be a little tricky at Turtle Shores," Brandi confessed, gazing sheepishly at the dirty sink inside our broken-down trailer.

No shit.

Considering the fact that I was now covered in mud that had spewed from the kitchen faucet, I'd say the woman was spot on.

I just wanted to fold into myself and cry.

I wanted to hug Sparkle to my chest and then text half a dozen semi-friends, frenemies or not, and even log onto their idiotic Tumblr accounts—anything to forget that I'd actually planted myself in the Land of the Lost and Incredibly Sticky. It wasn't enough that they'd already covered me in red goo, now the mud made me smell like the bottom of a swamp! What was I going to do if the plumbing didn't work?

"Cheer up!" Brandi smiled. "You can always clean yourself up with a few baby wipes and rat your hair, like me. A little hairspray goes a long way, honey. Did you know that I do hairdressing on the side?" Her green eyes got particularly bright. "Along with my late-night shift at the Moo & Brew Drive Thru—we specialize in banana splits and beer. I get really great tips when I wear these rhinestones." She sashayed her hips happily. "Here, try a hush puppy."

She handed me a plate that had been sitting on the kitchen table and offered one to my dad on the sofa, too. "Lorraine over by the dogwood trees fried these up for lunch, with real cheese and bacon inside. She don't leave her trailer much, on account of her eyesight, but she's a wonder with a fryer. She does most of the cooking for us at Turtle Shores."

Brandi pulled out a handkerchief with the word *Graceland* embroidered on it and dotted mud off my lips. I wondered where on earth she expected to wash it.

"You do realize that's how everything works here, right?" She added. "On the barter system?"

I saw my dad nod while he relished his hush puppy. I took a small bite of one myself and was stunned by the intense rush of flavor. Cheddar cheese, bacon and onion, all rolled together in a soft pillow of corn meal with a crispy crust. It was nothing short of . . . divine.

"See, most of us here are pretty low on cash," Brandi said quietly, as if that glaring detail was any kind of secret. "And to be honest," she crunched into a hush puppy and chewed, "we can't really get into the other trailer parks. Some folks claim we're too loco, if you know what I mean. But they'll talk trash about anybody! So we just take care of each other: I do hair, Lorraine cooks, Granny gives the best advice in the whole county, and Bixby repairs leaky roofs and siding—when he's not huffing paint, that is," she sighed. "Just be careful not to light any cigarettes near his trailer, okay? Oh, and the Colonel and the TNT Twins keep guard against nosey cops and criminals, and especially the exes. Ain't no secret 'round here that old boyfriends and girlfriends always cause the most trouble!" She chuckled a little. "Creek provides pretty much everything else you could ever need."

"Creek?" I asked.

"Oh, you'll find out soon enough," she winked. "Chances are, he's already done more for you than you could repay him for in a lifetime. Here, I think there are some tissues in this drawer." She opened a bin beside a rusty oven and handed me a packet with *Buckeye Motel* written on it, like it had been stolen. "A few swipes of these around your face, honey, and you'll be as good as new. Call me if you need anything!"

"Wait, what's your cell number? I left mine back at the—"

"T'ain't no phones, silly!" Brandi roared, rocking back on her kitten heels. "They don't work here anyhows. You just open up your door and let 'er rip." She turned the door handle and leaned outside. "Howdy-doodle!"

Her voice echoed through the woods, but I didn't exactly hear a reply. All I could detect was the sound of the TNT Twins blasting yet another target in the distance. And if I wasn't mistaken, I thought I saw a man swing from a rope through the trees.

"Criminy," Brandi sighed. "Bixby must be huffing paint again. And I wanted him to fix my toilet, too. Take a number, I guess."

She shrugged and patted me on the back. "Well, if you need any help, sweetie, I'm in the silver Airstream to the right of the biggest maple tree over there, covered with thatched branches and leaves. Our trailers are all hard to spot, if you get my drift," she grinned. "But don't ever think that means we don't know what's goin' on. Toodles!"

Brandi wiggled her fingers in my face before she headed out the door. "I'll be back in the morning with some of Lorraine's sausage and cheese grits. You're gonna think you died and gone to heaven."

"Right—heaven," I mumbled uncertainly.

I tried to force a smile as she hopped down into the mud from our trailer that was barely half the size of my old dorm room at Pinnacle. All of a sudden, I craved my dry bed there with its overly starched sheets and aroma of industrial cleansers everywhere. At least it was clean! I gazed around our grubby trailer, which was so small that I could touch the kitchen table, the range, and an overhead bunk bed without moving an inch. Not to mention that it was covered from floor to ceiling in shades of "burnt orange", "avocado" and "harvest gold" like some sicko shrine to reruns of *That '70s Show*. I was afraid that if I squinted, my father in his pimped-out leisure suit might actually disappear into the sofa's retro, hallucinogenic hues. Shaking my head, I folded my arms and glared at Dad.

"All right, start talking," I demanded.

He looked at me, confused.

"How is it you're so familiar with this place? Every time I turn around, you're practically lip-synching with these people, like you're totally used to their drill. Do you have relatives here or something? You always said our ancestors were English lords who came over and topped Cincinnati's social register. Not backwoods bumpkins—"

My dad flinched.

No, more than that. A pained expression came to his face, as if my words had somehow pierced his . . .

His . . .

Soul.

Oh my gosh. Who was this guy, anyway? Just yesterday he was *the* Royle McArthur—the loudest, baddest, most infamous law-shark of the Tri-State region. He had no soul! And now all of a sudden he seemed like a total stranger?

To my astonishment, tears rimmed the corners of his eyes. My dad reached out his good hand and ran his fingers along my dark, jello-coated hair.

"Bootifull . . . bootifull baybee gurrll," he said with a quiet sincerity, admiring the long strands, despite their stickiness.

I choked up in an instant.

For once in my life, I was utterly speechless.

"Go to the layk, Wobbin," he whispered.

It took a moment for him to roll his tongue back into position to talk again.

"Everrthin be all rite. Jus go to the layk."

Chapter 4

I shook my head as I walked alone through the thick woods, bewildered by my dad. It was like he'd put on a completely different face with me, one I'd never seen before. And he was so insistent that I go to the lake. Maybe he knew it was my only hope for a bath, or he thought I'd calm down once I cleaned up? Either way, it didn't help matters that every time a twig snapped, I was terrified the TNT Twins might be at it again. Fortunately, I didn't need a map after all to navigate their holes. The yellow circles of dry grass that polka-dotted the ground were enough to highlight their traps. I stepped gingerly around each one, keeping an eye out for any stray Attack Geese, when I spotted the sandy trail that led to the lake. Brushing aside a few honeysuckle branches, I pursued the path past a long bramble of twisted bushes and fallen sticks, when all of a sudden I saw it—

The setting sun.

Glowing gold across the water and shimmering on the wet sand.

It was so beautiful it took my breath away.

Before I realized it, I'd pressed my hand to my chest. Releasing a sigh, I let the sight fill me up for a few moments, feeling as if it could actually make my heart glisten inside. I closed my eyes for just a second, relishing the quiet. Then I glanced around.

There wasn't a soul by the shore, or even in boats on the lake. It was as if I'd stumbled upon my own, private retreat.

I walked up to the water's edge and sat down on the sand and stretched out my legs, allowing the warmth of the waning sun to soothe me a little, both inside and out. After such a crazy day, it felt good to let the calm of the gentle, lapping waves slowly seep into my bones. Leaning my head back, I heard the lonesome call of a bird overhead. When I glanced up, I saw a heron flapping its wide, gray wings.

My dad was right. Everything was okay now.

Remaining still, I noticed that the tree shadows had stretched into long lines across the lake. The darkening sky was inching towards twilight, so it crossed my mind that if I wanted to rinse myself off, I'd better go for a swim now before night fell.

Taking a deep breath, I stood up and slipped off my shoes and socks and walked out into the water.

It wasn't nearly as cold as I'd expected.

Wiggling my toes in the soft, silty soil, I got bolder, and I took a few steps into the lake until I was up to my waist.

I waded deeper to my chest. Then to my shoulders.

And I began to giggle.

Not only was I up to my neck in some forgotten lake in the middle of nowhere, but there wasn't a thing anyone at Pinnacle could do about it! With a giant thrust of my legs, I glided forward, feeling completely . . .

Free.

Free for the first time in my whole life.

There were no nannies or chaperones anymore. No society snoops masquerading as fundraisers or home room parents who secretly criticized every little thing I did. I was totally on my own out here.

And I loved it!

The only problem was that my heavy wool cardigan and pleated skirt felt like dead weights against my skin. I had half a mind to peel them from my body and let them float off into oblivion.

Feeling mischievous, I peeked around. What would it hurt? Absolutely no one was here, and the sky had gotten dark enough that a few stars had begun to twinkle. Scanning the horizon, I spotted a light shining over the tree tops that I was pretty sure marked the entrance to Turtle Shores, so I felt confident that I could find my way back. Giggling again, I peeled off my thick sweater, then unbuttoned my polo shirt and pulled it over my head. Wriggling my skirt from my hips, I was down to my Pinnacle-issue bra and underwear, which covered more skin than most old ladies' swimsuits. I clutched my heavy uniform to my chest and swam awkwardly back to the shore and tossed the bundle onto the sand. With a few strong breast strokes that I'd finally mastered after years of enforced swim lessons, I headed to the middle of the lake, relishing the feel of the smooth water gliding over my skin. Pausing for a moment to catch my breath, I glanced up at the rising moon and smiled.

"Hello, beautiful," I said, just drinking it all in.

"That's exactly what I was about to say."

I whipped around, swallowing way too much lake water. It tasted like lukewarm algae—

Oh my God—it was HIM!

Golden hair slicked back by the water. Rough-cut features that appeared dewy in the twilight. And there was no mistaking those piercing blue eyes and that deep scar across his cheekbone that crinkled into the shape of a dagger when his lips curled into a smile. The way his eyes lit up at the sight of me made everything all too clear—

All of a sudden, I realized it was no accident that he was beside me in Bender Lake.

He must've been stalking me!

Instantly, I curled my knees beneath my chest and thrust the biggest kick of my life in order to do a mad freestyle for the shore. Within seconds, I felt the guy's elbow slip around my neck. He hugged me tight against his hard chest and engulfed me with his other arm until I couldn't thrash at all, his powerful legs slowly pedaling to keep us afloat. Our heads were bobbing face to face, and I felt his rope-like muscles clamp down on me as tight as a cocoon, making me tremble. My chest heaved in a panic against his—cool skin against skin—but his strong arms kept me from moving an inch.

"You took my bank," he said.

His words were barely above a whisper, but the fact that we were nose to nose and skin on skin made them ring inside my head like an alarm bell.

"It wasn't your bank!" I cried, wriggling as fiercely as I could and feeling like a caged animal. "As I recall, you dared me to do it—"

Ha! I saw his intense, sapphire eyes narrow at that one, along with an indignant crease that formed over his eyebrows as he carefully studied my face. Sure, he might be drop-dead gorgeous in the twilight and scary-as-all-get-out, which was enough to unravel any young woman, but as his eyes searched mine, it hit me—

He has no idea that the bingo lady gave me the money.

So he must think I'm some kind of master criminal.

Go, Geisha girl, go!

I love being a good actress at times like this! With a proud, upward thrust of my chin, I squinted my eyes in my most mysterious gaze, then put on a cocky smirk, just to drive him crazy.

"You know what the best part is about being an expert bank robber?" I said in a gloating tone, adding a wink to rub it in, "no one ever knows what you're about to do next."

With that, I sunk my teeth into the black tattooed snake on his forearm and thrust my foot into his chest, giving him a fierce shove.

Okay, so he was way too tough to scream. But his hold did release a little, and that's all I needed. With laser focus, I broke free and headed to the shoreline like my life depended on it, my muscles burning with adrenaline. Two strokes, four strokes, hopefully all it would take was ten more! By the time I could feel the shore beneath my feet, and I stumbled to reach for my clothes on the sand, my heart was pumping so hard I thought it would explode. Quickly, I stood up and glanced over my shoulder for a second just to see how close behind me he was.

But there was no one to be found—

Anywhere.

The lake was just as empty as it had been when I discovered it, the surface still as glass.

Almost as if I'd imagined the whole thing.

Gulping down breaths, I shook my head and leaned my hands on my knees for a moment to get my bearings, hoping I hadn't somehow lost my mind. Out of the corner of my eye, I thought I saw one of the tree shadows waver a little over the lake. Laughter began to echo across the water.

"Go ahead, try to run, Silver Spoon," a voice called from somewhere in the twilight. "Where the hell do you think you're gonna hide?"

My feet drummed beneath me in the dark woods, and even though I'd thrown on my freezing cold and wet Pinnacle uniform in a rush, I still felt like my lungs had caught on fire. All around me were crooked silhouettes cast by the moonlight that I swear looked like those creepy trees from *The Wizard of Oz*. I half expected flying monkeys to zip by, when suddenly I heard an owl's hoot that scared me so badly I had to stop in my tracks to keep from tripping. Regaining my balance, I swiveled on my heels and glanced up to search the evening sky. Where, oh where, was that outside light for Turtle Shores? Just minutes ago it was shining as bright as daylight above the trees. What kind of total idiot would turn it off at night? Unless—

Unless—

Stalker Guy shot it out on purpose with a slingshot . . . or something deadlier?

All of a sudden, my mind began swimming with horror film images, picturing my body strewn in pieces on the forest floor . . .

Stop it, Robin! I ordered myself. Don't cave in to fear. If that guy wanted to kill you, he probably would've done it by now. So why didn't he, what does he want?

To scare the crap out of me?

Check. He aced that one.

To make me run in circles so he can laugh his ass off?

Check, he's got that covered, too.

To follow me around and play mind games till he figures out how I got the money from the bank?

Bingo!

Pardon the pun, bingo lady, I thought, resuming my brisk pace through the woods. But if I have any brains whatsoever, I'd face the fact that Stalker Guy is probably watching me right now. Watching me and waiting patiently so that he can . . .

Light my way home?

What the—

To my astonishment, I'd stumbled upon a clearing where there was a long row of illuminated, white paper sacks. Each one had a little candle in it, creating a warm glow that struck me as . . .

Enchanting.

I gasped, my hands rising to my cheeks like a little girl, as if I'd discovered a secret fairy glen. The lanterns were so simple, yet lovely, that I felt goose bumps alight on my skin. In the stillness of the forest, with only the sounds of crickets for company, the sight seemed almost—

Sacred.

Each soft light reminded me of the pretty votives that flickered beneath the gothic angel statues in the chapel back at Pinnacle. A bit wary, I took a couple of steps closer, only to realize that the lanterns had been strategically placed to shed light on where the TNT Twins' traps were, so I wouldn't fall in. If I followed them, I might find my way back to my trailer in no time.

Or, Stalker Guy could be there waiting for me at the end of the line.

Don't be stupid! I scolded myself. You don't know what this guy's up to, and you don't want to lead him anywhere near your dad, so you'd better *not* do what he expects.

Swallowing a deep breath, I took a hard left away from the clearing and started to run again. All right, so maybe I can't see very well out here, I thought, but unless he's got infra-red goggles, he can't either. And at least that makes us even. I dodged half a dozen tree trunks in the moonlight, when I skidded in a patch of mud and found myself crashing into something very big and hard and black.

Ouch. Christ almighty—

I slumped to the moist ground, my head ringing.

Crap. Just after I'd gotten cleaned up, too. Leaning forward, I rested my arms on my dirty knees for a second and rubbed my sore forehead.

"For crying out loud," I groaned in the darkness, "why can't somebody just shoot me already?"

Frustrated, I stretched out my muddy hand to feel what I'd run into, my fingers detecting a smooth, wooden panel. Then I brushed up against a long, thin arc with spindle-style spokes like a . . .

A wagon wheel?

To my surprise, a strange, orange glow hovered above me, almost like a firefly. It swiftly disappeared, and I could smell smoke—rich and musky and a little bit sweet, like my dad's favorite brand of cigars.

"I see you met Creek," a rocky voice commented from the shadows.

I nearly jumped out of my skin.

How I leaped to my feet in less than a hundredth of a second defied the laws of physics. But as soon I was standing, I felt something hard hook around my neck, applying a sharp yank to keep me from bolting.

"Hold on there, missy!" A woman's voice cackled with a laugh.

The more I struggled, the more I choked on the smooth curve of wood that kept me anchored in place, like a . . . a . . .

Shepherd's crook?

What was this, some sicko fairy tale?

When I grabbed at my neck to try and pull away, the woman gave me another jerk just to show she meant business. She tweaked my ear hard for good measure.

"Ow! Ow—okay, okay!" I yelped, afraid she was about to clap me upside the head.

"So, you fixin' to mud wrestle with me all night out here?" the woman growled. "Or are you gonna come inside my wagon for a warm cup of tea?"

I stiffened for a moment.

Hmm . . . ear tweaking, or tea with Crazy Lady?

For a split-second, I considered trying to kick myself free— if only I wasn't still gagging on Loony Bo Peep's hold around my neck. With that thought, she gave my ear another mean twist.

"Ow—Tea! Tea!!" I cried.

The woman cackled as if she were accustomed to such outbursts, which weirded me out even more. Thankfully, she released my ear and unhooked my neck, then wrapped her arm tight around my shoulders to guide me forward.

Swell. There's nothing like taking a little stroll in the middle of the night with a freaky stranger to keep your heart pumping. And just my luck, it was too dark to spot an escape route, let alone to see Stalker Guy any more.

"Don't you worry 'bout a thing, missy," the woman said, as if she'd heard my thoughts. "Creek ain't gonna hurt you so long as you're with me."

I sighed, exasperated. "Who the hell is Creek? And can you please tell me why I should care?"

The woman fell silent.

I could hear her open a heavy door with a squeaky hinge, presumably to her wagon.

"Well, I reckon them ain't quite the right questions," she said rather mysteriously.

The orange glow lit up again and filled the night air with spicy smoke. To my surprise, the woman set a heavy hand on my shoulder and gave me jiggle, as if to wake me from a deep sleep.

"What you really oughta be askin' by now is—who in tarnation are *you*?"

Chapter 5

"I'm *Robin*," I said defiantly, though the strange woman gave me a scrunched stare like she didn't believe me. She puffed on her cigar, and I tried to wave away the smoke.

"I see," she replied, her lips curving into a smile.

She set down her shepherd's crook in a corner of her cramped, gypsy wagon that was filled with hanging herbs, dusty books, and jars of icky things like lizard's feet and entrails. I watched as her black lace-gloved fingers skimmed a crystal ball on a shelf, and for the life of me, I thought I saw it cloud over. She turned to stare at me.

Her eyes resembled a timberwolf's. Their color was a peculiar, translucent gray with yellow in the middle, and they turned up slightly at the edges, as if caught in a permanent, predator's glare. At this point, I was beginning to think stepping inside her wagon might have been the biggest mistake of my whole life.

"Here, take one," she insisted, picking up a deck of scuffed cards and handing them to me. She motioned for me to sit down at her rustic table while she did the same. I had to push aside a candelabra she'd lit with blood-red candles to make room for my elbows, paying special attention to avoid the flames with my hair.

"I'm Granny Tinker, by the way," she said, her voice a mixture of warmth and gravel.

I'd noticed nobody used their last names around Turtle Shores, so her words gave me a start. The woman caught the look in my eyes and winked.

So that must not be her *real* name, I realized. And she's probably no grandma, either. Come to think of it, in the warm light of the candles, she looked more like a beautiful, aging rock star. Her thick, salt and pepper hair spilled luxuriously to her shoulders, and she wore a burgundy top hat with a peacock feather in it. Her black-velvet dress was held together by a long row of pearl buttons from her neck all the way down to her cinched waist. Overall, her appearance screamed boho— including the crimson granny boots she had on that laced up nearly to her knees.

"It's all right, Dooley," she said, stealing a glance at the card I'd picked out and set face down on a paisley scarf on the table. "You can come join us now."

To my astonishment, a tow-headed little boy peeked from behind an old trunk. He had to brush aside several embroidered pillows to clear a path to stand to his feet, and that's when I sucked air.

Oh. My. God.

He looked just like—

Stalker Guy!

Same messy blonde hair, same piercing blue eyes.

Holy Christ, he even had a matching snake tattoo on his forearm.

I couldn't help it—I jumped to my feet. This had to be some kind of wacked-out circus act I'd wandered into.

Before I could make a run for it, Granny Tinker grabbed me by the sleeve and gave me the coldest stare I'd ever seen in my life, so mesmerizing it was as if she'd clutched me by the throat and squeezed. Every fiber in her being seemed to say: *Don't you dare leave now and hurt this boy's feelings, or I will personally kill you.*

Stunned, I gulped several breaths and found myself settling back down in front of her table before I knew what hit me. The silence in the wagon was so thick now that I feared I might somehow drown in it. Nevertheless, the little boy took a timid step towards us.

"W-Which card did she take, Granny?" the little boy asked, his eyes as pure as an angel's, in a way that Stalker Guy's would never be.

The woman flashed him a generous smile, removing her cigar. For the first time, I noticed that one of her front teeth was gold.

"Hmm, the Wheel of Fortune," Granny said without even taking a look. She glanced over at me. "Ain't that so, sweetheart?"

I turned the card over, feeling my fingers tingle.

Whoa, she was right! There was a large wheel on the front, the kind you see at carnivals, surrounding a beautiful, blindfolded woman. People appeared to cling to the wheel, while at the top sat a perfectly peaceful angel. The edges of the card were decorated with a striking gold.

But how did Granny Tinker know—were the cards marked?

"No, honey," she said, as if she'd already read my mind. "It's your *soul* that's marked."

My heart began to race.

What was that supposed to mean?

"Pick another card, sweetie, and I'll tell you."

My forehead broke into a sweat. The little boy sat down on a wooden stool next to me and stared eagerly at the deck. I had no idea why he was so invested in my choice, but by this time I was afraid to refuse this scary woman. Biting my lip, I spread the cards out a little on the silk scarf and picked another one at random.

"Ah, The Lovers," Granny smiled, her gold tooth really shining now. She nodded. "History shore has a way of repeatin' itself, don't it?"

"W-What do you mean?" I asked.

Turning over the card, my heart leaped to my throat—on it was a young man and a young woman holding hands and staring with dreamy fascination into each other's eyes.

At that moment, I felt Granny's lace-covered fingers pat me gently on the hand.

"So tell me, what's he callin' himself these days?" Her eyes looked oddly fatigued.

"Who?"

Granny sighed. "Why, your Pa, of course! Let me guess, rhymes with Doyle?"

I gulped hard and nodded. "R-Royle."

Granny didn't even blink. "Figured as much. He always did go on about royalty, like their blood runs purple, not red like the rest of us."

Her gaze fell on the burning candles between us. I had to move my arm to escape the dripping, hot red wax.

"But, how do you know all this—"

My words were abruptly cut short by a loud ringing sound. I glanced up and saw a silver bell, about the size of my palm, hanging along a kind of trip wire near the door. It shook violently.

"C'mon!" The little boy grabbed my hand. "We gotta go. Cops!"

"Operation Groundhog," Granny sighed, like she was used to it. She shot a glance at the old trunk in her wagon. "Better follow Dooley quick, while I distract 'em. Unless you feel like bein' arrested tonight."

"A-Arrested?" The word got caught in my throat.

"Hurry, before it's too late!" Dooley urged, tugging me now with both hands towards the trunk. He threw open the lid.

Inside, I saw faded quilts, which Dooley promptly pushed aside, and then . . . stairs?

I shook my head for a second to make sure I wasn't seeing things.

The wooden steps led down to a well-lit room, with a sofa and a kitchenette and everything, like someone had managed to bury a trailer underground.

"Git a move on!" Dooley cried, scampering down the steps ahead of me.

I blinked hard, then carefully negotiated my way behind Dooley, allowing the trunk lid to close after me with a thud. When I reached the bottom, I saw puzzles and picture books scattered on the sofa, the kind meant for a child around six years old, which I imagined the boy to be.

"These are mine," Dooley glowed. "Creek brung 'em for me."

"Creek," I tested out the word on my lips, pretty certain we were both talking about Stalker Guy, so I decided to fish a little. "He must be . . . your, um—"

"Brother!" the boy piped up, clearly proud of him. "Wanna see the truck he got me?"

He settled on the couch and picked up a shiny firetruck that lit up like Christmas and squirted water from a hose at me with the mere touch of a finger. I rolled my eyes. If I hadn't been damp already, I would've been thoroughly annoyed. Before he could press a button for the siren, I held up my hand.

"Sh, Dooley," I said in my loudest whisper. "I think somebody's with Granny now."

Sure enough, above us I could hear the murmur of men's voices in low, demanding tones, like maybe they were questioning her. Then it fell quiet for a minute, until there was a loud thump and rattle, as though someone had pounded on her table.

"No siree!" I heard Granny's voice boom over our heads. "I ain't seen no such folk at all 'round here. If you wanna find a loose lawyer, though, I expect you oughta check Rhonda's strip joint up the road. She attracts 'em like flies."

Holy Saints in Heaven, it suddenly hit me that Granny Tinker was covering for me and my dad. What, out of the goodness of her heart? Right away, my thoughts turned to my father. The poor guy was all alone, half paralyzed, and he didn't even know where I was! What if some cop had managed to find our trailer?

At that moment, a small, warm hand slipped onto mine.

"It's okay," Dooley said, giving me a squeeze. "They cain't hear nothin' down here. And Creek's got everything taken care of."

Near as I could tell, his sweet, blue eyes seemed incapable of lying.

"Just like those candles out in the meadow tonight. Creek let me help set 'em up, you know. So you could find yer way home. Warn't they pretty? Don't worry, he'll treat yer Pa right."

"M-My dad?" I sputtered, aghast that Creek might be anywhere within twenty feet of my father.

"C'mon, I'll show ya."

With a tug, Dooley led me through the trailer to a back room that was piled to the rafters with canned goods and boxes, like a warehouse. On a top shelf that rimmed the ceiling was a long row of . . . wigs? Black, red, blonde, silver—one in every shape, color, and style.

"Brandi started chemo a while back," Dooley said, his big eyes registering my surprise. "She cried and cried when she went bald, so Creek brung her these. They look real nice on her. And Lorraine's downright crazy about Albers' grits." He pointed to a large, red and white case on the floor. "She makes 'em for everybody—even the Attack Geese. I like her cheese ones best. But the TNT Twins, well, Creek don't get mixed up in their explosions much, so he just hauls in potatoes for 'em." Dooley's finger aimed at a burlap sack on the ground.

Something about the skin on the boy's forearm caught my eye, and it wasn't simply the black snake tattoo. Below his elbow, I noticed he had a string of round, brownish dots, like maybe he'd had chicken pox? Yet when I squinted, I realized that they were more like scars—as in, burn marks—from somebody's cigarette. Shocked, I seized his arm.

"Dooley! What on earth happened—who would do this to you? Granny? Creek? Did Creek hurt you?"

"No!" The boy squirmed like mad, his eyes the picture of horror, but I held onto him with all my might.

"Tell me the truth, Dooley," I insisted. "What kind of sick, horrible human being would deliberately—"

"Time to come up. NOW." Granny Tinker had opened the hatch and bellowed in an iron tone that I swear could have leveled a building. Not since Mother Superior had I heard so much mettle in a woman's voice. "Our visitors done skedaddled."

Dooley slipped out of my hand like he was made of liquid and rushed up the stairs.

Shaking my head, I slowly climbed the steps, only to find Granny sitting at her small table with two steaming cups in front of her. Dooley was nowhere in sight.

"Sit down," she said.

I didn't get the impression I had a choice. "B-But I have to get back to my dad," I pointed out, "he's all alone, and probably scared—"

Granny's eyes narrowed, unrelenting, and she shoved a teacup towards me. She glared until I picked it up. Nervous, I lifted the warm liquid to my lips, praying to God it didn't have any lizard's feet or magic 'shrooms in it, and I took a careful sip. To my surprise, it tasted wonderful—like raspberries with cream and honey.

Granny folded her arms and smiled.

"No need to fret, child. Yer Pa's perfectly safe in his bunker—with Creek. He built one for all the trailers in Turtle Shores, just like my wagon. The Colonel and the TNT Twins blasted out the bunker holes with their explosives, and then Creek finished the rest. It was all his idea."

I could tell her eyes had picked up on my fear of Stalker Guy. She shook her head.

"Honey, Creek would rather die than hurt that little boy. Matter of fact, if it weren't for him, Dooley wouldn't be alive right now." She squinted at me, leaning closer. "And neither would yer Pa. Thems weren't cops that were just here. We can buy them off easy any day of the week. They was the mob. Said some high-falutin' guy hired 'em to flush out yer Pa. Like he owes him or somethin'."

All of a sudden, I felt the tea cup rattle in my hand.

"Doyle's got himself up shit creek this time, ain't he?"

"Royle!" I said adamantly. "Y-you've got him confused with somebody else—"

"Suit yourself," Granny Tinker nodded. "But I tell you this," she picked up her cigar from an ashtray and pulled out a pearl-handled switchblade, clicking open a long, shiny knife to cut off the cigar tip. "I ain't seen those mob boys up here for quite a spell. Surprised Doyle came back to Bender Lake to try and hide."

"It wasn't his idea—it was mine! And what do you mean came back?"

"He ain't never told you?"

Granny lit a match and leaned against her chair, puffing her cigar till it glowed. I could feel her studying me, her timberwolf eyes tracing the contours of my cheeks and nose, the waviness of my long, chestnut hair that never went completely straight, even with a hot iron. Then her gaze met mine, as if she were reading my dark brown eyes.

"Yep, you look just like her."

"Who?"

Granny let out a cackle that could have stirred the dead. "Why, the one that got away, darlin'. Must've been eatin' at him his whole life—"

"Who on this planet are you talking about?"

Granny's gaze rested on the candles between us, as if she could somehow see the past or the future in the flames. She watched them dance for a second, then cleared her throat.

"Well, I reckon a mirror can fetch ya a better answer than I can," she said softly, confusing me all the more. "And speakin' a mothers, a few years back, Dooley and Creek's Ma got herself mixed up with the meanest, son-of-a-bitch boyfriend this side of the Mississippi. You can blame him for puttin' those burn scars on their arms—and in their hearts. One night he knocked Creek's Ma around so bad she didn't live to see the morning. If it weren't for the way Creek hides Dooley, and the rest of us when we need it, those boys would've become wards of the state long ago. And half this trailer park would probably be in the loony bin. See, Creek's our angel. So long as we keep our traps shut."

Granny ran her black-laced finger along the steel of her switchblade and held it up to the candlelight, admiring its shine and brutally sharp edge. She stared me dead in the eyes.

"We got an understandin'?"

I nodded, grasping the stakes now. Maybe there were no guns at Turtle Shores, but that didn't mean Granny Tinker wasn't extremely well armed.

"S-So what ever happened to that s-super mean boyfriend?" I managed to spit out.

Granny inhaled a long, deep breath, releasing it slowly.

"Let's just say Creek made sure he won't never bother us no more."

With that, she sliced her switchblade across the candelabra so fast that the upper halves of each candle landed perfectly on her table, their small flames still flickering.

And I froze.

Suddenly, I felt cold to the bone, and not just from my wet clothes anymore. I think my mouth fell open, but I'd completely forgotten how to speak.

Trembling, I couldn't make up my mind what scared me more: The fact that Creek might have offed that guy, or the fact that if Granny had pushed her knife any closer, I'd be dead.

You know, a sane girl might've taken this moment to turn over Granny's table and give her an expert karate chop to the head.

But since I never took karate, and I'd pretty much maxed out *all* of my Geisha skills for one day, I simply sat there quaking like an idiot who didn't even have the good sense to run screaming out into the dark. Instead, I muttered something that I never dreamed would come out of my mouth to a total stranger.

"I—I really want to go home to my daddy right now. P-P-Please?"

Without another word, Granny got up and walked over to the trunk in her wagon. I watched her open it, hoping she wasn't reaching for another knife, crook, or some other secret weapon. Instead, she pulled out an old quilt. Returning to the table, she wrapped it around my shoulders and helped me to stand to my feet.

"C'mon honey," she said gently, slipping her arm around my waist to bolster me up. "Let's get you back to yer trailer. It'll be right nice to say hello once again to my good ol' cousin Doyle."

Chapter 6

My gondola floated serenely through a canal in Venice while I admired the crumbling, Old World buildings and blue sky. I leaned back, listening to a group of musicians along the bank, their violin notes dancing lightly on air. Then my eye caught the sight of a nun strolling by the water, who glanced up with a sad yet wistful look, as if she might know me. Her face was beautiful, and in the sweetest voice I'd ever heard, she called out "Mia bella!"

I gave the pretty nun a kind wave, then swept my hand over my ivory dress that made me look just like that chick singer in the NeoRomantix' latest video. Holding up a goblet for a toast, I nodded at the hunky gondolier and took my first ever a sip of champagne—all bubbly with a hint of sweetness!—and offered him a shy smile. This is the *life*, I mused, happier than I could ever remember. His eyes twinkled at me, and just as he leaned down to steal a kiss, a bomb exploded right in front of us and toppled our boat.

I screamed and bolted upright.

Only to discover that I wasn't covered in balmy, Mediterranean water, but rather, in a faded, army-issue blanket.

Good God—

I glanced around, realizing I was inside a rusty, old trailer.

So it hadn't all been a weird nightmare.

I really *was* in a trailer park, with only my dad and three-hundred-and-fifty bucks of bingo money to my name.

Brushing back the hair from my face, I vaguely remembered Granny Tinker walking me home the night before, where we found my dad asleep on the couch. Granny had wrapped my quilt around him to keep him warm, and then she helped me out of my wet clothes and tucked me into the back bed.

Another blast shook our trailer and echoed outside.

Cautiously, I peeked out the window just in time to catch a man in a boulder costume hurling through the air, his arms and legs flailing. Thank God he was wearing a helmet—

"JUSTIN! JASPER!" I heard Brandi's voice holler. "Now cut that out. The Colonel done told you not to launch each other from the trebuchet. Besides, yer cannons are gonna wake the new neighbors."

"But it's already noon!" one of the TNT Twins whined.

Astonished, I reached into my pocket for Sparkle to check the time, only to recall that we'd dumped her all the way back in Cincy. Oh yeah, and I had no pockets—I was still in my underwear.

Sighing, I leaned my hand to the floor to feel for my damp Pinnacle uniform, but instead, my fingers detected a dry stack of clothing and the rustle of . . . paper?

Beautifully thin bills of paper, as in *cash?*

What the—

I rolled out of bed, rubbing my eyes to make sure it was true.

There, on the floor, was a folded pair of jeans and a shirt with a stack of bills on top.

I grabbed the money and began thumbing through it. Each bill featured my all-time favorite Founding Father—Benjamin Franklin!—and his ever-so-lovely denominations at a 100 bucks a pop. Swiftly, I counted one hundred, two hundred . . . could there really be seven-hundred freakin' dollars here?

I gasped, nearly giddy, and I wanted to run and tell my dad the good news, until I looked down at my Pinnacle-issue bra and panties that reached nearly to my armpits. Heavens, I didn't want to scare him.

But my old uniform was nowhere in sight.

So where's the bingo money that was in my pocket? I wondered.

Maybe Granny Tinker dropped off the dry clothes last night, I thought, and hung my uniform out on a line? But why would she have doubled my money? With a shrug, I slipped on the skimpy, white tank top with lacy straps, noticing that it barely reached my belly button. My old French teacher would've called it a "camisole," but I was thinking more like "boob bandage." Then I threw on the ripped jeans that fell super low on my hips and had holes in the knees. As I zipped them up, I realized that they fit liked they'd been sprayed on.

And unless I rolled down my underwear, I'd look like freak of the century.

So I tucked in the waistband and slipped on my shoes, then bravely stepped over to a cracked mirror on the wall.

My mouth slung open.

Holy Cow—

I looked like a total slut!

More brazen than CeeCee Stone ever dreamed.

But I had curves—

Honest-to-goodness, flaunt-'em-if-you-got-'em *curves!*

I busted into giggles, staring at my bare midriff and cellophane-tight top.

Wow, welcome to Trailer Trash! With a few bold tattoos and navel piercings, I might actually win a six-pack at a local Karaoke bar.

Swiveling to the left and right, I tried on my best rebel scowl, full of bad-ass attitude, and let the new look sink in. Never in my entire life had I been allowed to wear a single shred of clothing that wasn't strategically designed to shout the McArthur's lofty status.

Or, I should say, what *used* to be our lofty status.

And that's when a shiver sped down my spine.

Who was my father, really?

Royle?

Doyle?

Had *anything* about our lives been real?

I took a deep breath and glanced over at the couch, where my dad was sleeping like a child, all wrapped up in Granny's quilt. Though he snored as loud as a hacksaw and drool dribbled from his chin, his face appeared amazingly carefree, with his secrets still tucked far, far away from me.

Yet strangely, a pair of men's dress shoes now sat on the floor beside him. I saw a note next to the shoes, and I tiptoed closer to pick it up. In handwritten scrawl, it read:

Silver Spoon,

Hope you like the street clothes and shoes for your old man.

Gotta blend in, you know. Oh yeah, and the Mazda fetched $700.

—Creek

"WHAT?!!!" I cried way too loud. "Creek sold my convertible??"

My dad merely yawned and tugged the quilt over his head, falling back into a heavy snore.

Spitting mad, I clenched my fists and dashed out of the trailer into the bright, noonday sun. All I found was an empty mud patch on the grass where my dream-came-true car used to be, along with another note on the ground.

Furious, I snatched it up.

By the way, that $350 that was in your uniform pocket went to pitch in for Brandi's treatment this morning. She doesn't know, so please keep it quiet.

—Creek

I have no idea how long I stood there, speechless.

At first I wanted to scream and bang my fists on something—or someone—and then I wanted to cry.

But how could I argue with the way he'd spent the money?

After all, bingo lady would've thanked Jesus with a heaven-busting shout if she knew it had gone to medical care. And then she would've called Creek an angel.

But since *when* do angels sport dagger-like scars on their cheeks and stalk teenage girls like me?

Unless . . .

This crazy, backwoods trailer park has got one hell of a Robin Hood on its hands.

Heaving a big sigh, I sat down on a log on the ground, thoroughly frustrated. For all I knew, Creek might be watching me this very second—and he probably had designs already on the $700 in my fist.

Just then, I spotted Brandi walking across the meadow out of the corner of my eye. She was expertly dodging the TNT Twins' holes with her red, high-heeled go-go boots. They matched the vinyl mini-dress she had on, as well as a cascading red wig that completed her look. I couldn't decide whether she resembled the red-head in that retro *Viva Las Vegas* poster that hangs at our local theater, or if she wanted to look like a firebomb waiting to happen. All I could say was, for a lady who had cancer, she sure knew how to dress out loud.

"Howdy-doodle!" she called out, wiggling her bright red fingernails at me. "I got ham and beans with your name on it. You don't even know it's lunch time, do ya? Not that I'm calling you a sleepy head or nothin'!"

Her voice was so grating I wanted to plug my ears, but who could argue with her smile as big as Texas? The woman glowed like good cheer on steroids.

"Look what you got!" she gasped, staring at my hand. Before I could stuff the money in my pocket, she'd snatched my wad of bills. "Oh Lordy, it's seven hundred dollars." I saw tears instantly well in her eyes. "You know, Creek mentioned that you might want to donate a little somethin' for my follow-up appointment tomorrow, but I just didn't believe him, seein' how we're brand new friends and all. My gosh, honey, you got yourself a heart of gold!"

"W-what?" I stammered.

Brandi hugged me so tight I couldn't breathe. How she managed it with a plate of ham and beans in her hand defied logic, but something told me her shifts at the Moo & Brew Drive-Thru had fine-tuned her finesse. When she released me, I gasped for air like a beached fish.

But I couldn't help catching the deeply shaken look in her eyes. Like she'd witnessed a train wreck.

I blinked for a second, but it was still there. Despite her day-glo green eyeshadow and stoplight-red lipstick, her eyes seemed filled with downright . . . fear.

And in the harsh daylight, not even her spackled-on foundation and sparkly cheek bronzer could completely camouflage the ashy tone to her skin. If I didn't know better, I'd say she looked almost like a . . .

Dead woman.

All at once, it hit me why Brandi wore such candy-coated outfits.

They were her armor.

The same way I used to hide behind my perfectly-crisp, pleated uniform, with my secret tool belt of Geisha skills tucked cleverly out of sight—so the mean girls couldn't get to me.

But Brandi was bracing herself against far more than snarky, trust-fund chicks. This was a woman who was fighting for her life.

Swiftly, I saw her wipe away the tears that had slipped down her cheeks, forcing a big smile.

"Aw, don't mind me!" Brandi chirped in a bright tone that didn't fool me one bit. "I just get weepy over the littlest old things."

She fluttered her hand as if she'd merely been over-excited, but I could see the raw courage in her eyes.

"Tell you what, darlin,'" she quickly changed the subject, "I'll go in yer trailer and serve these vittles to yer Pa right now.

After all, one good turn deserves another! And maybe with my help, he'll polish off the whole plate."

Brandi looked over my skin-tight clothes and gave me a sly wink. "See, we take care of our own here at Turtle Shores. And if you ask me, you look like you're fixin' to go out on a date." She gave me a sassy click of the tongue. "So you just git along now, and I'll make sure yer Pa's all taken care of. Might even persuade him to play a round of poker. Catch ya later!"

Before I could get a word in edgewise, Brandi had breezed past me and into our trailer, shutting the door so hard she made it rattle.

And I was left standing alone in my tracks, reeling.

In what felt like a nano-second, I was back to square one. No, worse than square one—not only were we broke again, but now we were missing *my* Miata!

"Ahhhh!!!" I fumed helplessly, kicking the dirt.

Across the meadow, a boulder popped up. A head peeked out and stared at me, wide-eyed, like I'd managed to figure out the secret pass code.

"You guys are nutso, do you know that??" I shouted with a hard stomp of my foot.

He simply laughed till his rock costume jiggled, and when his boulder buddy popped up beside him, they did a fist bump.

"That's it! I am soooo outta here!"

I stormed off into the thick forest, a good distance from the meadow, before I was tempted to throw something at the TNT Twins. Knowing them, it might start a firestorm.

Besides, I just wanted a few minutes to cool down, regroup a little, and plan my next move. The last thing I needed was to allow the TNT Twins to see me get flustered—or worse—see me break down and cry.

But as my legs marched like pistons through the dense woods and underbrush of honeysuckle, it occurred to me that I was being followed.

Because every time I took a step, I thought I saw the forest shadows beside me darken a little, and it wasn't like the sky had gotten overcast or anything. Then my skin began to tingle, and I even felt the small hairs stiffen on the back of my neck, as if something—or someone—was hovering way too close.

Just like that time at the bank.

Okay, I thought, it never did a girl any good to panic and try to hide from the alpha chicks at Pinnacle. They just saw it as a sign of weakness, and they'd hunt the poor girl down with their dirty tricks until they managed to crush her soul. So even though I did cave last night for that scary-crazy Granny Tinker, it was only because I was dead tired. Now that I've had some sleep and gotten my mojo back, it's time to meet this Creek guy head on.

I stopped and took in a deep breath to jack up my fortitude, then folded my arms.

"LISTEN MISTER," I said really loud, "I know you're out here."

I turned a little, just to see if I might catch a glimpse.

But there was nothing.

Frustrated, I let out a huff.

"And you should've asked me before you sold *my* car!"

Silence.

Not even the leaves dared to rustle.

"That was my frickin' car!!"

Still nothing.

I decided to go for the jugular—always my best tactic at Pinnacle. Find the soft spot and press until it really, *really* hurts.

"So, how would you like it if I took something of yours? I know where you hide Dooley! Nothing's stopping me from calling Child Protection Services right now—"

In a split-second, the mystery man had dropped in front of me, leaves falling all around us, as if he'd jumped down from a tree.

"You do that and you're *dead*—"

His large hands were around my neck in a heartbeat, all heat and hard muscle pressing down upon my skin, fully prepared to crush my throat.

And I'm pretty sure my pulse ceased right then and there. I was so scared I felt like my brain had flatlined.

But if I've learned anything from my incarceration at Pinnacle, it's to stare down the enemy, no matter how terrified you are. Then kill 'em with a smile.

"So, you gonna do me in the same way you knocked off your mom's boyfriend?"

I deliberately curled my lips into a wicked grin.

"Aw, come on, can't you show me some originality?"

Creek's whole body appeared as tight as a coiled snake. I swear to God, I could feel the heat of his anger radiating off his skin in waves. But his absurdly blue eyes—the kind that only belong to winged, celestial figures in Renaissance paintings—grew twice their size.

Ha!

I knew I'd found his tender spot then! He may be an incredibly tough customer, but at least he did have one bottomless wound that I could liberally dust with salt.

"You did kill that guy, didn't you?" I pressed viciously, trying hard to keep myself from trembling like jello. "Or is that just a nasty trailer park rumor?"

Creek's hold didn't loosen a bit. But his eyes narrowed as he studied mine with the same intensity of Granny Tinker, as if he could somehow read the darkest corners of my heart that even I might not be aware of. Yet in his grip, all of a sudden I felt like we'd become one creature—one tense, balanced-on-a-razor's-edge being—and if he dared to hold me much longer, I might just be able to see right into *his* most secrets places, too! With that thought, I felt the barest shiver run from his fingertips into my skin.

So, I smiled to myself, who's the predator and who's the prey now?

To my total surprise, Creek's grasp seemed to ease slightly with my line of thought as if it had vibrated through my skin. And he very cautiously released his fingers one by one, leaving only the sweat from his grip that lingered upon my neck. His gaze seared into mine.

"I had that asshole on his knees," he seethed.

Creek's eyes were blue flames, so fierce and so very full of . . . rage.

"But Dooley came."

His words hung in the air between us—bitter and painfully fresh—as though the incident had happened mere moments ago.

Slowly, Creek raked his hand through his messy, blonde hair. His gaze never flinched from my eyes.

I stole a deep breath—my first in what felt like a minute—and seriously considered making a run for it. But I knew my odds of escape at this point were infinitesimally slim. Instead, I swallowed hard, my mind racing to do the math.

"So . . . you were about to finish the guy off, when Dooley . . ."

I played out the scenario in my head.

"Walked in?"

Creek's jaw clenched, then twisted.

"And you let him go, rather than allow a child to . . . witness something like that?"

"Smart girl, Silver Spoon."

I nodded, grateful to be breathing. But I didn't kid myself for a second—now was the time to negotiate some kind of pact with this guy, or spend the rest of my trailer park days trying to outrun him.

Dig out your trump cards, Geisha girl!

"You know," I said with every ounce of bravery I could muster, thrusting up my chin, "looks like we're in the same business then, doesn't it?"

Creek cocked his head. His eyes appeared hard.

"How's that?"

"Well, we're both trying to take care of people we . . . I—lo—"

I stumbled over the word, feeling prickles surface on my skin.

"Love," I finally spit out, embarrassed.

Honestly, I'd never mentioned that term in connection with my dad in my entire life. And I wasn't sure if I really meant it, or if I simply wished it were true.

Because dealing with my father had always been like stepping into a hall of mirrors at a carnival. Every time I thought I was getting close to him, his reflection changed on me, and even now I wasn't sure who the hell he was.

"It seems to me," I pressed on, hoping Creek hadn't caught a whiff of my uncertainty, "that we both might be more effective if we joined forces to help our family members. You know, combined my female intuition and charm with your, um . . . street smarts? After all, I did beat you at the bank. Sometimes a soft touch works wonders! We could be the next Bonny and Clyde, like—"

"Partners?" Creek said, incredulous.

He wasn't exactly wide-eyed anymore. In fact, he was—

Laughing.

A grin had burst on Creek's face, as if the idea were beyond preposterous. And he rocked back on his heels with his thumbs in his front pockets as he let out a deep, throaty chuckle. His tousled hair fell loosely about his shoulders, pure gold in a shaft of light that had broken through the trees. And for the first time since we'd met, his face glowed with a warmth that was downright guaranteed to bowl most chicks over, even if it was at *my* expense.

It was enough to make a girl . . .

Pretty much keel over and drop dead of a heart attack.

Seriously, this guy was public enemy number one, a pure menace to women's health. There simply ought to be a *law* against anyone that beautiful running around wild and temporarily . . . unkissed.

And I couldn't help licking my lips, fantasizing about what it would be like to seal that kind of deal.

When suddenly, I spotted it—

A bold scar on his right bicep, inside a tattoo of a big, red heart.

Like he'd scratched out someone's name. And even more to the point: the name of a former girlfriend.

Creek swiftly folded his arms, covering it with his large fingers so I couldn't see. A hint of red flashed on his cheeks.

Ah, so you've got more than *one* deep wound, I realized, feeling as evil as those she-monsters who used to torment me at Pinnacle. But I have to admit, now that I'd tasted a little of their power, it felt truly intoxicating.

Especially when the handsomest creature in the solar system was standing right in front of me with sunshine glinting off his flaxen hair and pure, unadulterated vulnerability in his eyes.

Creek stiffened his back and swelled his chest a little, appearing tall and tough as nails, like usual. But I knew his secret now. He had a heart that had been broken once, and might still be in pieces—and I intended to exploit each and every shard in my favor.

"Just what do you propose we do as partners?" Creek persisted with an edge to his voice, a bit too eager to divert my attention from that scar on his arm.

I sucked up a deep breath.

Oh, maybe make out till next Tuesday! I wanted to say, hoping he hadn't somehow heard my thoughts on a breeze.

But really, that face and physique all in one package? Truly God does display a twisted sense of humor on us poor girls.

I shook my head to try and regain my focus.

"Um . . . how about rob banks?" I blurted in a quick save, hardly believing those words came out of my mouth. "I mean, think about it—after just a couple of big hits, we could be set. Right? No more money troubles."

"Like that whopping three-hundred-fifty bucks you got from Home and Hearth?" he taunted, shaking his head. "High roller, Silver Spoon."

Boy, oh boy—I was pissed off now.

"For your information, that three-fifty was better than what you hauled in, as I recall. And if it weren't for the Miata I, uh—borrowed—you wouldn't have gotten the seven hundred, either. So don't be callin' me Silver Spoon. I've earned my keep."

"Then what should I call you?" Creek interrupted, leaning in closer to me. I could feel his eyes traveling over my ridiculously too-tight clothes, lingering on the tender curves they revealed, as if they'd been freshly picked just for him. Then the warmth of his breath brushed against my ear, sending every nerve ending I had on high alert.

"Jail bait?" he whispered.

Until that very moment, I didn't think it was scientifically possible for every single skin cell in my body to blush in unison. Nevertheless, I'm quite sure that even my bare midriff had turned a bright, cherry red.

Dammit! Creek had totally derailed me with that one. But I still had some fight left in me.

"Isn't that what you wanted?" I replied, slipping up my hand to skim the scar on his bicep. "After all, *you* brought me these threads."

There it was—a slight pink to his cheeks again. And I was all ready for round two, when I saw Creek's blue eyes narrow a little.

"Look, your little private-school getup was a dead give away," he stated flatly. "And so was that shiny, red convertible—it had an electronic tracer. You're lucky the cops hadn't caught up with you yet, Hot Pants."

I blushed in equal measure.

"But I do kinda get your point," he said grudgingly. "We both have folks to look after here, and we're the only breadwinners they've got left. So listen up. I'll try giving you a test run. There's a small store with an ATM that has lousy surveillance up the road. I've been casing it for weeks, and it's an easy hit. With any luck, we could get a decent haul—if we play our cards right and don't use weapons while we're still young enough not to face federal time."

F-Federal time? I thought, queasy at the very sound of the term. That's right, I realized, this is hard-core crime we're talking about.

Up until now, it had all been kind of a lark for me—a rollicking daytrip away from the iron chains that had kept me imprisoned at Pinnacle. But with all of the deep shit my father was in right now, and the fact that I couldn't even qualify for a job that didn't include peddling drugs or turning tricks, suddenly robbery seemed like the cleanest option.

"You're on, partner!" I burst emphatically, before I could dare to let myself chicken out. I mean, what other choices did I really have? "But from now on, you call me Robin."

"Sure," Creek replied casually, even though he was staring me down with his glacial blue eyes to test my courage. "So meet me back in these woods tomorrow morning at six o'clock, sharp. No more sleeping in till noon. We've got work to do."

He turned and walked away.

And I absolutely hated myself for thinking it, but even his back side was beautiful.

Just as he'd entered a really dark patch of shadows, and I thought he might slip away entirely, he hesitated for a moment and glanced back.

"By the way," he said with steel in his voice, "I man the getaway vehicle from here on out. Got that? 'Cause you drive like shit."

Chapter 7

By the time I found my way back to the clearing at Turtle Shores, I was still shaking. Holy Moses, near as I could tell, I'd just closed a deal with the Devil! He was a drop-dead gorgeous Devil, I had to admit, and I think that's what scared me even more.

But if I didn't do something serious about my cash flow, these trashy clothes I had on weren't just going to be a trailer park joke—they'd be the story of my life. And I'd probably end up pregnant at 16 with a dozen crummy tattoos all over my body and only two teeth left after getting strung-out on meth.

Yet as I neared our trailer, the thought *did* occur to me that if it hadn't been for Creek hiding him in a bunker last night, my dad might've been nabbed by the mob. Or cops could've traced us to the Mazda, and we'd both be in the slammer.

Why did everything have to be so complicated? Creek was good/bad, bad/good—which one was it?

I halted in front of our trailer door and shook my head.

Maybe that's not the right question, I thought. Maybe I just need to shut down my emotions and get all the money I can, as fast as I can, and sort out reality later.

I took a deep breath and braced myself to face Brandi before I opened the door, knowing she was probably playing a rousing hand of cards with my dad by now. Hopefully, it wasn't strip poker.

But when I swung the door open, Brandi was nowhere to be found.

In fact, my dad was all stretched out, asleep again on the couch. I noticed that the plate of ham and beans sat empty on the small table beside him, so Brandi must've succeeded in feeding him something. Stepping inside, I gazed at my father, who looked so cozy with Granny's colorful patchwork quilt wrapped around him like a cocoon. His face appeared sweet and innocent, with none of the "Crocodile Cunning" that had made him so famous at Tweedle, Beckman & McArthur.

Hesitantly, I crouched down in front him and pushed aside a wisp of hair that had fallen across his forehead. It felt strange to stroke his warm skin and feel the slight perspiration on his brow—to touch his face at all, for that matter. I mean, this was the man who'd never even bothered to give me a fatherly peck on the cheek, let alone read me a bedtime story or tuck me in at night.

"Was I really so unlovable, Daddy?" I whispered, my voice splintering a little. "Or were you just too obsessed with work all those years to ever notice me?"

Inside, I half-hoped he might fess up for once to his role in our pathetic family tragedy, even though he always pretended it didn't matter, since he made more money than God. So when his breathing hitched for a second, it sent my heart racing.

I leaned in closer, eager to hear if he might have some witty explanation for himself. But all he did was release a long, slow breath, accompanied by a ragged snore.

Of course!

Who was I to think that the great Royle McArthur, the most blood-thirsty law shark ever to circle for the kill in Cincinnati, would lower himself to give *me* an answer?

That is, if there even was such a thing as Royle McArthur.

Or shall I say, *Doyle*—

I stared at his crumpled, sleepy face and slid my hand from his forehead down to his cheek, gently patting it with my palm.

"Who are you, Daddy?" I asked, secretly wishing it was possible for me to feel his soul before he woke up and put on one of his clever masks again. No sooner did my fingers release his cheek when I heard him mumble.

"Alay-seeee-ahhh," he said, somewhere between a call and a moan.

"Myyy . . . Alay-seeee-ahhh . . ."

In that moment, his expression became stern, and I swear his voice sounded rocky and almost a little . . . haunted, as though his mind was searching for something precious he'd lost.

And I couldn't tell if maybe he was having a nightmare, or if he was physically ailing.

"Daddy?" I jiggled him a little. "Y-You okay? Should we get you to a doctor?"

His lashes fluttered. Then I saw his eyes barely open a crack. He appeared groggy, as if he were somewhere very far away. As he struggled to focus on my features, taking in the curve of my forehead and cheeks, all at once his eyes grew as big as silver dollars.

Bolstering himself with his good arm beneath him, he managed to pitch his body upright.

Whoa—my dad stared at me, wide-eyed, like he'd just seen a ghost.

"Alay-see-ahh?" he gasped, his face turning a little pale.

There was such a sad yearning in his voice, like his heart was . . . breaking.

"Amorrrey . . . amorrrey mio!"

Beads of sweat shone on his forehead now. Shaking, he reached out his good hand to touch my cheek, a bit wary, as if he wasn't quite sure whether I was real.

"Myyy . . . Alay-see-ahh . . ."

With a deep release from his chest, my father sighed as though the mere sound of those words had filled him up with a golden light. And for the first time ever, I saw his eyes actually sparkle, as if he'd just caught sight of an angel.

Oh Lord, I thought, if only I could bottle the way he's looking at me right now, and keep it till the end of time.

Because it was pure . . . *love*.

And I wanted to throw my arms around him right then and there.

But I couldn't, because I was too mesmerized by the way it felt to have my very own father caress my cheek, like . . . like—

He genuinely cared about me.

And then his eyes welled up.

"Where . . . arrrrre . . . yooou?" he struggled to say. A couple of tears slipped down his cheek, slowly dripping onto his purple paisley collar.

"I-I'm right here, Daddy," I answered, my eyes moistening up, too. "It's me, Robin—remember? We drove from Cincinnati to Bender Lake. Yesterday."

"Baby?"

My dad's gaze traced the inside of our trailer for a few seconds before returning to settle on my face.

"Baby girrrl?"

"Yeah, Daddy," I snuffled, struck by the tender way he'd said those words, as though maybe he'd kept me cradled in his heart all along, but I just never knew it. "I'm your daughter. Your Robin. Do you feel all right?"

Without warning, the color in my dad's face blanched from a shallow pink to an almost green. And before I could stop him, he began to hurl at the orange shag rug in our trailer, covering his brand new shoes with regurgitated bits of ham and beans.

"Oh, Daddy," I cried, "you've emptied your whole lunch! And you got your nice shoes all messy, too."

Fortunately, Granny's quilt had escaped his path of vomit. I swiftly grabbed a towel that was hanging on the oven handle with the words *Buckeye Motel* printed on it.

"Here you go," I said, vigorously wiping off his brown, lace-up oxfords. Underneath the puke, I could see they were a burnished mahogany with dapper wing tips—they must've cost a fortune.

"They look as good as new, now. Creek brought you these shoes," I paused, still feeling scared to death and yet grateful to the guy at the same time. "So you wouldn't have to go barefoot anymore."

"Gooth . . . booey," my dad nodded with a smile.

"What?"

"Goood . . . boyyyy," he repeated emphatically.

Oh—good boy, I realized. "Um, yeah, I guess," I shrugged, giving his shoes a few extra swipes. "Kinda depends on how you look at it."

My dad stared for a while at his feet, admiring the luxurious leather while I mopped up the rest of his goopy vomit. I held my nose and tossed the towel into a trash can. Reaching for a paper towel on the kitchen counter, I cleaned off my hands as best I could and dropped it in the sink, then gently patted my dad on the knee.

"He, um—he hid you last night, didn't he, Daddy?"

"Whoooo?" My dad replied.

I stood up and swallowed hard, refusing to fall for one of my dad's slick maneuvers again. This was exactly the kind of evasive response that he always resorted to whenever I asked him a direct question during my childhood that he didn't feel like answering.

"You know *who*, so don't start acting dumb with me," I said flatly. "Creek. He hid you from the mob last night, huh? So what have you gotten yourself into this time, *Doyle?*"

Immediately, my father tilted up his chin, and I saw his face magically turn to stone—a granite composure that I'm quite sure he'd used a bazillion times to beat down his Cincinnati law competitors. And he might have appeared unreadeable to the ordinary layman, but I was his daughter— and I could see the cornered possum look in his eyes. Mean as sin, like usual, but equally scared.

He didn't fool me at all.

I had the upper hand now, and he knew it.

Folding my arms, I sighed. "You can start by explaining the name Doyle, Daddy. Apparently, there's a forty-plus chick around here named Granny Tinker who claims she's your cousin? As in, you grew up in these woods?"

I was hoping to make him crumble. To make him confess his roots and illegal pursuits and spit out our real family history, if our surname was even McArthur at all. And who on earth was my true mother, anyway? He'd always dismissed her as some high-society floozy named "Bitsy" who'd taken off with a Chilean mountain climber right after I was born. And he claimed that she and her Latin lover had fallen to their deaths in the Andes at 12,000 feet into a fissure of ice.

So of course there were no graves, or even markers! How could I have been such an idiot and bought that ridiculous story? I should have known it was just another one of his tall tales.

Tapping my foot, I kept up my unyielding glare at my dad. All the while, I couldn't help wondering if my real mom could be this Alessia he'd been dreaming so passionately about? Or had I simply been placed in a basket and dropped off one day on his doorstep by some forgotten lover? Good God, she might have even been a white trash chick from Turtle Shores . . .

I was close to vomiting myself now.

And knowing my dad—or who I used to think was my dad—anything was possible. But unfortunately, I wasn't about to find out now. Because instead of caving in to my demand, my father's gaze froze into mine with the most rigid stare I'd ever seen in my life. It actually made me shiver.

And then his lips tightened and puckered a little, as if he were working with all his might to form his words just right.

"Wobbinnnn," he said in a weighty growl that I'd honestly never heard from him before. He lifted his good arm and swallowed my fingers in his. His grip became so tight that it made me wince.

"Creeeek . . . a . . .verrry . . . goooood . . . boy."

He sucked on his lip for a moment and inhaled a big breath.

"Gooood . . . boyy."

His lower lip quivered in a small spasm, then jerked awkwardly back into place so he could talk again.

"Don't . . . break . . . hizz . . . hearrrrrt."

My father's words kept ricocheting around in my brain as I carefully escorted him across the Turtle Shores compound. What made him think I could possibly break Creek's heart? I mean, the guy was a backwoods Adonis! Had my dad somehow spied that scar on Creek's heart tattoo and made a quick assumption, like I did? Or was this his weird way of telling me that he thought I'd grown up to be pretty?

I sighed and kept a firm grip on my father's elbow, unable to sort out the mystery behind his meaning. Like usual, whenever I tried to understand him better, he always played a slick shell game on me.

Figures, I thought. No wonder he was a successful lawyer.

Glancing up, I peered across the meadow to try and find the whereabouts of Lorraine's trailer. I was hoping she might have a little more food left for my dad, because I feared he might grow too weak on his now empty stomach. Maybe she had something less heavy than ham and beans—like chicken soup, or crackers? Squinting hard, I studied every tree, bush, and boulder that lined the perimeter, wondering which ones might actually camouflage Lorraine's place. All the while, I had to watch our every step to make sure we didn't slip into one of the TNT Twins' holes. But by the time I managed to slowly shuffle my dad across the entire compound without plunging into a single vat of pudding or jello, I still hadn't spotted a thing. Then all of a sudden, I felt my dad stiffen and tug on my arm. He leaned his body to the left with all of his weight.

"Thizzzzss . . . wayyy," he insisted.

"Okay, this way?" I nodded, allowing him to pull me towards a large stand of maple trees. As we grew closer, just beyond them, I could see an old pile of chopped wood that was stacked six logs high and covered with moss. Behind the wood pile, for a fleeting second, I thought I saw sunlight glint off a piece of chrome beneath some overgrown bushes. My dad continued towards it like it was due north on his internal GPS, and sure enough, the most glorious aroma on earth wafted past us.

Oh my Lord —

Warm apples . . . with a hint of cinnamon and vanilla . . . followed by the rich, buttery scent of a golden-baked crust.

Sweet Mother of God, it smelled like paradise!

I was weak at the knees before I even knew what hit me — and ready to compete with my dad in the drool department — because I hadn't had a single thing to eat all day. And in my eagerness, I pressed on past the woodpile to the bushes, lugging at my dad to get closer to the source of what surely must be homemade apple pie. Just when I was lucky enough to spot another hint of chrome that I thought for certain revealed

Lorraine's trailer, I stumbled over a metal trip wire covered by leaves and bit the ground. Within seconds, a fleet of orange beaks were ripping at my knees and elbows.

"Ow—Ow!" I yelped, flailing my arms. I forced myself to peek past the geese to locate my dad, who was fortunately still standing and out of harm's way. "Attack Geese! Back off!" I cried, covering my face. "Tell them to back off, Daddy!"

"ZZZSSSSSSSSSSS!"

I heard a gigantic hissing sound, and instantly I feared that the Colonel might have unleashed boa constrictors to aid his bizarre animal defense squad. Just my luck, to get squeezed to death after being bloodied by a blur of beaks in this crazy Trailer Park from Hell—

"ZZZSSSSSSSSSSS!"

The sound was even louder and more insistent this time.

And to my surprise, the Attack Geese backed up, honking indignantly.

Panting, I sat up on my elbows, eyeing the hostile flock that reluctantly stepped a few feet away from me with their wings raised and surly looks on their faces. Another big "Zzzsssssss" cut through the air, and I glanced at my dad, shocked to discover that *he* was the source of the sound.

Then, in a dramatic, sweeping motion, my father lifted his good arm like a mighty, outstretched wing. The geese honked nasty retorts, tossing their beaks in offense. But when he reached over to grab his limp arm and hiked it up, hissing again as he let both limbs fall back to his sides in a big wave, it sent the geese flying. They stormed off into a thicket of bushes, rattling the leaves until they were out of sight.

Shaken, I stood to my feet and dusted the leaves and dirt off.

And then I couldn't stop myself from giggling.

I mean, really Daddy. Playing "Alpha Goose," complete with hisses and pretend wings? Where'd he learn that one, from Old Mother Hubbard? The nasty expression that still clung to his face made him look like the fiercest, badass gander ever to hit these boondocks.

And just then, my dad caught the amused look in my eyes and started to chuckle, too. He smiled and winked at me, clearly proud of himself.

"Geezss . . . arrr . . . dummm," he slurred.

Geese are dumb—

Yep, I nodded, scanning the red welts on my arms. But that didn't mean their bites hurt any less.

When I glanced back up at my dad, he pointed to a tall mound of bushes.

"Low-wayne," he asserted.

He rubbed his tummy as if he were a happy Buddha and motioned to the bushes once more.

Oh, Lorraine's place, I comprehended. And just as I'd hoped, he aimed at the nearby overgrowth of honeysuckle laced with about a million strands of ivy. I stepped over to my dad and grabbed his elbow again, directing him to the source of that heavenly aroma. When we reached the bushes, my dad pushed aside the dense foliage to reveal a metal door painted in shades of green and brown.

Camo colors, I realized. Reaching out, I tried to pull open the handle, but it was locked. Then my stomach growled impatiently, so I gave the door a hard knock.

Nothing, not even honking Attack Geese this time.

"Um, well, I guess she's not home," I said apologetically, feeling awful that I'd made my dad walk all that way.

My father rolled his eyes and sighed.

And when I lifted my hand to knock again, he grabbed it and shook his head like he thought I was simple.

"But you *said* this was Lorraine's place," I reminded him, confused.

My dad nodded, appearing weary.

He released my arm and made a big fist. Then he knocked on the metal door slowly three times, before giving it a series of hard, sharp raps in rhythmic succession, almost like Morse Code.

I bit my lip. Could that be a secret signal?

Hesitantly, the metal door squeaked open.

"Creek? That you?" A shaky voice remarked from the darkness inside the trailer. "You got that sack a flour, hon? I wadn't expecting you in broad daylight."

A woman peeked her long nose out, stepping forward so that the sunlight sliced across her face. I could see she was mere skin and bones, in her forties maybe, wearing an old t-shirt and jeans that were swimming on her. Her dishwater-blonde hair was pulled back in a bun and her eyes were as flat as gray stones.

That couldn't be Lorraine, I thought. With the way she cooked, I'd assumed she was a bubbly, 400-pound gal in a tent-sized, tropical moo-moo.

Suddenly, the woman lifted her nose to the air and sniffed. She turned to my dad, but her gaze seemed to travel right through him. Then she leaned a little closer and inhaled another deep whiff. Her nose twitched for a second, as if she were detecting something unusual, and her face crinkled into a wide smile that revealed no teeth.

"Well I'll be damned—if it t'aint Doyle McCracken!"

McCracken?! I gasped, horrified at the hillbilly-sounding name.

The woman reached out her skinny arms. "How you been, cousin? Up to no good, I expect!"

She gave my father a surprisingly tight squeeze, considering her fragile frame. Then she swept her bony fingers over his face, lingering on his forehead, nose and chin. When her hands settled upon his temples, she seemed to register the limp muscles on the right side of his face. Her wrinkled cheeks fell slack, as though she'd been able to read his whole life story in that single moment. I saw my dad's face turn red in shame.

"Family is forever, honey," she asserted kindly, patting him on the shoulder, "no matter what. Don't you never forget that."

My father nodded, but I couldn't help noticing that he refused to look my way.

And the God's honest truth was, I was trembling in my shoes.

What the hell?

Who on earth has a name like McCracken?

Not a single designer label in the universe had a name that hokey, much less anyone at Pinnacle. And it didn't escape my attention that my dad knew exactly where Lorraine's trailer was, as well as the secret knock. How could Lorraine and Granny Tinker both be my dad's cousins—was *everyone* in this backwoods Freakville related?

I leaned over and clutched my knees for all I was worth, feeling like the wind had been knocked out of me.

Oh my God, I panicked—if my last name really is McCracken, then what about my first name? Is Robin a lie, too?

Straightening up, I began to hyperventilate and my forehead got all sweaty. Just when I thought I was about to pass out, I felt Lorraine's hands caress my hair. Her fingers gently sifted through the strands like she thought they were made of fine silk.

"Lordy, Doyle," she said in a hushed tone that was so sincere it bordered on religious, "did you bring back our sweet Alessia?"

I almost fainted in shock.

That was the very same name that had been so passionately on my father's lips.

And when I turned to my dad, I discovered that he had tears streaming down his cheeks.

He shook his head resolutely, squeezing his eyes shut, as if he were trying to block out the whole world—including his mysterious past. His silence seemed to speak volumes to Lorraine.

Without warning, Lorraine pressed her fingertips hard onto my forehead, kneading my skin as if she were working dough. Naturally, I jerked back little, but she held my head firm, probing my cheekbones, jaw, and chin as though she could read the map of my soul. Her hands felt surprisingly strong, and yet soft, too—perhaps conditioned by years of handling bacon grease and lard. Finally, she traced the bridge of my nose and fanned out her fingers to cup my cheeks.

"No . . . yer skin's much too smooth, darlin', like a Georgia peach. An' young as a brand new day. Our Alessia would have to be in her thirties by now, I reckon. So you must be that girl who's the talk of Turtle Shores."

"The-the talk?" I said, startled.

"Yes ma'am. You're the one Granny Tinker's been prayin' for. She told us all a few weeks ago you were comin'—to help Creek take care of us. She done some special kind of voodoo to conjure you."

Now it was my turn to blush.

And even though Lorraine was as blind as a bat, her mouth broke into a big toothless grin, as if she'd expected to feel the heat coming from my cheeks. She gave my chin one last tweak before she finally released her hands. I saw her ball them into fists that she perched onto her bony hips.

"Well don't jes stand there!" she ordered good naturedly. "Sit yer bag o' bones down right now and help us peel some more apples."

Lorraine pointed to a couple of old rockers with chipped paint that sat in a gap in the bushes near her trailer. I hadn't noticed them before, but a very shaggy man in a gray jumpsuit with crazy, google eyes and hair the color of dust sat in one of the chairs. He had a long, scary hunting knife in his hand, and he waved it at me before he bent down to pick out fruit from a wooden barrel.

"Bixby cain't hardly keep up with all the apples Creek brought yesterday," Lorraine smiled. "So I aim to jar a heap of applesauce tonight after I'm done baking. Believe me, soon as you taste a slice of my apple pie a-la-modey style, I guarantee you'll be happier than pigs in mud."

Chapter 8

I pounded on Granny Tinker's gypsy wagon door with everything I had in me, and then I gave it a swift kick.

"How dare you voodoo me here!" I hollered, mad as hell. "You had no right! My life used to be wonderful. Do you hear me? Wonderful!!"

My chest heaved to catch my breath because I was on a roll now. Two whole pieces of Lorraine's pie with ice cream on top had energized me enough to face an army. And I intended to make Granny pay for this.

"Wonderful, eh?" A husky voice replied from out of nowhere. "Then explain to me why you ain't hitchhiked outta here yet?"

I nearly leaped to the moon.

"Unless you're a lyin' sack a you-know-what. Somethin' tells me you wouldn't know wonderful if it came up from behind and bit you."

"Huh? Where are you?" I demanded, whipping around so fast I got dizzy, only to stare at the same old trees and bushes. The curtain to Granny's wagon window was closed, and it didn't seem like the sound had come from there. I peered between the nearby bushes, but I didn't spy so much as a quivering shadow. Stomping my foot, I shook my fist in the air.

"C'mon, you coward—show yourself!"

Another quick one-eighty, just for good measure, turned up nothing. Then I felt a tap on my shoulder.

Jumping back, I clutched my chest, relieved to see it was just an acorn that had toppled to the ground. After all, Granny Tinker could be awfully spooky up close.

But then two more plop-plops hit my shoulders, followed by a heavy thunk to my forehead.

Blinking a couple of times, I rubbed the sore spot, when I heard a familiar cackle along with a surge of childish giggles. Suddenly, my face met a shower of acorns.

"Hey, stop it!" I yelped, expecting to see a vast troop of vicious squirrels—nothing about the Colonel's animal defense squad could surprise me anymore.

But I should have known. Instead of scrappy squirrels, I spotted Granny Tinker and Dooley perched on top of her gypsy wagon. They were sitting cross-legged with burning incense sticks beside them, like they'd been . . . meditating?

"What the f—"

"Don't you dare say a word like that in front of this child!" Granny Tinker scolded, covering Dooley's ears. "Do you want me to wash yer mouth out with my lemon-spider leg soap?"

I gasped and shook my head violently.

"Then I suggest ya clean up your speech right now and git on up here."

"Huh?" I said, floored. "Why?"

"Don't ya wanna new perspective?" Granny Tinker smiled, her gold front tooth glistening in the afternoon sun. "Honey, if you don't git some understandin' pretty soon, yer never gonna find out who you are or why yer really here. So I suggest you climb up my ladder, pronto."

Granny released that cackle again—the one that could send shivers down my back in an instant and quite possibly scare zombies.

I shook my head, feeling completely insane, and stepped up to her rickety, wooden ladder on the side of her wagon, afraid that if I didn't follow Granny's orders, she might cast even more creepy spells my way. Hesitantly, I tested the first rung with my foot, and it seemed to hold my weight okay, so I scrambled to the top before the ladder could snap. Breathless, I stood on Granny's roof, surprised to see that she'd covered the entire length with her faded quilts. In the center was her crystal ball within a circle of smoking incense sticks and shriveled animals' paws that looked like they'd been mummified about a century ago. The sight made my breath hitch, and then I saw her crystal ball turn a deep, blood red—

"Welcome home, *Rubina*," Granny said with a roll of her tongue. "I ain't seen you in broad daylight since the day you were born. And even that was through my crystal ball."

She didn't laugh at me this time.

In fact, her gray and yellow eyes seemed like a world of . . . sadness.

And I'm pretty sure that's what slayed my heart the most and made the tears brim my eyes. Because other than my dad earlier that day, I'd never seen a single person in my whole life look at me so piercingly, as if she already knew me to the bone.

"Ru-Rubina?" I stuttered, trying to adjust to the sound of that strange word. I slowly lowered myself down to sit on her rooftop before my trembling legs could buckle beneath me. "P-please don't fool with me, Granny," I begged. "Is th-that my real name?"

Granny reached out to gently stroke Dooley's white-blonde hair, giving him a loving smile.

"Sweetheart," she said to him kindly, pointing across the compound to Lorraine's trailer. "Look over yonder. Bixby and Doyle sure could use yer help peeling all them apples Creek brought. Why don't ya git along now and give 'em a hand?"

Dooley nodded, and in a flash he sprinted across the length of Granny's rooftop and leaped into thin air—

And I screamed till I thought I was going to puke my guts out.

Cringing, I covered my eyes, because I couldn't bear to see what had become of poor Dooley! That is, until I felt Granny Tinker's strong fingers rip away my hands and yank me to my feet.

"For Heaven's sake, child," she said, standing before me. "Look with yer own eyes."

She motioned to the tree canopy, level with her wagon rooftop, where Dooley was skipping happily along wooden planks that connected tree to tree, like the suspended boards you see at zoo exhibits for chimpanzees. My mouth dropped in shock, until I felt Granny's lace-covered fingers lift my chin and set it back into place.

And there was that cackle again.

"Jes' like yer Ma!" Granny smiled. "She always did scare a bit easy, comin' from that high falutin' family an' all. Amazing what folks will try to conquer fer true love."

"My mother?" I gasped.

I don't know what came over me, but I bravely grabbed Granny by her black-velvet shoulders and shook her in desperation. "Who was she Granny? Is she still alive? Is her name Alessia? Tell me the truth!"

To my astonishment, Granny held herself erect and sealed her eyes tight, as though she were meditating on some far-off radio signal that ordinary mortals couldn't hear.

And when she opened her eyes, she studied my face for the longest time, till I got so nervous I could feel my palms breaking into a sweat. Her lips curled into a knowing smile, flashing her gold front tooth.

"Have you done *earned* the truth?"

"Earned?" I replied. "What kind of question is—"

Boldly, Granny grabbed my jeans by the belt loops and spun me around to face the compound.

"Tell me what you see," she commanded.

I wanted to spit out *A freaky white-trash wasteland*, but I didn't dare. I took a deep breath and glanced around, scanning the bizarre number of wooden planks and tree stands that rimmed the forest canopy, which I'd never really noticed before. Not to mention the homemade catapults, trebuchets, and spud cannons that lined the compound on the ground. But from this height, I suddenly realized it was easier to identify where all the trailers were, each one covered in live shrubs and vines like an overgrown Chia Pet.

Granny gave me a forceful jiggle, making my mind race to figure out what she wanted to hear.

"Um, well," I confessed, "I can see everybody's trailer, plus a couple of cars up on blocks and an old, rusty washing machine."

She swiveled me around to stare me in the eye.

"Lord have mercy," Granny sighed. "Right there's yer trouble. You don't feel anybody."

"Feel?" I shook my head, bewildered. "Granny, I'm not exactly psychic, like you—"

"Ain't you gotta heart?" she barked defiantly. Granny gave me one of those looks again that could cut right through your chest and lay your soul out in pieces.

I nodded, trembling a little. "Yeah. I mean, I think so."

"Then prove it. Look again, honey."

And God knows why, but she took what appeared to be loose ashes out of her pocket and promptly blew them into my face.

Coughing, I fanned frantically at the smoky air. Then I tried to swallow and focus, squinting again at the compound just to get this over with.

And before I knew it, goose bumps sped down my limbs.

Because all of a sudden, I saw them.

I mean, really *saw* them—

There was Bixby and Dooley and my dad sitting on old rockers. They were laughing their heads off around a wooden barrel as they threw their apple peels for distance like they didn't have a care in the world. Lorraine ducked her head out of her trailer and yelled at them to stop their racket and hurry up, but that just made them laugh all the more. Dooley finally fell off his chair in a fit of giggles.

And then there was the Colonel at the edge of the meadow, waving a big stick in the air at his Attack Geese until they fell into single file. He blew a whistle, and they obediently trotted through a ridiculous little obstacle course made out of rocks, sticks, and mud tunnels. Afterwards, he bent down and patted each one on the head. I could have sworn I saw his geese smile.

Oh, and at a very loud count of three, I heard the TNT Twins furiously ram a narrow log into one of their cannons, tumbling head over heels when they struck the end. For a second they looked delirious, and then they scrambled to their feet and let out a whoop, celebrating with an awkward-looking Boogie. God only knows what they were going to blow up next.

Yet surprisingly, the only one who didn't appear to be enjoying herself was the usually effervescent Brandi. I saw her stretched out on a faded chaise lounge in the shade, her limbs flopped at uncomfortable angles, as if she didn't so much as lay down for a nap as she collapsed. Her fire-hydrant red wig had slipped a little, revealing her pink, bald head.

"Wow, I guess everybody's pretty busy," I said, turning to Granny. "Except, you know, Brandi—"

"That's 'cause she's plum exhausted," Granny cut in, "with her chemo and all. She's dying, honey."

I swallowed hard, feeling a lump rise in my throat because I knew it was the truth. I'd seen Brandi's gray pallor myself. And as much as I pretended not to like her overwhelming friendliness, she had been nice to me. I mean, genuinely nice— with no mean-girl thought of kickbacks later—for no good reason other than it was in her nature. And try as I might, I couldn't think of a single person at Pinnacle who'd ever bothered to treat me that way. I sighed, feeling Granny set her hand on my shoulder.

"Why in tarnation do ya think Creek works so hard?" Granny said. "And even started casing banks? We're a family here at Turtle Shores. But if we cain't get more money soon for Brandi's treatments, she ain't gonna be with us much longer, darlin'. You know, Brandi's the one who raised Dooley like her own ever since Creek's Ma passed. And she's always been the first to pony up any time somebody needed a cavity filled, or a new engine part, or just more food on the table. A big heart like hers deserves better'n this."

All of a sudden I shivered a little, even though we were standing together in the heat of afternoon sun, and my thoughts started spinning. This was a whole new world to me—one without health insurance, or any guarantees for that matter—but where people actually cared about each other. Even if it meant breaking the law.

And it couldn't be farther from my uptight life at Pinnacle than the other side of the moon.

I looked down at my feet, studying a star pattern on one of Granny's old quilts beneath my sneakers and wondering how it was possible that I'd landed in a place that was the polar opposite of everything I'd ever known, almost like yin and yang.

And that's when I felt Granny's lace-covered hand grab mine and squeeze, as if she were imparting strength.

"Ain't you missing something, honey?" she said, her voice low and insistent.

I lifted my gaze and shrugged my shoulders, unsure.

Granny turned to stare at Bender Lake. "That there's a mighty big big body of water in front of you."

I nodded, taking a deep breath. She was right—the lake stretched out before us like a sheet of glass. Not even a ripple broke its smooth, shiny surface.

"Once you cross over that lake with Creek tomorrow, honey, yer life ain't never gonna be the same."

"B-But how did you know about our pact?" I gasped. Then, from the corner of my eye, I spotted her crystal ball, which was slowly changing color to a sky blue like it had been saturated with spooky ink. It was the very same hue as Bender Lake—

Granny stared into my eyes.

"Sweetheart," she said gravely, "it warn't me who prayed you here. It was Creek."

She waited for her words to trickle into my brain, watching the astonishment surface in my eyes.

"He needs help like nobody's business to keep us all together, he just won't admit it. But any fool can see it takes more'n one person to get the kind of cash Brandi needs to survive. So let's just say maybe I helped him along a little with what I know."

Granny's eyes twinkled at the spirals of smoke that rose from her incense sticks, even though they'd nearly burned down to their brass holders.

"Besides," she said with a mischievous grin, "bringing you back to yer real home, where yer Pa found the only true love of his life, was the very least I could do fer our dear Alessia."

Chapter 9

"Alessia . . ."

"Alessia . . ."

I let the word roll softly off my tongue over and over again like a prayer.

For some reason it comforted me, even if the whole "mother" idea turned out to be nothing but wishful thinking, or knowing my dad, a downright hoax. The name just sounded so lovely on my lips, as if it belonged to an angelic being with shimmering wings who might offer protection when I least expected it.

And an angel was precisely what I needed right now.

Because at almost sunrise, the woods around Bender Lake were blacker than the inside of a broom closet—I know this for a fact from the time mean-girl Bree Cox locked me behind the janitor's door before fifth-period Biology at Pinnacle. And with every stick that split beneath my feet, my heart bolted inside my chest, and I wanted to rocket as high as the stars that still twinkled overhead. To make matters worse, the closer I got to the spot where Creek said we were supposed to meet at dawn, the more I heard a peculiar, whispering sound.

It could be just the forest leaves scuffling in the breeze.

Or the noise of birds as they rise and stir in their nests.

Unless Creek had stationed the TNT Twins and the Attack Geese to patrol my every move, and they were getting downright restless.

Feeling paranoid, I rotated on my heels just to make sure no one was sneaking up behind me. It was a reasonable maneuver, considering how many times I'd been pelted or bitten in this God forsaken place.

But who was I kidding?

I couldn't see a soul in the ink-black darkness, and for all I knew, I might've just ventured in circles.

Then I felt something soft whisk across my cheek.

Startled, I reached up and grasped a . . . feather?

I stroked it between my fingers, struck by how silky it felt, when I saw a warm, shaft of light glimmer between the trees.

Thank God there was something I could still depend on! The sun—my oldest and most loyal friend—had faithfully inched a little over the horizon, just enough to cast a thin ray that peeked through the forest at my feet.

And that's when I noticed another feather.

Small and white, like the first one. And the very second I leaned down to pick it up, I heard the whispers again.

Oh Lord, I begged, please don't let it be Granny Tinker casting another weird spell.

I glanced up, fully prepared to see a whole network of planks and platforms high in the trees with Granny, Dooley, or Creek staring back at me, probably laughing.

But all I saw was another feather swaying ever so slowly to the ground.

As if it had fallen from a wing—

An angel's wing.

And again, more whispers.

Where were they coming from?

No sooner did I have that thought when another shaft of light pierced through the trees. Suddenly, I could see a trail of small, white feathers illuminated on the forest floor, as though quietly leading me toward dawn.

And before I could blink, there he was.

Creek.

Backlit by the soft rays of the rising sun.

I knew he was facing me, but his features were shadowy in the lingering darkness. Yet there was no mistaking the broad silhouette of his shoulders and strong legs, or the golden hues created by the morning rays on his wayward blonde hair.

I stood in my tracks, unable to say a word.

He was so devastatingly beautiful, his form highlighted in the early light, as though he'd somehow been created fresh, just for that very moment by a higher power.

A cruel higher power who knew exactly how to tear a girl's heart out.

I shifted my weight and straightened up as tall as I could, a pillar of strength so no gorgeous piece of Trailer Trash could possibly get under my skin.

And I saw him take a bold step towards me.

He whispered something and held up his hand to release another white feather, watching as it was swept up by a soft breeze.

"She hears you, you know," he called out.

The forest was so quiet that I felt as though his words had delicately slipped into my ears, echoing softly. And I hated to admit it, but I already adored the sound of his voice—so smoky and serious for a guy his age, compared to the flippant, arrogant tones I always heard from the boys at Breton. I clenched my fists, hoping to barricade my heart a little, when I saw Creek lean his head back, relishing the simple warmth of the sun that had begun to envelop him in light.

I swallowed hard, just savoring the sight.

Because it took all of my willpower not to be slayed by his handsome presence in that pastel light. Drawing in a deep breath, I worked up my nerve to respond.

"Who?" I taunted, crossing my arms to act tough. "Who hears us out here—the sun?" Maybe he scatters feathers for a morning ritual, I thought, that Granny had taught him to bring good luck. There was no end to her mysterious ways.

Creek raked his hand through his long hair, warmed now to the color of butter, and he shook his head.

He allowed the silence to hover between us, waiting.

And in that moment, the morning air suddenly felt heavier to me, as if the particles of mist that had collected at my feet had started to swell. A few birds chimed, their voices sharp and eager for dawn. Then a gentle breeze picked up and tousled my hair like unseen fingers—

"Your mother," Creek said.

His words sliced straight into my heart. And then twisted.

What the hell would *he* know about my mother?

"There are no secrets in trailer parks."

Creek took brisk strides towards me, and in that instant, I wished I could sink into one of the TNT Twins' holes after all. Tingles rifled my cheeks, but I stood my ground, realizing the sun was probably illuminating every feature of my face by now, so I'd better not cower. I slung my hand on my hip, pretending to be nonchalant, until he walked up to within inches of my face. He cupped both hands and held them out to me like an offering.

And in them were feathers.

Downy and white, with sand dusting their edges.

"Prayers," he nodded.

His voice was so tender that I felt as though he'd invisibly caressed my cheek.

"Because they hear us, Robin. Our mothers—nothing can break that bond. Go ahead, take one," he urged.

His striking blue eyes held mine, and I swear to God it didn't cross my mind to blink for at least a minute.

And my fingers began trembling out of control—

God damn him!

He'd totally nailed the deepest hurt inside my hardened, Geisha-girl heart—the one that'd been hemorrhaging ever since I was old enough to realize that I didn't have a real mom, like other kids. Just surly caretakers and mercenary gold-diggers who couldn't wait to get rid of me.

But of course I wasn't able to stop my hand from picking out a feather from his palm. I cradled it for a few seconds, like it might actually be a silent message from a mother I could call my own. Then I let it go, watching as it was lifted by a delicate breeze. The feather twirled and rose up in a band of sunlight, shining white, and I found myself hoping that somehow, somewhere, whoever was or is my mother might sense my presence, maybe even feel the beats of my yearning heart.

And when I glanced back into Creek's eyes, for a split-second, I thought I saw them actually glisten.

He blinked and steeled himself, thoroughly rejecting anything that might have remotely looked like . . .

Tears.

Tears?

Good God, everything this guy just said is either for real, or he's by *far* the most accomplished sociopath I've ever met, beating out the worst of the alpha Pinnacle chicks by a mile.

My teeth clenched together.

"Tell me what you know!" I spit out, in no mood to be manipulated by Creek or anyone else, regardless of how handsome or clever they might be. "Is my real mother dead? 'Cause that sure as hell has always been the line I've been sold."

Creek's gaze fastened to his boots, and I saw the snake tattoo on his arm tighten and then ripple. Even the bruise I'd left on his skin from biting him in the lake shimmied a little, making me proud.

"No," he replied.

His jaw stiffened. He appeared to be selecting his words very, very carefully.

"I mean, I doubt it . . ."

He paused and glanced up to search my face. His gaze felt as intense as a spyglass, as though he was doing more than just checking for my reaction. He was scrutinizing my *soul*.

"I can tell by your dad's eyes," he finally said. "They still have . . . hope. Rare quality in these parts."

"Then where *is* she?" I sunk my fingers into his tattooed arm before I could stop myself, digging into his bruise. "Why would she leave me or my dad?" I asked a little too desperately.

Creek studied my eyes as if carefully testing my mettle.

And his silence felt downright endless . . .

But I waited for what seemed like forever without a word, eager for some honesty—the kind I knew I'd never get from my dad.

Then I saw the ragged scar on his cheek shift just a little, as if he was measuring his response.

"She left because she loves you too much," he finally said. "Both of you—enough to want to protect you. Believe me, I know something about how that feels."

He turned to face the morning sun, as if the rays strengthened him a little, and all of a sudden his features lit up with gold.

He was utterly breathtaking. But that didn't prevent me from wanting to slap him right then and there.

"What do you mean?" I cried out, trying to make my tone sound more menacing than desperate this time.

"It was over fifteen years ago," Creek replied. "Folks around Bender Lake say your mom was rich and beautiful, from Italy. She fell in love with your dad, a stockboy at her family's pasta sauce plant in Cinci, and she got pregnant. Her father wanted to kill him."

"Kill my dad?" I smirked. "Get in line! Who doesn't want to murder my father—he has that effect on people."

I might've been wisecracking, but inside I was trying to hide the fact that a deeper part of me was sucking air.

My mother—Italian?

And my dad a mere stockboy?

How is it that everyone in my life had a way of playing musical chairs with their identity lately? Including *me*?

This was too much. My whole body betrayed me by trembling right in front of him.

"Here," Creek said in that soft, smoky way he had that could reduce a girl's heart to warm liquid, "you look cold. Put on my jacket."

He took off his frayed jean jacket and wrapped it around my shoulders, and I eagerly slipped my arms inside. It was still warm from the heat of his body, like an embrace. My breath hitched—it even had his *smell*. Traces of spring leaves and campfire smoke and something sharp and invigorating, like maybe tree sap. I'd never been allowed to be this close to a guy my age before, let alone one who was so . . . intoxicating. Swiftly, I glanced aside, hoping he couldn't read my thoughts.

But Creek clutched my shoulders and swiveled me to face him. His blue eyes burned into mine.

"Alessia's dad forced her to put you up for adoption before they left the U.S., like you never existed at all. But Doyle—he tracked you down and broke in one night and stole you back. With Granny and Lorraine's help, of course. They say she could see back then."

My hands clamped over my mouth in total shock.

"We don't never abandon nobody at Turtle Shores."

Creek's eyes narrowed.

"Say what you will about your dad, but he risked his *life* to get you. And Granny says he's been beatin' himself up ever since, trying to become rich enough someday to win back your mom. He still loves her."

"D-D—" I stammered, trying to compose myself, "Does he know where she is?"

"Probably Europe somewhere. Rumor has it that her father had her locked away in a convent so she couldn't stain the family reputation any more."

"With a name like McCracken?" I added, still stumbling over the sound of that word.

Creek shoved his hands into his jeans pockets. I could tell he was getting cold, but toughing it out. He cast a glance at the lake, which we could see now through the trees, its ripples sparkling in the morning light. He nodded.

"When we cross that lake, Robin, you ain't *you* anymore. Understand that? You won't be just out for a joy ride. You'll be considered a criminal, like me. And there's no way to go back to your old world—they'll smell you in a heartbeat. You'll have the stink of Turtle Shores."

I leaned back on my heels to ramp up my courage, then flashed my most brazen smile.

Oh, how you underestimate me, Creek! I thought. I'm still a Geisha girl to the core, just like my dad who passed us off at Indian Hill for the last fifteen years. And I am so gonna enjoy proving it to you.

"Sure," I replied, lifting my chin. I winked just to keep him guessing. "I'll try to keep that in mind."

But Creek surprised me by grabbing my hand—and a shiver sped through my body, which I refused to reveal. His large fingers felt warm but calloused, and he began to lead me carefully through the woods. The whole time his grip remained firm, as solid as a clamp, as if he thought I might bolt. And I have to say, I *loved* the feeling of his skin against mine, the way he slowly picked his way through the brush and made certain to guide each step so I wouldn't trip or fall, as if he knew every inch of the forest blindfolded. No one had ever paid such attention to my welfare before, but I wasn't about to yield my heart too easily.

As soon as we reached the edge of Bender Lake and stopped, I yanked back my hand just to remind him that I was a free agent—and my soul remained tethered to no one. For a minute, I scanned the dark blue lake with a cottony layer of mist still clinging to its shores. The sight was so lovely that I felt completely absorbed in its hushed beauty, hardly registering when Creek pulled up a small wooden boat on the sand. He stood beside it, waiting.

Then I felt his eyes travel slowly over my body and linger, his gaze settling on my cheeks now warmed by the sun, as if—

Just maybe . . .

He thought *I* was breathtaking in the morning light, too!

Quickly, I bit the inside of my cheeks to hide my smile.

After all, the first thing a girl learns at Pinnacle is how to perfect the fine air of indifference.

Cold.

Calculating.

All the while falling *madly* in love.

Yep, my heart was thrumming faster than a race car engine at full throttle.

Until I caught the sight of something bright flickering out of the corner of my eye.

It was a white pillar candle, cemented in a pool of wax and surrounded by a loose ring of feathers, nestled in the bottom of Creek's boat. I swear, it looked almost like . . .

An altar.

The gold flame danced in the breeze. When I looked closer, I realized that Creek had assembled small tokens around it—a copper bracelet, a lock of brown hair in a turquoise barrette, dangly silver earrings—that might have once belonged to his . . . mother?

And then Creek's gaze met mine.

Raw.

Brutally honest.

And fiercely challenging—

Without even the slightest hint of upper crust pretense.

And in that moment, I could see all of his built-up pain, simmering rage, even all of the fragile hope he still had left in him—right there in his piercing blue eyes that didn't know how to hold a single thing back, or maybe never wanted to.

So very opposite of everyone I'd known at Pinnacle.

And I understood, in that instant, that if I got into Creek's row boat, I was going to be stripped bare of every shred of soul camouflage that I'd ever counted on—at least when I was with him. Because somehow, in Creek's presence, it seemed utterly impossible to remain phony for long.

But that didn't mean I didn't have a few tricks left up my sleeve.

Bluntness being one of them.

"Creek, did you *pray* me here?" I blurted, hoping I'd cut to the bone.

I saw the flame on the pillar candle leap at my words.

But Creek didn't flinch.

In fact, his stare was so unwavering that I felt like he'd swallowed me whole, and was still game for dessert.

"What I prayed for," he replied defiantly, "was help to take care of Brandi."

He steadied one foot in the small boat and boldly stretched out his hand to invite me in. A wisp of a smile passed over his mouth, just enough to make his cheek scar crinkle into that scary dagger again.

"Guess God's got a sense of humor," he added.

"B-But why do we need to get into a boat to rob a bank?" I asked him, reluctant to take his hand. "Don't tell me you've found one that floats."

Creek's cool gaze scanned the sandy beach beside us. He shook his head and waited for me to get a clue.

Footprints . . .

The sand was completely covered in our footprints, I realized. Each one a tell-tale sign of exactly where we'd been and where we were headed next. I watched as the lake water gently surged onto the shore, erasing the last of our tracks like we'd up and disappeared.

And with a jolt, Creek yanked me into the boat—no more waffling on the beach and spewing out my lines of bravado any more.

As I stumbled to regain my balance and plopped down on a wooden slat in front of his candle, for a brief second I closed my eyes.

Dear God, I prayed earnestly, *I have no idea what the hell we're doing. I'm just trying to help my dad and some folks at Turtle Shores. So if you don't mind, please don't let us get shot today.*

I trailed my finger in the cool lake, watching the slim line I'd made disappear back into the water while I listened to the lapping sounds Creek made as he rowed us to the other side. Oddly enough, it reminded me of the dream I'd had yesterday of riding through a canal in Venice. But my "gondolier" this time turned out to be even *better* looking—except he had a whole lot more on his mind than flirting and champagne.

In fact, Creek hadn't said a word at all.

He simply stared at the candle that had burnt halfway down to the wooden slat between us, his eyes studying the pooled wax, preoccupied over our next moves.

Every time a bird glided past us in the morning mist and let out a hoarse cry, it made me jump a little and jostle the boat.

But Creek just kept on rowing.

When we reached the opposite shore, he closed his eyes briefly and blew out the candle, setting down his oar. Then he pulled out a plastic bag from behind his feet. Opening it up, he took out two wigs, presumably Brandi's. One was long and blonde, like a hippie-boho chick, and another was short, black and spiky.

"Dibs on the Goth wig!" I insisted, grabbing the black one before he could stop me.

Creek shook his head.

"No way. You have to be even more . . . sexy."

I'm quite sure my cheeks flashed as red as a traffic light.

What did he mean by *more?*

He grabbed the black wig and thrust the blonde one into my lap.

"You're the . . . um, distraction," he said. "Every Wednesday at seven am, an armored car delivers cash for the ATM at Bob's Beer & Live Bait about five miles up the road."

I slipped on the blonde wig and tucked in my thick, curly hair. It fit so tightly it made my scalp itch. Twirling a few stiff, Swedish-looking strands, I noticed that they nearly reached to my hips. Geez, I thought, all I need is to put on some white go-go boots, and I could probably make a killing in Vegas.

"So," I replied, "are you saying want me to sashay my hips and flirt with the armored car guy, then try and grab his money?"

Creek sighed impatiently. His eyes took on a wolfish concentration.

"Sweetheart, the fastest way to get dead is to mess around with an armored car guy. They shoot first, then maybe ask questions later."

The chills that raced down my spine broke a land record for speed. I straightened up, trying not to look too scared.

"I've been casing Bob's place for weeks," Creek continued. "He's a real asshole who rips off everyone at Bender Lake, and he doesn't exactly hire the brightest bulbs to work for him. So after the armored car guy makes his drop, then it's up to the store employees to actually load the ATM cartridge."

"And they can be," I shimmied my shoulders with a glint in my eye, "easily diverted?"

Creek nodded with a sliver of a smile.

"I should've known you'd turn me into a working girl," I taunted, seizing the black wig on his lap. I thrust it over his impossibly soft blonde hair, just wishing I could take a minute to stroke a few strands, but instead I dutifully stuffed his locks inside. Releasing my fingers, I sat back down in the boat and gasped. By the look on my face, Creek could tell I thought he appeared . . . vicious.

His eyes seemed an even icier blue with the contrast of the black wig and his black t-shirt, and the color brought attention to every scar and tattoo that marred his skin, making him look hard and mean.

Creek climbed out of the boat and pulled it to the shore. He briskly extended his hand to me, and I could already feel the change in him. All of a sudden, he was no longer the tender guy I'd stumbled upon in the woods who whispered prayers at dawn. He was totally focused, like a warrior heading to battle, and his whole demeanor had become cold and determined. Biting my lip, I took a deep breath and stood up to grab his arm.

Good morning Life of Crime! I thought, studying his hard features. So good of you to lend a hand.

Hanging onto him, I leaped out of the boat and onto the sand, mentally preparing for my new future.

To my surprise, Creek dug into his jeans pocket and pulled out one more white feather. I saw his Adam's apple chase down his neck as he placed the feather in my palm, then folded over my fingers. His hands engulfed mine, but this time they were cold.

"Keep this in your pocket," he insisted in a voice made of flint. "For protection."

There it was—a flicker of that softness in his eyes again, like I hadn't been imagining things. For a moment, he gazed at me with what looked like genuine . . . worry.

I nodded, taking his feather by the quill and studying its thin, tapered edge. But of course, knowing me, I couldn't resist messing with him.

"Don't worry, I can take care of myself," I smiled, lifting the feather to trace a sassy curve along his scarred cheek.

Creek seized my wrist so fast it hurt—hurt hard. He met my gaze with a frighteningly rigid stare.

"We'll just see about that. You keep your wits, you hear? I don't want to have to report the worst to your dad.

Releasing my arm, he turned away and strided to some nearby bushes, pulling out a motorcycle that had been completely concealed in the leaves. It was old and rusty, and it had metal casings that extended halfway down each wheel with the word *Indian* barely legible on its motor. Creek gave it a kickstart, and the engine sputtered for a few seconds, then roared to life, spewing out black smoke like an angry dragon.

"Creek!" I coughed, waving at my nose. Just then I noticed that the seat was as wide as a platter and looked like it had been ripped off from an old tractor. "We're going to wake up everybody at Bender Lake—"

"About time they got up before noon!" he shouted back, climbing onto his motorcycle. He nodded at me and smirked like he was Satan. "Get on!" he ordered.

I didn't think it was actually possible to shake from my forehead to my toes, but I swear that damn cycle was so loud that it made even the sand quake beneath my feet. I clenched my hands into fists, hoping to keep from wobbling as I bravely stepped towards Creek's monster. Slipping behind him on the tractor seat, my body began to jostle so hard that I feared my molars might tumble out. I closed my eyes and flung my arms around Creek, locking my fingers together in a death grip.

And in that moment, I felt his whole body stiffen, like perhaps it had been a long time since he'd had a girl so close. And I know this sounds crazy, but in spite of the earth-shaking engine, I could've sworn I felt a subtle ripple run through him and then linger in my hands.

"Robin," he turned to say into my ear, "are you okay?"

I tightened my knuckles until my joints hurt, squeezing my eyes shut and feeling utterly petrified.

"Fuck you," I replied.

Chapter 10

We careened like some crazy snake on fire through the woods, dodging trees and shrubs so fast I had to bury my face into the back of Creek's t-shirt so my scream wouldn't reach all the way to Cincinnati. But when I felt our motorcycle sputter and slowly rumble to a halt, I finally worked up the nerve to poke my nose out.

Hacking, I fanned at the fumes and opened my eyes. Before us was a wide field covered in vibrant green shoots that sparkled in the morning dew. The blanket of color was so rich that I half-wished I could eat it, the way I used to want to devour the emerald baubles I spied at Tiffany's. I felt Creek's ribcage swell beneath my fingers, as though he'd taken a deep breath, struck by the sight, too.

"Spring cornfield," he called out over the engine noise, shifting in his seat to steal a glance at me. "Still green, like you. Hold on—we've got one more mile."

He turned the motorcycle onto a narrow gravel road that bordered the field and accelerated, bulleting down the lane at what surely must've been 90 miles an hour.

"Creeeeeeeeeek!" I hollered, carving my nails into his waist. "Do you have to go so fast?"

The motorcycle slowed down a little, and I nearly fell off as he slid it to a stop.

"Nope," Creek shouted to me, cutting the engine. At once, the world became as quiet as a church sanctuary. "'Cause we're here."

I glanced around, seeing only more cornfields.

"Here?" I said, surprised.

"Yep, time to ditch the cycle before we hoof it."

We hopped off, and Creek cleverly hid the motorcycle in some overgrown brush. Then we walked along the gravel road until we came to an intersection. Up ahead was a tacky building with cars up on blocks beside it and buzzing neon lights advertising cheap cigarettes and lottery tickets. The sign over the store said *Bob's Beer* with the words *& Live Bait* crossed out. To the right was added *Quick Loans & Paychecks Cashed* in red spray paint.

"Bob chucked selling live maggots and worms a while back," Creek said. "He decided to become a maggot himself and fleece half the county with his crummy loans. Practically everybody I know is paying him in blood."

At that moment, a bulky gray truck hastened down the road and came to a stop, screeching its wheels.

"Here's our armored car," Creek folded his arms and nodded. "Right on schedule."

We watched as a man in a black jumpsuit hopped out of the truck and threw open the back, pulling out a small gray bag and darting into the building before we could say "money drop." Quick as a flash, he returned and climbed into his truck, scribbling something onto his visor before he roared out of the parking lot like he was going to catch hell if he was more than 30 seconds late.

"Bob's too cheap to pay Amos' Armored Car Company the extra ten bucks a week to load his ATM cartridges," Creek pointed out. "So that money's just sitting behind the counter right now, waiting for us—"

He startled me by stripping the jean jacket he'd loaned me off my back.

"Here's the plan," he said, his black spiky wig only magnifying his intense gaze. "You go in first and loiter inside the store for a while. I'll be right behind you, keeping a low profile. Then you act sexy—you know, hot to trot. When the guy steps out from behind the counter to flirt with you, make sure you occupy his sole attention."

A smirk rose to Creek's lips, flashing that infernal dagger scar again.

"For a girl who looks like you, that shouldn't be too hard."

A wave of heat rose from my cheeks to my forehead, but I simply squared my shoulders and straightened my blonde wig, refusing to break my Pinnacle code of coolness now. Nevertheless, I dug my fingernails into my palms to the point of pain to keep from showing my reaction.

So Creek really does think I'm a looker! I thought, floored. What a nice little Ace to slip into my back pocket for later.

"What happens if you get into trouble when you try to grab the money?" I said casually, pretending my part in all of this was a piece of cake.

Creek's eyes transformed into blue ice.

There it was—his warrior demeanor again—accompanied by a cold stare so penetrating that most people wouldn't mess with him if their lives depended on it. Goose bumps shimmied down my spine.

"You just worry about you," he replied with a tone as sharp as a knife. "I'll take care of the rest."

I nodded and turned away, chewing my lip, and sauntered off with fake confidence ahead of Creek, swinging my hips in my low-slung jeans. Part of me was just dying to know whether he thought I'd actually achieved "sultry" or not. As I approached the front door, I hiked up my lacey camisole straps to bare more midriff. The thought occurred to me that I'd never worn such skimpy clothes in public before, let alone to lure the opposite sex, but I didn't dare let on my rookie misgivings. Instead, I poured it on like a Victoria's Secret supermodel, moistening my lips into a sullen pout and fluffing my blonde wig until my hair appeared wild and windblown. But when I opened the door, I noticed that the red-haired guy behind the counter with the yellow plaid shirt glanced aside when he saw me, heaving a sigh. He appeared to be downright . . .

Bored?

No, worse than that. More like . . . annoyed.

As if he thought I was as sexy as a concrete cinder block.

He just doesn't want to surrender, I told myself, feeling sorry for him.

I stood in my most vampish pose by the door, judging my prey to be maybe nineteen or so. Quickly, I made a beeline for the donuts on the counter. It was only a little after 7, but I was already starving. I boldly opened a box of donuts with white powdered sugar and lifted one for a provocative bite, allowing my lips to linger on its pillowy edge. Thrusting up my chest as I chewed, I glanced down at my cleavage.

"Oh my," I said in my breathiest, sex-bomb tone, "Look! I've spilled sugar all over my shirt."

With that, I slowly loosened the top lace of my camisole until I thought my breasts might spill out, and I began to seductively lick the end of the lace, when I heard the swoosh of Creek opening the door behind me.

I assumed the boy's eyes would be glued to the tender white skin exposed over my Pinnacle issue bra.

But I couldn't have been more wrong.

He only had eyes for Creek.

"You're going to pay for those donuts, right?" the guy sniffed, locking his gaze on Creek's chest with a hunger never intended for fifteen year-old girls.

"Uh, sure," I replied, flustered. "L-Let me go get some milk—"

I sped over to the back of the chips aisle where Creek was killing time.

"What do we do now?" I whispered, shooting a glance at Mr. Salivating behind the counter. "He doesn't even know I exist."

Creek's eyes fastened on mine.

"He will now."

Clutching me by the shoulders, Creek moved in for a full-blown kiss!

His hands roamed up the back of my camisole, and I wanted to freeze—to try and keep my wits just like he'd instructed—but I couldn't.

Instead, my bones had melted into simmering butter, and there was nothing holding me up any more except the grip Creek now had on my waist.

No one had ever prepared me for the fact that when the hottest creature in the continental U.S. decides the moment's right for a total lip lock, a girl's brain is pretty much going to wash downstream.

And I couldn't help myself—I reached up and grasped Creek's face and poured myself into him with more passion than I'd ever daydreamed possible under Pinnacle's ever-present security cameras.

Take that, Mother Superior!

I wrapped my leg tantalizingly around Creek's, treating the jeans fabric between us like nothing more than tissue paper. Then I ran my hot hands up his miraculously-tight chest beneath his t-shirt, until I swore I could feel sparks actually alighting from my fingertips. All of a sudden, I felt Creek's lips break a little and mumble against mine.

"Jealous yet?"

"Huh?" I managed to reply, keeping my lips glued to his. I peeked behind us, but the red-haired guy was busy wiping the counter. He coughed and turned to straighten postcards on a rack.

"Nope—not at all. I don't think he's even bothered to notice."

"Then slap me," Creek ordered, barely loud enough to hear.

"Are you serious?" I whispered, breaking off my lips this time.

"Go for it!"

I stepped back from Creek's embrace, hardly able to believe his imploring eyes. He nodded at me, so I hauled off and gave him a thwack—

"You asshole!" I cried, my Geisha skills revving up to full force now. I stole another glance at counter guy, whose eyes were riveted to Creek now like a hopeless puppy-dog crush. "You know better than to kiss me after hitting on my brother and openly admitting that you're . . . you're GAY!"

For the first time since I'd met him, I saw Creek's eyes become as wide as the Moon Pies that hung from the peg board beside him.

Ha! I thought. So Creek doesn't figure out everything after all.

I winked at Creek and moved in for the kill, tearing off his jean jacket and running my hands up his impossibly toned chest, then lifting up his black t-shirt over his head, leaving his ripped abs completely exposed.

"Well I'm not going to share you with every freewheeling cowboy in this county, mister! And it's high time you gave me back my favorite t-shirt," I hissed, shoving Creek into the beef jerky turnstile until he toppled over with a clatter. "Take that, you traitor!"

In a fury, I marched up to the front with the black t-shirt wadded in my hand and glared at the counter guy. "No donut or milk money for you today," I fumed, pointing back at Creek. "You want payment? Then send two-timing Sir Lancelot over there the bill!"

Just as I suspected, the guy couldn't wait to dash over to Creek, suddenly becoming Mother Teresa in his shit-kicker boots and Wrangler jeans.

"You okay?" they guy gasped, tenderly petting Creek's black spiky wig. "Here, let me help you up—"

And frankly, at this point I didn't hang around to hear the rest, because I was too busy marching out the front door with an awkward bag of money stuffed up my camisole and padded by Creek's t-shirt, making me look like I'd suddenly bloomed into a teen mother-to-be.

And although it was a total drag to try and jog across the gravel parking lot with a few thousand dollars bumping against my belly, the adrenaline pumping in my veins helped me reach our motorcycle tucked in the brush in seconds flat.

Luckily, my heart was charging so fast I barely noticed the deafening roar of the engine after I'd managed to kickstart the Indian all by myself.

And with one last glance at Bob's, I cringed and blew a kiss in Creek's direction. "Please take care of him!" I prayed to God earnestly, hoping that angels or maybe even mothers on high would help him find a way to get out of there. Then I tore across the cornfield, sending loose dirt and those pretty, green shoots flying.

All the while, I could feel my smile begin to stretch as wide as the open road.

Last time you call *me* green, Creek, I thought as the stiff strands of my wig lashed against my cheeks.

Chapter 11

"Take off your clothes," a voice whispered at the edge of the lake like a ghost.

It was still a bit misty out, and I thought I felt a warm breath against the back of my neck—

I whipped around. There he was!

Creek, stripped to his torn jeans with his blonde hair dangling against his shoulders again, as if the powers that be had somehow beamed him right in front of me.

And he was grinning from ear to ear.

"You were a *very* bad girl today," he remarked.

Unable to control myself, I hugged him with all my might, elated that he'd made it out of Bob's place okay through God knows what kind of messy miracle. And Lord, how I wanted to kiss him again! But I felt like a fool with a bag of money and a t-shirt still bulging over my belly, because I'd been too preoccupied to remove them till I'd succeeded in hiding the motorcycle.

Creek broke away from me and gazed at my tummy with a laugh.

"You rocked it!" he said, patting my stomach.

"B-But how'd you get here so fast?" I gasped.

Creek's lips slinked into a smile. He shook his head. "Sweetheart, it ain't hard to get a lift in these parts when you're not wearing a t-shirt. Now we gotta move—"

He slipped both his hands under my camisole, removing the money bag and t-shirt and letting them fall with a thump to the sand. To my surprise, he threw off my blonde wig and traced his fingers beneath my camisole straps, tenderly lifting them over my head.

My heart ricocheted inside my chest. Oh my God, I thought, is this the part where we have post-heist sex?

Creek's eyes arrested mine. They were still that hard blue, broken by shards of glass in the middle like a guy totally focused on his mission. But there was a softness at the edges as well, as if maybe he wanted to . . .

Protect me?

And *kiss* me at the same time—

Both urges warring inside him.

Well, I decided, no time like the present to test that theory!

I rushed my hands up his firm chest and clutched his face, pulling his lips to mine for as much Heaven as I'd ever been allowed on this silly, spinning planet.

And spin I did! Inside, I felt as if I my whole being had gotten lost in a dreamy whirl. All traces of thought evaporated, only the smell and feel of his hard skin and soft hair overwhelming my senses. I was tumbling end over end, because no one had ever informed me that . . .

When you touch someone this beautiful—

It's like falling into a pool of light.

And all of a sudden,

You're that beautiful, too . . .

Creek's hands surged up my bare back, and I couldn't stop from pressing my breasts against his chest—my scratchy, Pinnacle-issue bra be damned—as my fingers nimbly undid the button and zipper on his jeans. I pulled them down his legs like they were as easy to rip from his body as saran wrap, and then I kicked off my shoes to do the same with my jeans.

Who was this girl??

I'd become a mighty blur—all animal on instinct and overdrive—who was determined to make both our bodies sing in the sunshine and sand that seemed to cry out for us to become one creature.

But then I felt Creek hoist my nearly naked body in his arms, hugging me tightly to his chest.

He kissed me uncontrollably for a few seconds, when all at once his lips broke free, and he rested his forehead against mine.

And he began to walk into the lake, gently carrying me, as though we were heading for some strange, a spur-of-the-moment . . . baptism?

"Bloodhounds," he said breathlessly, his gaze full of alarm. "Bob's got bloodhounds—"

From out of nowhere, I heard the echo of a chorus of dogs, their deep resounding barks growing closer by the second.

With one last kiss, Creek released me to the water, sailing me forward. The cold shock rushed to my neck, constricting my lungs and leaving me heaving for air.

"Swim, Robin!" He ordered, pointing to an inlet of the lake covered in shadows. "Swim with everything you've got!!"

"But what about you?" I cried, astonished and dog-paddling like crazy.

I saw Creek rush to the shore to grab the money bag. Then he pulled out a black trash sack from his jeans pocket on the sand and filled it with our clothes, my wig, and several heavy rocks. Tying a knot, he hoisted it with the money bag and dashed into the water after me.

"Go!!" he cried, doing a furious breast stroke, lugging the two bags with him.

I focused on the dark inlet and tore ahead, my arms slicing into the cold water until I thought my heart might rupture. A bam-bam! rang out over our heads, scaring me so badly I accidentally swallowed gulps of lake water and turned to peek back, my stomach lurching. On the shore stood a barrel-chested man pointing at us with a shotgun, surrounded by a chaos of gangly brown dogs racing back and forth on the sand, sniffing and howling in frustration.

"Keep going!" Creek yelled. He appeared to drop the trash bag with the rocks midway in the lake, because all of a sudden his strokes were so fast he was nearly next to me—

And he grabbed me by the hand and pulled me toward the inlet with a force that left me reeling.

There we were, in the dark shade of the inlet like a blanket had been thrown over us, making us disappear. Creek pulled me closer to him and grabbed me by the shoulders.

"Take a deep breath, the very biggest you can!" he commanded.

And without another word, I was under water—we both were—and Creek was towing me along with the money bag, his strong legs kicking forcefully through total darkness.

I couldn't even see him anymore. It was as though we'd fallen into a black hole. I could only feel the pull of his hand through what must be some cave or tunnel under water. I kicked and kicked, when I saw the liquid ahead of us begin to appear gray, with a little shafts of light filtering through. My lungs burned, but I kept kicking, until I felt Creek pull me up—

Air!!

I gasped and gasped, my lungs feeling as if they'd nearly collapsed.

"We did it!" Creek burst, his eyes sparkling now. "Jesus Christ, we really did it! No one's ever gotten away from Bob's bloodhounds before!"

He wrapped his arms tightly around me for a victory hug, and I slumped against his hard chest, still craving more air.

"What?" I finally gasped. "You never told me about Bob's bloodhounds!"

Creek threw his head back and laughed. "Sweetheart, why do you think nobody dares to rip off his piece of shit store? There's a reason he can leave that much cash lying around."

To my astonishment, Creek gazed at me with a look I'd never seen from him before. No longer a single trace of coldness, as though his eyes had been bathed in sunlight. They were so warm and radiant now that I wanted to fall into them, like the shimmer of a heavenly spring sky. He lifted me up and swirled me in his arms, our two bodies entwined and swooshing through the water as we both began to laugh. When we stopped, he stared into my eyes and brushed a wet strand of hair from my forehead.

"Oh my God, Robin," he said, somewhere between admiration and total awe. "We're legends now."

Chapter 12

"Total self control is always the key," instructed the visiting speaker in a bright purple kimono for our 3rd period Asian culture class. Her pasty, white makeup and blood red lips made her face look like a mask, and her black hair was piled high onto her head in an elaborate chignon, held together by chopsticks. "You must understand that Geishas embody perfection: beautiful, poised, mysterious. And as you go out into the world to lead multinational corporations, be aware that in Japan, and to some extent China and Singapore as well, businessmen will expect certain, shall we say, attributes—even from top female managers. Learning such skills will serve you well in Cincinnati, too." She winked provocatively, running her hand down the suffocatingly tight sash that cinched her waist. "But don't for a second think that means you have no *power*."

Sister Beatrice giggled with a shy smile, covering her mouth. I noticed that between her formal nun's habit and the guest speaker's kimono, the two of them looked eerily alike.

"And that power comes from your inner treasure box of emotions that is *never* revealed, and keeps your coworkers guessing. This is the art of getting ahead in the global marketplace! Let them *think* you're giving something, while you're actually taking what you need. Each stop is merely a way station on your rise to the top. So take your cue from the time-honored wisdom of the Geisha. Though they may serve tea, dance, and engage in casual but always leading conversation with their best clients, they never betray their real feelings."

All of a sudden, the guest speaker broke away from the front of the classroom and walked straight up to my desk, her wooden sandals clacking. She began to remove the chopsticks that held up her chignon until her hair spilled down to her shoulders, becoming wavier and oddly more brown. Then she grasped the edges of her cheeks and yanked at the white skin, peeling it from her face like puddy to reveal . . .

An utterly breathtaking woman.

So beautiful she appeared to be sculpted from a dream, just like that lovely one I had of floating down a canal in Venice. Her hair was tousled by a warm, soft breeze, and her kind, chestnut eyes held a sadness that broke my heart.

She reached down to pick up my pencil from my desk and wrote something in my school notebook. Swiveling it around, she tapped the paper for me to read:

Never betray your real feelings.

Except when you truly fall in love.

I glanced up at her in shock, and the woman's eyes met mine.

Only now, she was wearing a formal nun's habit, like Sister Beatrice. Her face was cocooned by the heavy black and white material that seemed to constrict more than just her cheeks. The look in her eyes made it appear as if her habit had also hemmed in her soul.

"Don't run from love, Rubina," she whispered to me in a heartbreaking Italian accent. "Embrace it."

With that, she reached out to cup my cheek. Her fingers felt warm and soft, kind of like arriving . . . home.

Startled, I jerked a little.

But instead of the woman's hand, all I felt on my cheek were two small feathers.

Holding them up, I trembled at the sight—one was black and one was white—like two roads I could possibly take in life. My vision was still a bit hazy, but I glanced around, realizing I was nowhere near my old classroom at Pinnacle. Instead, I was high up in the trees of Bender Lake on a wooden platform that was covered in the delicate spring petals from a blossoming dogwood nearby. Beside my feet were scattered an array of twenty-dollar bills, still drying in the late afternoon sun.

And then there was the nearly naked body of the handsomest guy I'd ever seen, his back to me, sleeping. A pile of dry clothes lay beside him and a couple of more wigs—items I knew that we would soon wear for more hits.

Because it turned out that Granny Tinker was right.

When I crossed the lake this morning with Creek, it was like the River Styx that we'd learned about in 7th period Classical Mythology at Pinnacle. My life was never going to be the same. I wasn't the Robin McArthur I used to know anymore.

I was a girl who'd actually kissed a guy—twice!

I knew how to start a motorcycle now.

And I was a criminal.

This underworld that I'd crossed into had more than its share of consequences. I sat up on the platform, my gaze shifting to Creek, who continued to sleep soundly. He'd told me earlier, when we'd walked back from the lake to the woods, that we were "vampires" now. Not the sparkly kind in teenage novels that I used to devour like potato chips, but the real ones who must sleep during the day and only come out at night because they're wanted by the law—as well as by guys like Bob, who Creek said "Play dirty as hell."

What he meant by dirty I didn't even care to know. It may sound strange, but even after the harrowing morning of our first job together, all I wanted to know was one thing:

Who was that woman from my dream?

Was she my mother? Or just some tortured, wishful fantasy of mine?

I stared at Creek, at the beautiful form of his tan back contrasted by the ugly burn marks that ran up his arm like a vicious dot-to-dot picture that told a story I would probably never hear. A story of darkness and abuse beyond my wildest comprehension. Then my eyes settled on the ornate red tattoo of the heart on his bicep that surrounded a particularly ugly scar. Clearly, it had contained a name that he'd held dear once, and at some point, painfully scratched out.

Who might Creek have loved? I wondered.

Did he give his heart for real, like the way that beautiful Italian woman had challenged me to love in my dream, in spite all of my aggressive Pinnacle training? Was this the advice of none other than Alessia?

Perhaps that was too much for a girl like me to ever know.

But as I heard the rappings of a woodpecker echo through the forest, part of me wished that I could magically heal Creek's wounds. Make him whole—maybe even innocent again—just like wide-eyed Dooley, the one he protected so fiercely. And I swallowed hard, daring to lift a finger to edge it closer to Creek's bare arm. Because by now, I'd pretty much already admitted to myself that I had a deep desire to . . .

Write my name there, too.

Oh God, I thought, am I actually falling in love?

Embrace it, my dream woman had said, as though she'd led her life full of regrets.

And didn't want me to be that way.

I held my breath.

For just one winsome moment, I wanted to touch Creek on that heart tattoo while he was sleeping—while he wasn't alert enough to put up any of those cold barriers between him and me, from a life that had been harder than I would ever imagine.

So I carefully—oh so carefully—skimmed my finger along the upraised ridges of that scar.

And Creek's strong hands were gripped around my shoulders in an instant.

I was so frightened I felt like the wind had been sucked out from my lungs.

"Don't *ever* touch me there!" he cried, glaring at me.

Wild eyed, Creek's expression was so full of adrenaline I thought for certain he was going to kill me.

I wriggled uselessly, his tight fingers pressing white against my skin that hurt like hell. Wincing, I muttered, "C-Creek, I j-just wanted to—"

"Wanted what?" He demanded with a cruel urgency that brought me to tears. I bravely fought them back, because in my heart I knew—

He wasn't even speaking to me.

He was speaking to someone else. Someone who'd really . . . hurt him.

"Ow!" I cried out finally, when I couldn't take the pain anymore, but Creek wasn't about to let go until he got his answer. He shook me a little.

"I-I just wanted to touch you," I explained. "I mean, when you aren't awake and you don't have those barriers anymore."

Creek blinked at me, incredulous. I could tell my words had begun to trickle into his mind a little. He shook his head as if shocked at himself—at his own kneejerk violence. He seemed to be just now registering that I wasn't at all who he thought I was.

His grip loosened like he'd been lost in a delirium, and he slid his hands down my arms, yet his eyes still seemed a world away.

"Who was she?" I asked, my heart in my throat. After all, it was pretty damn clear to me that she was sitting right there between us, like a blockade.

Creek's whole body stiffened. He let go of me and folded his arms, all tough as steel again. Then his eyes locked on mine, now rife with bitterness.

"She was someone who could walk away from Turtle Shores and waltz right back into her cushy life again, any time she felt like it."

In that instant, goose bumps danced over my entire being.

But I'd had enough—

Creek's life might have been rough, but mine wasn't exactly a picnic lately, either. And nothing gave him the right to hurt me.

"Well I don't get that privilege anymore. Do you hear me? It's all gone! Everything I ever had at Indian Hill. And as far as I'm concerned, I've earned the right to know her name."

Creek's eyes narrowed, studying mine. "What makes you think that?"

I crossed my arms and held my ground. "Because you know all of my secrets now. In fact, you've known them most of your life—with Doyle, and Alessia, and God knows who else from my family has been around here fucking things up. But I don't know yours."

"You know plenty," Creek scoffed, grabbing a dry pair of jeans from the clothing pile he'd stashed on the platform. He slipped them on and stood up, as if taunting me.

And I stood up right along with him.

"But I want to know everything," I pressed. "You said there are no secrets in trailer parks—except from *me*, is that it? Just because I was raised posh in Cincinnati by a white trash dad done good, you get to treat me like a second class citizen now. Isn't that a little hypocritical?"

I tugged on a pair of dry jeans as well and zipped them up.

"Look," I said, feeling a bit silly with just my Pinnacle-issue bra on top. "If we're going to keep doing this—"

My breath snagged at the harsh reality of my life for a second.

"You know—robbing places—that means we need to have each other's backs. And be completely ru-ruuuu—"

I didn't just trip this time—I did a full-blown belly flop over that word.

Good God, I thought, I don't believe I've ever said the term *real* to someone before and actually meant it, especially with my cold upbringing and steady Geisha brainwashing. It was like all of those other words I'd never gotten to really experience before in life: love—bonding—family. But for some weird reason, I was starting to believe that mysterious Italian woman from my dream was right, mother or not.

"We gotta be real with each other," I spit out bravely. "Didn't you notice that Bob shot at us today? With a real gun? So if I'm gonna risk my life with you for the people at Turtle Shores, I deserve to know as much about you as you do about me. Including what her name was."

I boldly poked at the scar on his arm this time, no longer giving a damn what he thought anymore or how tough he was. Because the way I saw it, either the stakes were even for both of us, or it was high time I grabbed my dad and hitchhiked to another trailer park.

Creek simply smirked at me and started to laugh.

"I know what this is really about," he nodded, that rotten scar on his cheek crinkling into a dagger again as if to intimidate me. "You're just riled up because I kissed you."

"No," I huffed, clenching my fists. "The issue here is—"

He leaned in closer, nose to nose—totally interrupting me.

"And you've never been kissed by a guy before," he hissed like an accusation, a giant grin spreading across his handsome face.

Shit!

Now Creek had that secret down, too—

Was it really so obvious?

I swiftly glanced aside, trying to hide my embarrassment, when I felt him run his hand gently down my long, curly hair, then cup my cheek.

Creek's body was so close I could feel the heat of his skin near mine.

"So if I do give you her name," he said tantalizingly, "do I get another kiss?"

I'm not sure I could've refused him if my life depended on it.

But just to be cocky, I scrunched up my nose and said, "Maybe."

For a second his eyes grew cold again, in that way I absolutely hated.

"Her name was bitch. You got that?" Creek stared me down. "No, make that bitch-of-the-fuckin'-century. But you must believe me, Robin. I know the difference between her and you."

He took a fleeting glance at the scar on his arm and closed his eyes for a second, as if shutting an iron door. He looked again into my eyes.

"She didn't have a heart, and you do. Never in a million years would she have risked her life to help take care of her dad—or anybody else for that matter—like you did today. And considering where you came from, and how you were raised, that's pretty damn amazing."

I felt my eyes glisten over with tears.

More than that, I felt them slide right down my cheeks.

No one had ever accused me of having a heart before! How could Creek see something in me that I'd never even admitted to myself?

He clutched my face and gently brushed away the tears from my cheeks with his thumbs. "So do I get that kiss now?" he whispered.

I nodded, and pressed my lips to his. They felt soft and luxurious against my skin, far more than the genuine mink collar I used to have on my Gaultier winter jacket. Such a thing seemed dead to me now, compared to the throbbing heart I could feel from Creek's firm chest against mine.

Goodbye bitch, hello Robin! I thought, absolutely glowing inside. And I couldn't help wondering if this meant we were boyfriend and girlfriend now, since maybe the cobwebs of our pasts had finally been cleared out?

But I didn't have the time to brave that question to him, because as I impulsively ran my hands through Creek's silky, blonde hair, I suddenly heard shots over our heads.

BOOM-BOOM-BOOM, they went, like a dozen guns.

I hit the deck, covering my head.

"Get down, Creek!" I shouted desperately. "Bob's found us!"

More boom-boom-booms filled the air, but between their echoes reverberating through the woods, I heard Creek . . . laughing?

He grabbed me by the arm and hoisted me to my feet, dusting me off a little.

"Those aren't shots, silly," he said, brazenly stealing another kiss. "They're fireworks."

He swiveled me around to see the sky through a gap in the trees.

Sure enough, I spotted a projectile racing into the air that exploded, sending colorful sparks spiraling down in a sky that I hadn't realized had already grown gray at the edge of twilight.

"Quick, get a shirt on. The TNT Twins are sending up their rockets!" Creek smiled. "You're about to be invited to your very first hoedown, girl."

Creek stole yet another kiss—

"Welcome to *real*, Robin."

Chapter 13

"Do you guys always celebrate robberies like this?" I asked Creek, fanning the smoke from the TNT Twins' homemade fireworks that stung my eyes and nose. I'd heard wild whoops that made it sound like they already knew we'd brought back a sack of cash.

"Hell no," Creek laughed, coughing. "If we did that every time some fool committed a crime near Bender Lake, there'd be a non-stop block party going on. But word's probably gotten out by now. Gossip 'round here is faster than chain lightning. Lucky for us, Bob and his bloodhounds have a healthy fear of the TNT Twins' explosives."

He turned to pick up a blouse from the stack of clothes on the tree platform.

"Tonight at Turtle Shores is kind of special. So I, um . . . brought something for you."

He handed me a lavender blouse. It felt like silk, the kind of designer item my stepmom used to try and buy me off with so I wouldn't rat to my dad about her affairs. But when I glanced up at Creek, though his features were tanned and scarred—some might even call rough—I could tell by the guarded look in his eyes that his heart was secretly on the line. As much as he'd ever allowed it to be, anyway.

So this blouse is actually a gift? I thought, amazed. That means something to him?

Does that imply *I* mean something to him, too?

I shuffled my feet for a second on the platform, running my fingers over the pretty flowers embroidered on the blouse's neckline.

Did Creek steal this? I wondered, my hands all of a sudden feeling tingly. I wrestled inside with whether that nixed any romantic currency.

Creek's lips tightened, as if he were a bit unsettled by my reaction, and his eyes checked mine. But this time they weren't cold or warm. They were . . .

Hopeful.

An expression I hadn't seen flash across his face before. And it pierced my heart.

"I, uh . . . paid for that," he mentioned with a glint in his eye, as though he'd suspected my thoughts. "With money I got for fixing Old Man Riley's tractor at the farm up the road."

Creek gave me a wry smile. "That's how I got the tractor seat for our motorcycle. He let me have it from his old barn."

He glanced at the blouse, clearly proud of it. "Go on," he said softly. "Try it on."

I held it up for a second and slipped it over my head. The blouse fit perfectly, and it had delicate ruffles down the front and at the bottom of the sleeves. The fabric was almost sheer enough to see through, but not quite. It felt heavenly against my skin, like the whisper of an angel's wing.

And I didn't need to ask Creek if it looked good on me. The warmth that bloomed in his eyes told me he thought I was beautiful.

Funny how we could kiss like the dickens in the heat of the moment, on a dare or just before swimming for our lives from

Bob's bloodhounds. But right now, with the sparks from the way he gazed at me racing up and down my spine, I suddenly felt self-conscious.

And I could tell Creek did too, because he folded his hands awkwardly for a second, like he didn't quite know what to do with them, even though we'd kissed only a few minutes ago.

Was it because we were finally going out on a real date? I thought. Well, in a backwoods, fireworks-and-hoedown kind of way?

"C'mon," Creek urged. He quickly threw on a dark blue t-shirt from the clothes pile and collected all the bills that had dried on the platform, handing half of them to me. "Stuff these in your pockets. Let's get down to Turtle Shores and see what all the fuss is about."

I carefully followed him down the tree-stand ladder to the ground, and we picked our way through the forest that was growing more shadowy by the second. Yet through the trees, I could see the reflections from the fireworks glowing on Bender Lake.

My heart skipped a beat.

Because despite the smell of sulphur and other obnoxious fumes I didn't recognize, the vibrant colors of the TNT Twins' fireworks on the dark water were . . .

Captivating.

But not half as exquisite as the twinkling white lights that greeted us like stars when we arrived at the Turtle Shores compound.

I stood at the edge of the meadow in shock.

The delicate lights criss-crossed from tree to tree over our heads like winsome fireflies illuminating the meadow.

And on some of the tree branches hung round paper lanterns in charming colors—the kind that usually appeared gaudy in daylight, like some sad remnant of a forgotten carnival. But here, in the twilight, they appeared . . .

Magical.

Creek saw me halt in place and gasp.

A big smile spread across his face, lit up by the orange and red and blue paper lanterns that hung above us.

"Didn't know the boondocks could cast such a spell, did ya?"

He took me by the hand and led me across the meadow in a confident, weaving pattern as though he had a psychic radar for the TNT Twins' traps. Music started up, a swift, toe-tapping melody with a banjo and fiddles that soared into the night air, filling the whole meadow with a cheerful sound. At the entrance of the compound, I could see folks starting to dance around a bonfire, their heads bobbing as they stepped in formations and then grabbed new partners. As we got closer, I realized that some of the boom-boom sounds weren't just fireworks, they were from people who were drumming on old pots.

And one of them was my dad!

He sat on a chair beside Dooley next to Granny Tinker's gypsy wagon with a wooden spoon in his good hand and a rusty pot in his lap. Wailing on that pot with all his might, he ribbed Dooley as if they were in a fun competition, the two of them making a racket that rivaled the TNT Twins' rockets. At a pause in the melody, my dad grinned on his right side like he was having the time of his life. He tousled the boy's hair, watching his young face light up. A twinge of envy struck me inside. Why hadn't my dad ever bothered to treat me like that? Like someone he could be at ease with and maybe just enjoy? At that moment, my dad glanced up and caught a glimpse of me with Creek. His arm went slack, and he dropped his wooden spoon to the ground.

Like he'd just spotted a wandering spirit . . .

And that's when I heard a familiar cackle.

"Ain't she the spittin' image of her Ma?" Granny Tinker called out, smiling as she got up from her rocker and walked over to me. Her gold tooth sparkled in the firelight. "Why, purple used to look so nice on Alessia. That apple don't fall far from the tree."

In her usual flamboyant style, Granny had on a wide-brimmed leather hat with a feather in it, and her long, green dress was made of heavy brocade, a bit odd for a spring.

"How you been, darlin'?" she said, slinging her arm around my shoulder. "Understand Alessia paid you a little visit this afternoon."

At once, all rational thought fled from my brain. And I believe my feet turned into cement.

How could Granny Tinker possibly have known about my strange dream today?

When I glanced into her eerie gray eyes, with their peculiar yellow in the middle, Granny turned and nodded at an old quilt that was spread on the grass by her wagon. There sat her crystal ball surrounded by sprigs of wildflowers and herbs. The reflections from the bonfire made her crystal ball look ablaze, until it began to mysteriously cloud over. Slowly, the face of a beautiful woman started to surface—

I blinked hard, but she was gone. And before I knew it, the bright music seemed to rise and swirl around us like a tide, pushing me even closer to Creek. I felt him tug at my hand.

"Don't pay attention to her," Creek laughed, pulling me away. "Granny just loves to spook people. C'mon, let's pass out that money now, and get this party fired up."

He led me over to the dancers near where Bixby was playing banjo with some men who sawed at fiddles. Beside them sat two large, covered kettles with a copper coil leading to an old barrel. Several folks were lined up with empty jars that the Colonel filled from the barrel with a clear liquid. He gave each one a smile, and they saluted him.

"Moonshine," Creek whispered into my ear. I gazed up at him in surprise. "The Colonel's special brew. How do you think we attract such a big crowd?" he winked.

Then he pulled some of the cash from his pockets, his mouth slipping into a smile. He cupped the bills and held them up like precious jewels. "Okay, we're gonna give out this money to whoever our hearts see fit." His gaze was so keen now it made me quiver. "But Robin, I want you take a really deep breath." He paused, waiting for me. "'Cause the feeling you're about to get right now—well, you're gonna remember this night for the rest of your life."

I nodded with flutters in my stomach, and we began to wind between the dancers, tapping them on the shoulders and holding out money, then watching as the glee erupted on their faces. At first, there were big hoots and hollers of joy. But it was the tears that followed that really tore me apart. And I soon discovered Creek was right—the authentic gratitude, even love, in these people's eyes was more intoxicating than any backwoods moonshine. One old woman hugged me with everything she had in her and said now she could get medicine for her granddaughter. Another man exclaimed he was going to fix his truck to go to work again, while the guy next to him just buried his head in his hands and mumbled thank yous to Jesus that he could finally pay off Bob. His words really rattled me, given our own brush with Bob's methods.

But it was Brandi who slayed my heart the most. I spotted her near the bonfire, hardly recognizing her. She was wearing a pretty calico dress and no wig this time. Her head was completely bald, shiny in the firelight, and she was barefoot, as if she wanted to feel the earth beneath her feet. She looked thinner than I'd remembered, and rather than dancing with the others, she was swaying her hips with her eyes closed, as though allowing the music to fill her up inside. Yet despite all of her health problems lately, she was smiling. As dancers whipped past her, Brandi seemed to occupy a quiet, still place, where only the warmth of the fire and the sound of the banjo and fiddles could enter. Then I saw her hesitate for a moment. As the music rose into a series of high sweet notes, she lifted up her arms like wings.

And I just stood there, heartstruck, watching her in awe.

Because for the last year and a half, I'd lived nearly every day of my life with the richest and unhappiest girls you could ever hope to find, who snarked, complained and blackmailed their way into anything they wanted. Yet here was this woman who'd practically had a death certificate handed to her, simply taking time out to cherish a moment.

And it made me feel like Bob's money was burning my hands into a crisp.

I only had four hundred dollars left, but I knew every little bit could help—

"Brandi!" I called out impulsively, trotting up to her and jostling her shoulder. She opened her eyes with a start. But when she saw the cash in my hands, her face didn't light up, like I'd expected. And she didn't even bother to see how much was there. She just stared at it with a faraway look on her face, then curled my fingers over the bills.

"Sweetie," she said kindly, lifting her hand to cup my cheek. The resigned look in her eyes frightened me to the core. "I believe my cousin Earl needs this a lot more than me. Hey, Earl!" She cried out to a man dancing nearby. "Our Robin's got something for ya—so you can git that new heater."

The man she called to stopped dancing with a curious look on his face. He walked up to us, spying the money in my palm, and immediately he grabbed me and lifted me in the air, swirling around so fast I got dizzy and begged to be set down. Then he insisted that I dance with him. Before I could resist, we were gallumpfing around the bonfire with bounding two-steps as he sang along to the brisk melody:

"We'll all go to heaven when the Devil goes blind,
But not till my baby puts her hand in mine,
And swings with me till the break o' dawn,
Saint Peter don't call, I got dancin' shoes on!"

He kept whirling me this way and that, and then he gave me a really hard spin. All of a sudden I broke loose, and I found myself stumbling . . .

Right into the arms of Creek.

"Whoa, hold on!" Creek laughed, gripping me tightly so I wouldn't fall into the bonfire. His face glowed from the flames.

"Looks like you got the hang of things. But don't lose your footing."

He enveloped me in his arms and began to sway a little—for a few, blissful moonlit moments—as the music slowed to a softer melody. Catching my breath, I glanced up and saw the stars flicker above us, so bright now in the clear night sky, and the way Creek's eyes seemed to match their light. His hold on me felt strong and enduring . . . and tingles began to spark along my skin. Something inside told me I was living out every teenage girl's dream—dancing with a hot guy most Pinnacle chicks would kill for. But even so, my heart started to wobble. How could I just lay my head on Creek's chest right now and pretend to have a romantic "interlude," after seeing Brandi? With the way she looked, she might not last another two weeks.

Creek pressed his cheek against mine, his feet moving slower now, as if he'd somehow been able to detect my thoughts. His grip on my hand stiffened until it hurt.

"We're gonna beat this, Robin," he whispered defiantly, glancing over at Brandi. "She's family, and we never give in. Tonight, we're gonna figure out a way to make a bigger hit."

"Family," I nodded, allowing the edges of that word to seep into my soul a little. The whole notion was completely foreign to me—not at all like the glad-handing and air kisses of people I'd known in my dad's world. This was more like a slow-burning coal, something that made me feel warm inside, yet nervous at the same time, because I knew couldn't just shake it off on a whim like so many plastic smiles. What Creek meant by "family" struck much deeper, in a place I'd never known existed before. A place he'd called my heart.

I swallowed hard, wondering if Creek could sense the conflicting thoughts that had run through my mind. When I searched his eyes, I realized they were that determined, icy blue again. And I knew right then and there that he meant every word of his resolve, and that we wouldn't stop until Brandi, Dooley, my dad—everyone at Turtle Shores—was taken care of.

Then I watched as a slight softness returned to Creek's face, while our feet swished in the grass. His eyes even became a bit cocky, with a hint of something more, as if he were withholding a secret. Puzzled, I noticed that the compound had grown quiet. Bixby had stopped playing the banjo, and I could no longer hear fiddles or the TNT Twins' fireworks any more. A hush had fallen over Turtle Shores.

"What happens now?" I whispered to Creek, feeling self-conscious in his arms in front of everyone, with no music to dance to. "Is the party over?"

"Not exactly," he replied with a smirk. "Folks 'round here don't waste good firewood on a bonfire unless it's something pretty important."

Just then, I could've sworn I saw his eyes twinkle.

"Happy birthday to you," he began to sing softly. "Happy birthday to you."

Startled, I opened my mouth to correct him—my birthday wasn't till May. But he quickly placed a finger over my lips. Then I heard other voices join in, their chorus swelling until the song filled the meadow.

And when I glanced left and right, I realized that standing around us in a circle now was a throng of people. I spotted Bixby and Dooley and even the TNT Twins' in their silly boulder costumes and helmets, plus a whole host of folks I didn't know. All at once, I heard Granny let out one of her raucous cackles.

"Here she comes—git on over and make some room!" Granny said, leading people to step aside.

The circle split open, and to my total shock, Lorraine appeared from out of the shadows of the woods. She was holding a beautiful white cake with sweet pink and purple roses, her arm linked around the Colonel's. The candles on the cake warmed her face, though I could tell by her blank expression that she didn't quite know where I was.

"A little to the left, my dear," the Colonel said, leading her directly to where we stood.

"Happy birthday, darlin'!" Lorraine gave me a gummy, toothless smile as they stopped, holding out the cake. "I made this special today, just for you—from scratch. It's my great-grandma's recipe with real buttermilk and vanilla bean."

I choked down my embarrassment and accepted the cake, every muscle in my body twisting. Oh Lord, how do I tell them all the truth? They'd gone to such trouble!

"Creek," I whispered through my teeth, shaking my head, "there's been a huge mistake. I was born on—"

In that second, I caught sight of my dad out of the corner of my eye. He was still sitting near the bonfire in the chair by Granny's wagon. But when his eyes met mine, he hung his head.

Like he'd just gotten caught red-handed.

"Robin," Creek whispered back, "it *is* your birthday." He stole a glance at my dad, too. "Maybe the whole thing about May was—"

I held up my hand to stop him.

"Got it," I snapped, staring down at the burning candles beneath my nose. "Yet another lie—"

I couldn't help myself; I began to tremble all over. And to be honest, there was nothing I wanted more in that moment than to walk up to my dad and take a swing, or at the very least, slam Lorraine's double-decker homemade cake right into his face—

But I couldn't.

Because as I looked around at everyone, their expressions so warm and genuine, I was completely overwhelmed by the kindness in their eyes. Yet it also forced me to admit one very brutal fact:

No one—absolutely no one—in my entire life had ever given me a birthday party like this unless they'd been paid extremely well by my father to do so. And after all those long, lonely years, it turned out they weren't even celebrating my real birthday after all.

Tears slid down my face, both from a gratitude to the people at Turtle Shore and my shame at learning the truth.

"There, there now sweetie!" Lorraine reached out a hand to brush the tears aside, as if she'd memorized the contours of my cheeks. "You're gonna put out yer candles if you keep that up. C'mon now—blow!"

I shook my head and motioned for Dooley to come over and help me. He trotted up, his face the very picture of hope.

"Make a wish," he said excitedly. "Granny told me it's your birthday!"

My breath halted as I tried to allow that information to truly sink in.

Then I nodded and closed my eyes for a wish.

Dear Lord, I prayed from the bottom of my heart—

I snuck a peek at my dad again, only to see him turn his face and study the ground.

Please help us get enough money to save Brandi.

And keep me away from sharp objects near my dad.

Or else I swear to you, I'm gonna go straight to Hell for burying him.

Chapter 14

"I'm really sixteen today?"

I leaned back against the tree that held our platform, snuggled halfway inside a sleeping bag Creek had provided, still trying to wrap my head around that idea. Before we'd left Turtle Shores for the night, I'd dutifully taken a piece of cake over to my dad to spoon feed him, glaring the whole time. But did he answer any of my questions about the actual date of my birth?

Hell no.

Like always, he played the slick innocent, suddenly unable to talk between chews due to what he called "duress." Or as he said in his slobbery, tongue-twisted way, "doo-weth." So after ordering him not to give Granny and the Colonel too much trouble for taking care of him in his trailer, I swiped a lick of frosting and landed a sticky smack on his forehead, cussing under my breath as I wished him good night.

"So what is the date today, anyway," I pestered Creek on the tree stand, hoping for a more honest answer. "March, April?"

With all of the craziness lately, I'd completely lost track. I squinted at Creek in the moonlight, counting on my fingers the days since my dad's stroke. "It's gotta be April by now. But April what—first? Oh my God . . ."

I sank into the sleeping bag in disbelief.

"Don't tell me I was born on April Fool's Day—"

Creek kept silent.

And I could've kicked him for that. But I pretty much took it to mean a yes.

"Seriously?" I gasped, hugging the sleeping bag up to my nose, as if I could hide from the truth. "Well that explains everything. No wonder my life's always been such a wreck—"

"Robin," Creek sighed, interrupting my rant.

He was just a silhouette beneath the moonlight now, like some beautiful phantom whispering secrets to me in the dark.

"Your dad had to protect you. He rescued you from the adoption agency, remember? So that means changing your name, birthdate, social security number. Guess he and I have a few things in common."

Chills skittered down my back as I thought of all the ways Creek must have guarded Dooley—if that was even their real names. How many times had they headed to the underground bunkers to hide from well-meaning social workers who would've split them up? Had they gone so far as to fake their own deaths to avoid the system?

"Creek, tell me something," I urged, my palms feeling clammy now. I was about to step over a line, and I knew it. "What's your name? I mean, your real one? Something tells me it isn't what you go by."

Creek didn't move, didn't make a sound.

He seemed like a big shadow cast by a rock.

But we had all night—and I wasn't about to budge, either.

So I took my best shot.

"I'm Rubina McCracken," I offered, like a manifesto of truth that I wanted to reign in my life now. "Born April first, sixteen years ago. How's that for starters?"

I saw Creek shake his head slowly in the dark.

"No. You're Rubina de Bargona," he corrected me. "The granddaughter of a Venetian Count. Your dad never got to marry your mom. So legend around here says Granny gave them a gypsy wedding in the woods. But that doesn't jive with Ohio law, or in Italy either. So technically, you're still a de Bargona."

I sat up straight, my mind spinning. I had Venetian blood in my veins? Were these people still rich, or had they squandered everything like my dad? Since I was illegitimate, maybe it didn't matter.

Just then, I felt something rustle beneath my hand on the platform.

Two stiff pieces of paper. I held them up and tilted them to the moonlight, my eyes straining to distinguish their features.

They were the cards I'd picked out from Granny's deck in her wagon. The Wheel of Fortune and The Lovers.

"What are these doing here?" I dropped them from my hands as if they'd been on fire. "Did Granny put them on the tree stand to try and voodoo me again—"

I heard Creek chuckle in the dark.

"My guess is it was Dooley," he replied. "He really wants us to be together."

Together? I thought. Like boyfriend and girlfriend?

"And to answer your question, my name is Creek. After Stone Cross Creek in Whistler Holler, where my mom grew up. She told me the happiest days of her life were playing in that sparkling water. I want Dooley to have that—to have something beautiful to remember. It's worth more to me than a thousand Italian aristocrats. So we stay near the lake."

His silhouette grew closer, and I could feel the warmth of his palm caress my cheek for a moment, and then his lips pressed softly against mine. He leaned back and brushed the hair from my forehead.

"What I just told you, Robin, you can count on—no matter what. See, I don't change every minute like your dad. 'Cause I ain't ashamed of where I come from, or where I'm going."

"Where are you—we—going?" I asked, my face flushing at my own boldness.

"Right now?" he replied. "Fountain Square. It's got the biggest banks. And there's one that has sloppy surveillance between two-thirty and three am, when security changes shifts. The new guy that just got hired likes to text a little too much. I've had my eye on him for months."

I felt my throat tighten.

That wasn't what I meant at all—our next hit. What I wanted to know is where we were going. As in, if there really is such a thing as a *we*.

And if I'd learned anything at Pinnacle, it's that fortune doesn't favor the weak. Only the strong get what they want, so it was time to ramp it up.

"Are we together Creek?" I asked, picking up the two cards that I'd dropped on the platform. I studied them carefully, hoping to prevent him from reading my gaze in the moonlight. Inside though, my heart was racing. What if he said no?

But I didn't have time to fret over his answer.

Because I felt Creek slip the cards from my hand.

"Hmm," he mumbled, resting his gaze on The Lovers.

Then he lifted the card and traced its edge slowly down the curve of my cheek and along my jaw to my chin, tenderly following the stretch of my throat. Hesitating, he descended to the swell of my breasts and lingered there, enveloping my lips in a kiss.

Not just any kiss.

That kind of kiss!

With the moon behind him, all I could see was his shadow as if he'd become a specter. But the warmth of is lips told me he was for real. And despite the darkness, I felt like my whole body had burst into light.

Creek broke away, even though I craved so much more—

"If we weren't together, Robin," he said softly, "I wouldn't be here right now."

How is it possible to soar without ever leaving the knotty wood slats of our tree stand?

But inside, I felt as if my heart had sprouted wings.

Wheee! I thought, my lips curling into a smile.

And I knew Creek was telling the truth, in a way that I'd never really trusted with my dad, because in spite of all of our bizarre twists and turns lately, he didn't play charades with my emotions. What you saw is what you got. Which is why my heart sank when I heard him clear his throat, as though there was something he needed to clarify.

"But if there's going to be any kind of we," Creek said, surprising me by opening up the flap of my sleeping bag and snuggling inside, "I want you to do something for me."

He wrapped his strong arm around my waist, and his whole body felt hard and warm, yet more like home than anything I'd ever known. I could feel his soft breath, moist upon my neck as he nuzzled even closer, as tight as a glove. His contours were a perfect fit—a piece of a puzzle that I'd never realized was missing before, but that now made me feel more whole. Yet deep inside, there was a part of me that still struggled a little. I'd never for a second wanted to be one of those pathetic, needy girls, like Laura Ritter, who was always waiting for somebody else to complete her while her own heart bled her dry. Girls like that always lost themselves in relationships, becoming nothing more than sad ghosts. So I decided to rib Creek a little, just to keep myself in the driver's seat.

"So what is it you want me to do?" I taunted, giving him a sly poke in the stomach. I shimmied my hips a little, trying to act sexy. "How about a full striptease for the guard in the lobby this time, so you can bust that bank in Cincy?"

Creek grabbed my hand—hard. Startled, I yelped a little, now all too aware that he was in no mood for kidding when it came to matters of the heart.

"Robin," he tightened his arm around my waist like a vise. "I want you . . . to forgive your dad."

I felt my whole body tense up, the angles of my bones digging into the tree platform.

"You can't truly be with me, or anybody else, until you do. 'Cause that anger, it kills something in people. It's what killed my mom."

I felt a trickle slowly slip down my cheek—

A total surprise to me, since I had no idea that my eyes had welled up. I gritted my teeth, willing it to stop and biting into my own flesh so Creek wouldn't hear. But who was I kidding? He was so close, he could probably feel my tears slide against his own skin.

And he just let them fall.

In the dark silence, in that eerie space he always seemed to know how to provide in order to let me be me. Or at least, to try and *find* me.

And a part of myself was a bit grateful for his quiet wisdom. But another part of me wanted to hit him.

How dare Creek accuse me of being bitter, when he knows perfectly well he'd slit the throat of his mom's old boyfriend in two seconds flat if he got the chance?

"Creek," I replied, my muscles tense now to the point of strain, "It's not fair for you to push me for forgiveness when—"

"It's not the same thing," he cut in, sensing where I was heading.

He waited for a second to let that filter in.

"The difference is that your dad really loves you. He's just had to do some pretty awful things to prove that to himself. But he did them for you."

"Then why doesn't he ever show it to my face!" I spit out, sitting up in the sleeping bag now. "You saw him—he acts more fatherly to Dooley than he ever has to me!"

I felt Creek's hand gently stroke my head, then run his fingers along strands of my hair to slowly untangle them. Although I was furious and didn't want to admit it, he had succeeded in calming me a little.

"Doyle doesn't think he can ever be enough for you, Robin. Can't you see that? You're Alessia to him—the woman he can't ever have. Maybe none of us can."

Creek was sitting beside me now. But the moon had shifted behind some thick trees. And without its light, he seemed to be made of total darkness all of a sudden, in a way that spooked me—like he'd somehow taken on my father's soul and managed to talk out loud. I thought about the Wheel of Fortune card, how Granny had told me that history was repeating itself with The Lovers, and shivers slipped down my skin. But just because Creek had kissed me, did that give him the right to trespass over all my family's pain? Why was it his business, anyway?

"Because I want to love you, too, Robin."

I sucked air.

Creek had said that in the barest whisper. But he might as well have shouted it with a megaphone to my soul.

And I sat frozen in the dark, breathless.

Feeling split wide open.

There was no hiding with this guy! No Geisha tricks that could work on Creek to defend myself.

He was pure and raw. And he demanded nothing less from me.

"You asked me earlier today about being real," he said, honoring my physical space by not touching me now. "Well all I know is that you gotta be the one to love your dad first. 'Cause he's all broken inside, Robin. And your anger is keeping him from healing."

"What—what do you mean?"

"I saw him grab a big, long stick during the hoedown tonight, while everyone else was busy dancing. He used it to pull himself up and try and limp around in the dark behind Granny's wagon, where he thought nobody could see him. But I did. And when he caught me watching, he started swearing. His speech was perfect, Robin."

Oh my God, how I wanted to slug my dad. Of course! He'd been playing up his disability all along, because deception is his superpower.

"And he struggled to walk over to me," Creek added. "It was hard for him, but he did it. He was trying to man up and face me—to be a real dad. And with every bit of strength he had in him, he shook that big stick at me and said, 'Don't turn her into a crook.'"

"Wha—?"

"It's true—that's what he said. He was slow, but his words came out clear as a bell."

I started to laugh. "M-My dad, advising anyone not to be a criminal? How on earth did you respond?"

Creek was quiet for a long time.

He gently tugged me back down to the platform, his hand easing my head onto the sleeping bag. Then he laid down beside me. We could see the stars peeking through the branches above us, and the moon had inched from behind the trees, glimmering pure white once again. It was so beautiful I wanted to hold the sight in my heart forever. But I was hanging onto Creek's every word.

Creek kissed my cheek before tilting my head onto his chest to use for a pillow. He caressed my hair for a moment. I felt his lungs rise and fall with a long breath.

"I told your dad it was too late for that," he finally answered me. "We already are crooks. And that's probably not gonna change any time soon. Then I told him something else, but that's just between two men."

I held my breath, wondering if there's anything else Creek wanted say to me.

He twirled a strand of my long hair around his finger for a few seconds before letting it fall back to my shoulder.

"Robin," Creek confessed, "I think I broke his heart."

Chapter 15

I climbed onto the Indian's cold metal seat in the dark, after Creek had silently rowed us in the boat across Bender Lake in the moonlight.

No candles this time.

Nothing that could give us away to Bob or anyone else who might want to track us down. Like Creek said, we're vampires now—nocturnal creatures who only strike at night. And after taking a quick catnap on the tree stand, and then stuffing in more of my birthday cake to tide us over, we were ready to set out for our next hit.

But as I wrapped my arms around Creek on the motorcycle, I felt him reach into his pocket before he started up the motor. He pulled out something and tucked it into my hand. From its softness, I knew immediately what it was.

A feather.

My throat clenched and I said a silent prayer for our safety.

Before the roar of the engine split my ears.

Then I blew the feather into the wind and hugged Creek's waist for all I was worth. The Indian lurched forward, and in no time we were bulleting through darkness.

No headlights.

Our journey lit solely by the moon.

Creek navigated the bike along dirt edges of farm fields and down abandoned gravel country lanes, where not another soul was traveling. For over an hour the wind whipped my hair as we wove past silhouettes of black forests and rolling hills, my nose filled with the scent of moist earth and the early burst of spring crops. Occasionally, I saw unlit farmhouses and barns that looked like big boxes in the night, until we finally saw the twinkling lights of Cincinnati. The closer we got to the city, the more the tall buildings rose high before us, sparkling like jewels.

My heart skipped at the sight.

Because all of a sudden, it came rushing back—

Only a short time ago, I was a bonafide city girl.

The kind of chick who had 3 designer handbags in spring colors and a diamond-rimmed cell phone.

And not a single real friend in the whole world.

But now I did.

I actually had a motley, makeshift family. They were the craziest group of people I'd ever met. But they were also nearer to my heart than all the paid staff I'd known for ages.

And I was about to commit a crime for them.

Flutters skittered in my belly until my stomach began to twist.

I felt Creek reach down to pat my leg, as though he'd sensed my nerves through the white-knuckled grip I had around his waist.

He headed the motorcycle beneath a big cement bridge at the outskirts of the city, and in the moonlight I could see we were entering a rough neighborhood full of junk cars and run-down houses with cracked windows that had iron bars over them. It was the kind of area my chauffeur would never have dreamed of going through, and I can honestly say I'd never seen this side of the city before. Then a dog charged at a chain link fence alongside us, barking viciously and rattling the metal gate so hard it made me jump.

Junk yard dog, I thought, spotting the high coils of razor wire.

A couple of dark figures lingered on the unlit street corner ahead, not even bothering to look up as we sped by with no headlight. What on earth were they doing on a sketchy street in Cincinnati at this hour?

Exactly the same thing we're doing, I realized—

Getting ready to commit a crime.

And that's when it hit me.

This is what poverty really looks like.

No wonder Creek keeps Dooley near Bender Lake.

The folks at Turtle Shores might be loony tunes, and well below even food stamp status, but at least they had the beauty of the lake around them—something that could nourish their souls.

And I never thought I'd say this in a million years, but around all the hard pavement, brick, and steel of the city, I actually found myself missing the soft, green surroundings of the lake.

Just then, Creek made a hard right at an intersection that funneled us onto a street leading downtown, and I prayed no cops would stop us for a broken headlight. But by now, I'd noticed that all of the roads Creek took were particularly dark—narrow alleys or back streets tucked behind buildings that had no street lamps. Clearly, he knew these shadowy night routes like the back of his hand. Then he made another turn onto a tight street sandwiched between two tall buildings. All at once, I saw a glow ahead of us.

Fountain Square.

Its central statue lit up with golden streams of water.

As we approached, the giant bronze woman at the top of the statue loomed before us. She held her arms outstretched like an angel, her hands spilling water. The needy bronze figures below her looked up with eyes of hope, as though her gift might save lives.

A lot like the way people viewed Creek.

I hugged him even tighter, as if that were even possible, wondering how many times I'd played beside this fountain as a little girl with nannies who didn't give a shit. I'd defy city rules and splash in the fountain pool on warm afternoons, getting my school uniform all wet, until I eventually got bored and would demand to be taken to Tiffany's.

Tiffany's!

Out of the corner of my eye, I spied the pretty teal overhangs opposite the square, lit up by soft floodlights.

"Stop!" I cried into Creek's ear, jiggling him.

He slowed the Indian to a pause and turned to me, but by then I'd already leaped off the motorcycle and started running—

Right into the arms of the loveliest place on earth.

I stopped in front of the windows, pressing my hands against the glass, just like I always did as a little girl.

But the displays were empty.

Of course! It was two-thirty am. Who shops for diamonds at this hour?

Creek was beside me in a shot.

"What are you doing?" he whispered hoarsely, clenching my arm. "We can't be seen here—"

"But the spring collection!" I gasped. Never in my life had I missed the new lineup of charms and bracelets and pendants. When I used to think I was born in May, I always had plenty of time to peruse the new spring catalog before demanding one as my birthday gift.

Creek grasped my shoulders and swiveled me to face him.

"You're not that girl any more!" he hissed, glaring into my eyes. "Just one—*one*—of those tiny gold rings in there would be enough to save Brandi's life." He shook me a little. "Do you hear me?"

Hear him? Was he kidding? His words hit me like a blow between the eyes.

If I still had my cell phone Sparkle, we wouldn't have to be trying to rob a bank right now. We could have fenced it for thousands of dollars.

That thought struck me in the gut, and I sank a little in Creek's grip. When I glanced back into Tiffany's, I noticed a few baubles were lit up in the innermost display cases of the store. Those shiny jewels used to represent a kind of hope for me. A belief that I could make life better for myself someday— somehow—if I just hung on long enough to survive my family's weirdness.

But now everything inside that store looked dark and cold.

Creek wrapped me tightly in his arms, as if he'd felt me shiver. "We gotta get out of here, Robin," he whispered, "into the shadows again."

I nodded, and he grabbed me by the hand and rushed me back to the motorcycle. But instead of kickstarting it, he walked the bike by the handlebars as we headed into the darkness beside a building, slinking quietly into the shadows towards the back of a bank.

And not just any bank.

Cincinnati Federal.

The richest, most glorious financial institution in the city—with crystal chandeliers in the lobby, Italian marble on the floor, and bank tellers who were forced to wear little black bowties and greet everyone, regardless of age, as either "Sir" or "Madam."

How do I know this?

Because Laura Ritter's dad is the bank president. And a month ago after school, she finagled a pass from Pinnacle for us to visit him under the guise of "career day." After he spent all of one minute smiling at us and giving me a handshake, he sent her off to give me a private tour of the bank so we'd be out of his hair. Which included entering the vault without a single adult around.

This is back when Laura thought we were going to become girlfriends.

As in, *those* kind of girlfriends.

And I completely led her on so she'd finish my crummy essay on "The Legacy of Geisha Power in Asian Culture."

Just a few kisses—okay, that led to a full-blown makeout session inside the bank vault where no one could see us—were enough to convince Laura that she could trust me. And her work got me an A.

As well as the code to the vault and the back door.

It wasn't hard. Laura's dad had made her name and beginning letter of their last name the password to the vault keypad, and reversed it for everywhere else. I could hear her proudly whisper "L-A-U-R-A—R" as she typed it in. Being her dad's only daughter, who he showered with expensive gifts instead of attention, I could tell Laura took the code as a grand sign of affection. How would she know any different? That same slick crap used to work on me, too.

And I didn't think much of it at the time, until now.

Little did Laura know she'd been kissing a future criminal. But I guess after copping a feel up my bra, she'd gotten what she wanted out of the deal.

"Creek," I said, grabbing his jean jacket to make him stop walking. "We don't have to con the security guard to this bank. I know the codes—"

"What?" he replied, floored. He moved towards a thin alley between two buildings that was as black as ink.

"Seriously, I know how to get in," I pressed. "I went to school with the bank president's daughter. Trust me."

Creek was silent. I could feel him weighing my words, weighing the consequences of altering plans that had taken him months to create. But then he very carefully opened up the bag he'd dragged with him all the way from Bender Lake and pulled out our wigs and coveralls.

I knew this was a big step for Creek. He was used to leading the way, controlling every second so nobody got hurt. But this kind of intel didn't come along every day.

I stepped into the faded gray coveralls that Creek had brought and slipped on a dowdy wig. It was shaggy and dishwater blonde, designed to make me invisible. Part of the plan was that we were to look like the cleaning crew—substituting for Jarrod's Cleaning Service that normally comes on Thursdays, but sometimes has another company fill in on Fridays. From observing the security guard for months who only covered Friday night, Creek knew the guy didn't pay much attention to his job for the first half hour. The minute he arrived for work, he liked to spend his time texting the strippers he'd just ogled at the Gilded Lily that closed down at two am. Creek said he always pestered the women with obnoxious phone calls while walking up to the bank, then feverishly sent them texts to follow up.

Which was exactly what he was doing right now.

"Hey Starla, what's happenin'?" we could hear him say, a dark figure striding slowly across the parking lot to the back of the bank. "What? Amber gave me your number. No, not to get me off her back—Starla? *Starla* . . . fuck it!"

I could see the guy shake his head and swiftly punch more numbers into his cell. Creek was zipping his coveralls after throwing on a short, brown wig and stuffing in his hair. Then he hid our motorcycle behind some trash cans and returned, clutching my hand and giving it a squeeze.

"Let's do this," he said in a rough whisper.

And he surprised me by giving me a kiss.

A deep, thrill-you-to-your-bones but utterly frightening kiss.

Because everything about it said, *If anything goes wrong, baby, just remember—I love you.*

And I'd never gotten one of those in my entire life!

As much as I wanted to melt right then and there into the pavement, I was too flat-out scared.

Creek broke away, his hands still wrapped around my cheeks, holding me steady. He just gazed at me, like he wanted to tuck my face into his heart. My pulse felt like a speeding bullet. Then we both took really deep breaths and turned to walk single file to the back door of the bank with our heads down like we'd planned, as though we'd been doing this crappy job for years and we hated it.

Gulping hard, I could feel the apprehension swelling in my throat as big as a fist.

When we reached the door, I lifted my hand to punch in the code, but Creek snatched my wrist—

"No," he whispered. "The cleaning crew wouldn't know the code."

Duh!

I nodded at him and bit my lip, spotting the buzzer. I pressed it and glanced again at Creek, memorizing the name "John" on his fake nametag. I was "Sue," and we "usually" worked for Sunshine Cleaning Service, but we'd "agreed" to fill in tonight for Jarrod. Creek had fake paperwork in his pocket that claimed we were bonded. I didn't even ask him where he'd stolen it from.

But it turns out we didn't need it, because the security guard was too busy chomping on a big bag of chips and finishing up a heated conversation on his cell to pay any attention to us.

"Yeah? Well screw that!" he grumbled, letting us inside the door. As soon as he saw our nametags, he didn't bother to ask for more. Creek merely muttered, "We're the fill-ins for Jarrod," as we stepped inside, and that was enough to get us rolling.

I quickly tugged on Creek's arm to follow me to the cleaning closet. It was a door on the right where Laura had first tried to kiss me, but I'd kept her at bay by slipping behind a bucket and shoving a mop between us. "This isn't quite the right place," I'd giggled at the time, like I was teasing her.

But now it was no joke.

Hands trembling, I picked out an aerosol can and a feather duster from the closet while Creek pulled out the vacuum. The thought occurred to me that I'd never used these things before, and I watched in awe as Creek appeared to know exactly where the cord was hidden on his industrial-sized machine. He yanked it out like a pro and plugged it in, nodding at me to continue down a hall. When he turned on the power, the vacuum roared like a freight train.

Perfect!

Now security guy wouldn't hear a thing.

And I felt my pulse calm down a little. So far everything was working out. I shook my duster at random surfaces, trying to act like I knew what I was doing, and headed towards the lobby, an area I figured most cleaning crews started with first. Creek followed behind me, running the vacuum over the carpet. We kept our noses to the grindstone and methodically covered the whole lobby, then slipped behind where the tellers normally worked. I wasn't sure whether there might still be cash in the drawers to steal—our original plan, since Creek had said this particular bank had gotten arrogant and sloppy and didn't even use dye packs. I reached up to try and open one to check. But then I felt Creek bump me so hard that I lost my grip.

Startled, I saw him shake his head and point towards a hall at the back.

The vault.

Looking into his eyes, I nodded. Why bother with cash drawers when I had the vault code?

We both proceeded toward a set of mahogany double doors. As soon as we stepped through, Creek braced the large vacuum against the doors and left it running.

Oh God, this is it! I thought, shaking a little as we headed down another hall. But I smirked while Creek walked towards an enormous, round steel door at the end, the kind of vault you always see in movies. Since the building was over a hundred years old, and a historical landmark in the city, most people assumed that it was the only vault. But Laura Ritter had shown me differently.

I whistled loudly at Creek, enjoying the surprise in his eyes when he turned around.

Pointing to a plain metal door on the side, I motioned him to come over.

"This is the secret vault," I said when Creek got close. It was very unassuming—in fact, everything in this part of the bank was kind of ragged, compared to the elegant entrance with its showy crystal and marble, designed to put customers in awe. The carpet here was threadbare, as if it hadn't been changed in decades, and the secret vault door was hardly state of the art. It looked like something designed years ago when maybe keypads were still considered "hi tech." Nevertheless, when Laura showed it to me, she was proud.

"All the employees think the other vault is the main one," she revealed with a knowing smile. "But here's where my daddy stores special deposits." She whispered her name as she typed into the keypad like an idiot. "Daddy lets me study in here sometimes, because it's so *private*," she said as seductively as the geekiest girl on campus could manage. "You know, if you ever wanted to meet me to study, we wouldn't even have to come in the front door." She licked her lips. "'Cause I just reverse the code for the back. It could be like our own little tryst." With a sly wink, she spun the turnstile handle and opened the vault door wide.

"What about security cameras. Wouldn't people see us make out in here?" I asked, pretending to be interested. In reality, I couldn't wait to split.

"Oh, nobody looks at those," Laura waved her hand. "The images are too fuzzy anyway. Get real—my dad said nobody's dared to rob his bank in over fifty years."

At that moment, I thought Laura's bragging was a total snore, even when she showed me some exotic gold coins her dad kept inside. But after holding my breath now beside Creek and typing into the keypad to open the vault, the bland gray interior all of a sudden looked like heaven to me.

Forget rare gold coins that could be easily traced—

What made my heart race were the bags.

Beautiful bags of cash.

God only knows who they belonged to. Laura had said most of the bank's safe deposit boxes were in the circular-door vault, with the exception of her dad's special holdings. But ownership wasn't exactly on our minds as Creek and I quickly picked up one bag each and stuffed them into our shirts inside our coveralls. Then Creek gripped my hand and yanked me from the room.

"Ow!" I yelped.

"Move!" he said. "The less time we spend in here, the less likely we are to get into trouble."

He slammed the door behind us and spun the handle, then tugged me down the hall towards his running vacuum.

I couldn't believe it—I actually had thousands of dollars of cash bumping up against against my Pinnacle-issue bra. Sure, I wouldn't have minded taking a few more bags, but I could see Creek's logic as he grabbed the vacuum and moved it from the double doors, proceeding to keep cleaning the floor while we headed our way back towards the bank teller area.

With my feather duster and aerosol can in hand, I sprayed and wiped with a fury, sneezing a couple of times. Secretly, I snickered a bit at the fact that this was the first time I'd ever cleaned anything. But my heart nearly leaped to the rafters when I saw the security guard slowly stroll into the lobby. He began to walk in little angry circles underneath the giant chandelier, cussing.

"Goddammit!" he fumed, typing into his cell phone.

I did my best to look haggard and bored, the way I assumed most cleaning ladies must, fluffing my feather duster over a cabinet and keeping my eye on Creek nearby. Casually, he continued to rake his vacuum beneath a desk.

"Three hundred lousy bucks into her thong, and the bitch wouldn't even talk to me!"

I couldn't help giggling a little, and I saw Creek smirk too, shaking his head. We were nearly home free. All we had to do was linger here a while longer—act like we were still doing a good job—and then head to the back door.

Creek gazed up and nodded at me to veer left away from the lobby, and I followed his lead, until I heard the security guy stop swearing.

His long silence froze me in place.

With a quick glance, I saw him staring directly at us with a disturbed look on his face, so I kept my eyes glued to my feather duster on a windowsill, swishing vigorously.

"Hey!" he barked over the sound of Creek's vacuum.

I thought my heart might explode—

"Don't you guys need some better light?"

All around us, the bank had recessed amber lights for a subtle radiance that enabled us to walk around the building and do an okay job cleaning, but hardly enough to pass a white glove test. Obviously, it hadn't been in our interest to throw on the daytime switches.

But that idea occurred to the security guy now.

All at once, the lobby was flooded with the searing white glow of the giant crystal chandelier. It was so bright it stung my eyes, and I threw my elbow over my face. As my eyes adjusted and I lowered my arm, I could hear Creek turn off the vacuum and drag it close to me to plug it into another socket. But before he could edge past me, I suddenly saw it—

"My house!"

I couldn't help it—those shocked words left my lips as I spied, right in front of me on the marble wall, a poster of my house in Indian Hill. It was supposed to be foreclosed and auctioned off when my dad's law firm went under. But instead, there was a picture of our mansion that had bright gold lettering below it that read:

❧ SPRING FUNDRAISER BALL ❧
April 3ʳᵈ at the elegant home
of Charles & Chloe Tweedle

"What?" I cried. "What the hell's Tweedle doing with my house if the law firm went belly up? That son of a bitch—he's the one who must've been embezzling . . ."

Despite the fact that my rage made me see only red in that moment, all at once I realized that it was so quiet now that you could hear a pin drop.

And before I knew what hit me, a pair of strong arms had grabbed me and practically thrown me from the lobby down the hall facing the back of the bank.

It was Creek. And all he said was, "Run! Run like hell!"

He was racing beside me, our money bags bouncing hard against our chests. My legs were moving as fast as I could carry them—while I was still coming to grips with my stupid outburst. How could I possibly have been such an idiot?

"Stop right there!" the security guard called out.

But we were mere feet from the door and not about to halt now. Creek shoved me in front of him, and that's when I heard a deafening blast—

The echo thundered against the walls, so loud I thought it might crack my head open.

It had to be a gun! Oh God, I was far too scared to turn around and check. I heard Creek's voice say, "Open the door!"

I wrangled with the handle and shoved my body against it, bursting into the cold night air when I heard another shot—

"Creek!" I cried, swiveling to see if he was okay.

But the guy I saw coming out the door was a bloody mess.

"Oh my God!" I screamed in shock as he raced towards me.

Creek yelled, "Move—move NOW!" His body only inches from mine—

But just then I heard another blast.

I felt him fall hard against me.

And that's when everything went black.

Chapter 16

"See, it's your *soul* that's marked," I heard Granny Tinker cackle. She was wearing black boots and a long, red velvet coat with white ruffles sticking out of her sleeves like some bohemian circus ringmaster. Oddly enough, she stood beside a giant Wheel of Fortune with a bullwhip in her hand. Cracking her whip, she looked at me like she meant business and gave the wheel a turn. "You can't run away from yer fate even if you tried, darlin'."

I glanced around at the gaudy, striped tent we were in with sawdust on the ground and the stale smell of popcorn everywhere. In the center of the arena was my dad in a colorful clown costume juggling burning torches as though he'd never been paralyzed. He stopped all of a sudden and slipped one down his throat. When he pulled it out again, he looked at me and smiled.

"Easy as one of Lorraine's pies," he declared in perfect English.

Dooley laughed, riding past him on top of a baby elephant, looking as happy as could be.

"Where's Creek?" I cried out, totally confused.

"Well, now there's somethin' we gotta talk about, sweetheart," Granny said, waiting for the Wheel of Fortune to stop spinning. She tipped her black top hat to me. "He's gonna need some of my very best herbs to heal, that's fer sure. But it's mighty hard to git a move on while I'm still asleep, if you catch my drift. So in the meantime, honey, yer gonna have to look after yer Pa."

At that moment, I saw my dad fumble and drop one of his burning torches. The dry sawdust immediately caught on fire. Before I knew it, flames were racing to engulf the arena.

"Daddy!" I cried, watching as Dooley scampered out of the tent on his baby elephant to safety. But I couldn't see my dad any longer in the flames and smoke.

I rushed into the gray, billowing clouds to try and find him.

"Rubina—"

"Rubina!" I heard a voice call.

From inside the smoke, I saw a figure emerge wearing a dark lace shroud. Her beautiful face was as pale as a ghost, and when her eyes met mine, I was mesmerized.

"It's not his time to go," she whispered, before the flames engulfed her, too.

And I screamed.

"It's okay now—it's okay," I heard Creek's voice soothe me, stroking my forehead.

But when I opened my eyes, I could taste blood upon my lips.

I screamed again.

What kind of nightmare was this, where were we?

I sat up and looked around, bewildered.

Everything seemed pitch black.

Yet as my eyes adjusted to the dark, I could tell Creek was behind the wheel of a truck, driving with no headlights again. I was beside him on a couch seat, and my thoughts raced in total panic.

"What happened to you?" I cried, just now noticing in the moonlight that he appeared to have blood all over his shoulder and arm. "Oh my God, we've got to get you to a hospital!"

I saw Creek smirk a little, keeping his eyes on the dark road ahead of us.

"And give away our location after the first successful robbery of Cincinnati Federal in fifty years?"

He pointed a thoroughly bloody arm at the truck floor.

There, on the mats, were two swollen bags.

I couldn't believe it. We actually made it out of there?

"But Creek, how did you—"

"Shhh, take it easy. You got a concussion," he replied, completely focused on navigating the backwoods gravel lane.

God, this guy is as tough as nails! I thought, my mind spinning. He doesn't even seem to notice that he's a bloody wreck.

I saw the moonlight cast a brighter glow on the road as we left a wooded area, and Creek glanced over at me.

"It's better than it looks, Robin. A nine millimeter doesn't hurt so bad, about like a baseball bat. Nothing like the pistol whipping I gave that security guard."

I immediately sucked air.

Creek just sighed.

"I could've shot him back," he said somewhat impatiently. "I was trying to protect you."

That's right, I realized—I had to have passed out by then. And Creek must've somehow jumped the guy and gotten his weapon to fend him off. Then he had to carry me, with the weight of our two money bags and a bullet or two in his arm, to safety. But where on earth did he get this truck?

"H-How did it all happen?" I stuttered, more than a little afraid of his answer. This was a side of Creek that scared the holy shit out of me—the very darkest side that was as mean and deadly as sin when he needed to be.

Creek swerved the truck onto an uneven dirt lane that rimmed the edge of a field.

"When the security guy got me with that second bullet, I stumbled and fell against you to the pavement."

He shook his head.

"What a fuck up—I don't even know why I did that. It was only my arm."

Holy Mother of God. Creek spoke about it as casually as if he'd been at basketball practice or something. But then, a part of me realized this was hardly Creek's first altercation.

"The guy came running up and I dove for him, knocking the pistol out of his hand pretty quick. He whined like you wouldn't believe when I held it to his head. So I told him to give me his truck keys and walk straight back into that bank. Then lock the door and never say a word about seeing you or me or anything. Or I'd show up at his shithole apartment at 247 Sycamore Street on the other side of the river. When he least suspects it, of course."

Creek nodded, still studying the road ahead.

"Let's just say I make it my business to know all about these guys before a hit. And believe me, that man didn't walk back to the bank; he ran for it like his life depended on it. Because it did."

My heart was racing out of control. I wanted to cover my ears—and a really big part of me wanted to cry, too. What the hell had we done? Who had we become?

I never wanted my mother so badly in my whole life, wherever she was.

And that really nasty nightmare I had just before I woke up didn't help matters much. Somehow, I felt like everything I'd ever understood about myself had gone up in flames.

Creek steered the truck from the dirt road into a forest, slowly traveling through the pitch black darkness like he knew exactly where he going. I could hardly see a thing now, but he appeared unconcerned as he wove between the trees. Then he gently stepped on the brake and eased the truck to a stop somewhere deep within the woods.

It was the kind of place you leave a dead body to rot and not be found for decades.

Or where criminals like us stash a getaway vehicle.

"Robin," he raised his bloody hand to my cheek, but it only made me flinch, "with those two bags, we're set. We don't have to do this anymore—we've got two hundred grand. But we do have to lay low for a very long time. And that means no sudden moves, just live in the tree stands each night until this all blows over. And of course, get rid of this truck tomorrow."

"But we're felons now, huh?" I said, feeling the moisture slide down my neck. Dammit—I knew I was crying. It was all so overwhelming.

Creek nodded.

He was quiet for longer than I thought I could bear.

And I hated myself for sounding weak when I said this, but I couldn't' stop. I was never going to be as tough as Creek was no matter how hard I tried.

"Is the security guy gonna be all right?" I burst.

Quietly, Creek leaned forward and kissed my forehead, then wrapped his arms around me and held me tight, rocking me a little. I hadn't known till that very moment that I was shaking all over.

"He'll be okay, Robin," Creek sighed. "He wasn't really supposed to shoot at two unarmed people, you know. But I do feel for him—he's gonna have to steal himself a different truck now."

All at once, I burst out laughing.

I know it sounds crazy, and I was probably hysterical at this point, but all I could do was shake my head and let the laughter spill from deep in my belly.

"Are you serious?" I said, gasping for air. "The guard drove a stolen truck? What kind of bank—"

"Hires a guy like that for security?" Creek shook his head, laughing now, too. "Only one that's gotten way too cocky and casual for its own good."

He loosened his arms from around me and brushed the tears from my cheeks. I wondered if he'd smeared blood on them.

"But we aren't gonna make those kinds of mistakes. So I have to fence this truck tomorrow. And Robin," Creek said, his voice sounding grave now, "we'll never breathe a word about tonight to anyone. Do you hear me? We just keep paying Brandi's medical bills on time from anonymous envelopes."

I nodded, feeling a queasiness rise in my stomach. This was a whole different ball of wax than keeping mum about CeeCee Stone's drug exploits at Pinnacle. I suddenly felt as if Granny's words had come true—that my soul *was* marked now. I had huge secrets to keep, and in one long violent night, my entire life had changed.

Creek grabbed the money bags from the floor and opened his door to step out.

"We have to hoof it from here," he said. "We can't leave a stolen truck too close to where we sleep."

I took a deep breath and followed suit, stepping out of the truck and walking up to Creek to take one of the bags from his grip. After all, I committed this crime too, so I should carry my fair share. But I was grateful when Creek grasped my hand to lead me through the dark woods.

And all the while, I couldn't help thinking that we ought to be happy. Our money problems were solved. Except that near as I could tell, Creek still had a couple of bullets in his arm and shoulder, which he'd probably end up taking out himself with a knife and some alcohol. And now, we were both permanent outcasts.

What was my sixteenth year going to look like? As a fugitive . . .

Had my dad done things like this all along too, even before he'd met Alessia? Did it run in my blood?

As I carefully stepped along the uneven forest path, I resolved to ask him.

Because Creek had told me my dad could speak just fine, when he really wanted to.

But before I could plan out some of my questions, I spotted a hazy glow in the distance.

Which was kind of strange, since the Colonel didn't usually leave the Turtle Shores light on at this hour.

Creek stopped in his tracks.

"Robin," he said abruptly. "Do you smell that?"

"What?"

I took a big whiff.

Smoke. It smelled a lot like the bonfire we'd had, but somehow less woody. More like burning grass and something weird, like maybe gasoline.

And then I heard explosions—

Shocked, we watched as giant fireballs climbed high into the night sky. Their sound was deafening.

Creek yanked against my hand.

"We gotta run!" he cried, pulling me in a mad sprint towards the inferno up ahead. "Turtle Shores is on fire! Oh God, when Bob strikes, he really fuckin' plays for keeps—"

Chapter 17

When we reached Turtle Shores, we couldn't see anything in the massive amount of smoke. Explosions were bursting everywhere, as if all of the TNT Twins' stashes were firing off at once. I screamed—all I could think of was my dad and Dooley and Brandi. Everyone had probably been sleeping when the compound was set on fire! Creek grabbed my money bag from my arms and threw both our bags to safety in an old barrel just beyond the entrance, then pointed at a scraggly tree.

"The bell!" he shouted. "Ring the bell!"

Thank God for adrenaline. Because I was able to gather my wits and do as Creek asked, dashing to the tree and spying a rope. I yanked and yanked on it, praying that everyone would wake up in their trailers and get down to the bunkers. Surely the sound of the explosions would tip them off? Oh God, but what if my dad couldn't get up?

I ran straight into the thickest smoke.

"Robin!" I heard Creek shout after me, but I didn't care what master plan he might have up his sleeve for rescue this time. This is my *dad.* And no matter what he'd done with his life, I wasn't about to wait and let him burn alive.

Twenty strides forward through the center of smoke, then thirty two more directly to the right—

This was how I'd learned to navigate the TNT Twins' holes in the meadow on the way to my dad's trailer. Would Granny or the Colonel be there, too, since they'd agreed to watch out for him? Could I manage to get them all down to the bunker if they were injured?

I didn't know these answers. All I knew was that I was going to do my damndest to try.

I kept dodging the flames that licked at my feet and coughing incessantly at smoke, holding my elbow over my mouth to try and deflect it. Three more strides to the right, I thought, and I should run smack into—ouch!

Holy shit! I'd made it, and I immediately sank to the dirt, my head ringing. I banged against the metal of my dad's trailer and ran my hand along the side to try and find the door. My eyes burned like hell, and I was coughing uncontrollably now.

"Daddy!" I cried. "Hold on, I'm coming!"

There it was—I could feel the metal handle to the trailer. I flipped it open and scrambled inside.

Only to see more smoke, everywhere.

He must've left his windows open—

"DADDY!" I yelled.

But I heard . . . nothing.

There was no silence more sickening to me on the planet in that moment.

"Daddy, where are you?" I begged, beginning to feel woozy from the smoke in my lungs, my eyes stinging like crazy. Nevertheless, I leaped forward to where the couch must be, patting it with my hands to try and feel for my dad. I reached up to the bunk rail but only discovered a pillow and blankets, so I sank down to the floor.

"C'mon, Daddy, where are you?" I cried again, feeling my fingers over the carpet. "Please—knock on something—anything—give me a sign!"

And that's when I saw her.

Hazy, through the smoke . . .

The woman with the dark lace shroud.

She was made of smoke, just like when I saw her in Granny's crystal ball. I swear I could've put my hand straight through her.

And her eyes were closed, as if she'd been . . . praying.

Then she opened them, seeming to look right through me.

And she held up a feather.

She let it fall from her fingers.

Then disappeared.

Stunned, I watched as the feather did little curls in the smoke and floated towards the back of the trailer. I stepped forward after it, my eyes following its twists and turns, until I saw it fall . . .

Right down on my dad.

"Oh my God!" I bent down and jiggled him, but he was as still as a corpse.

"No!" I cried, coughing madly. "No, you can't die!"

There was only one thing to do. I tilted his head back and mashed my lips to his, blowing hard.

I broke away and thumped his chest with all my strength.

Again—then again—

Furiously, I kept trying to resuscitate him, when I felt his good hand grab my arm.

"Ow," I cried. Damn, he still had that iron grip!

My dad coughed hoarsely, so I lifted him up to a sitting position, then threw my arms around his chest and tried to drag him across the floor.

"The bunker!" I screamed, kneeling on the floor to try and feel for the handle. "Where is it?"

"Thust go, Wobbin!" I heard him sputter between coughs. "Thust go!"

And he collapsed in my arms.

No, not like this! I thought, patting the floor frantically. Then I remembered that in Granny's wagon, the stairs to the bunker were at the bottom of a trunk.

But there was no trunk in this trailer.

Except there was a couch—

I dragged my dad over to the old couch and pushed up at the cushion, feeling a metal panel beneath it with a handle.

And I could lift it!

Glory be, there they were—the most beautiful plywood stairs I'd ever seen. Embracing my dad from underneath his arms, I lugged him down the stairs very carefully, taking backward steps and trying to keep my balance. When I'd finally gotten his feet through the opening, I saw the metal panel underneath the cushion slam hard above us and seal off the smoke. I breathed a sigh of relief.

And just then, I heard my dad utter a soft moan.

He was still *alive.*

I stumbled a little and leaned against the wall to steady myself, then dragged my dad to the bottom. I could see his chest rise and fall, giving me hope he might really make it. The very second I was able to hoist him into a recliner and make sure he stayed upright, I ran to a water cooler and got him a drink.

"Here you go," I said, still hacking but tilting up the cup so he could take a sip. God bless him, the air was clear down here. For just how long, I didn't know, but something told me Creek probably had oxygen tanks somewhere if we really needed them. Luckily, after swallowing a little water, my dad hacked for a few seconds like I did, then took deep breaths of the clean air.

He stared into my eyes.

"Sank yoo," he said.

His eyes didn't dart from me, like they often did when he was spinning his usual lies. Instead, he lifted his good hand to his mouth to push his tongue over a bit to the left. I saw him close his eyes for a second, as though trying to concentrate.

"Thaaank . . . yooou," he said deliberately, in perfect King's English.

Tears swelled in my eyes.

He did it! He'd just proved to me that he's actually trying to get better, not just relying on his slick victim routine to manipulate me even more.

I wanted to hug him in that moment.

Hug him and grab a washcloth and wipe some of the smoky grime from his face. But the very second I had that thought, I heard a violent, crashing boom—

I assumed it was another one of the TNT Twins' stashes exploding. But after that, we could hear the peculiar sound of rushing water.

And to our surprise, we saw a little stream of water begin to trickle down the stairs.

"Where's this water coming from?" I gasped. "It wasn't even raining outside."

My dad clutched my arm.

His eyes appeared less than alarmed—more like relieved.

"Waaaater Towwwer," he enunciated very slowly.

Water Tower?

I shook my head, unable to picture what he was talking about, when I heard the metal door to the bunker creak open.

"You okay down there?" The Colonel poked his head in and shouted. He spied the two of us with his one eye, looking us over carefully, and then nodded. "Better check if Creek's got some mud boots stashed, 'cause Turtle Shores is gonna be a swamp for a while. Creek done blowed up Bixby's homemade water tower to put out the fire."

Holy Smokes, I thought—he always did find a way of thinking big.

"Too bad about all that money you got," the Colonel continued, looking at me. "Everyone in the compound's fine, even my Attack Geese made it down to the bunker. And we only lost one old pop-up trailer to the fire. But them poor money bags just got all blown straight to hell."

Chapter 18

"What?"

I dashed upstairs and out into the compound quicker than the Colonel could say "incendiary device."

Only to see clouds of steam hovering over the entire meadow at the cusp of dawn, with pieces of confetti falling all around me like rain.

Green little pieces of confetti.

As in, our cash—

I sank to my knees in the gooey mud that had at least a quarter inch of water still on top. Desperately, I grabbed at the stray bits of damp paper.

Surely we could paste them together, I thought, coughing at the mix of steam and smoke. Somehow tape all those little pieces into bills once again?

I rose to my feet, swiping at some of the bigger shreds that floated down among the ash, my sneakers squishing in mud. Then I saw a corner of paper with the number 50 on it, convinced it was a good sign. I snatched it from the air, feeling victorious.

But when I glanced down at the small handful of pieces I'd collected, I suddenly realized how ridiculous I was.

They looked like someone had put our cash through a blender.

And at the entrance of the compound, I spied what used to be the barrel Creek had put our bags in, now just a dark hole in the ground with shards of metal everywhere.

"Oh God," I moaned, slumping into a crouch in the mud with my head in my hands. "Why didn't we just drop our bags back in the woods?"

"'Cause they would've gotten stolen. Or worse, we'd be arrested," I heard a familiar voice behind me say. "Those bags had our finger prints all over 'em."

I whipped around—it was Creek!

I hardly recognized him. He was a filthy, dirt-splattered mess.

But I threw my arms around him anyway and gave him a kiss, a mud and confetti-soaked kiss.

"Ouch!" he winced.

Oh geez, I'd completely forgotten that he still had a couple of bullet wounds in his arm and shoulder.

"It's okay—it's okay," he reassured me, giving me a half-smile that made his cheek scar crinkle into that wicked dagger I'd come to love. He pointed to his other cheek away from the bad shoulder and gave it a tap. "Here, maybe?"

Yes! I gave him a big smooch, so grateful he was okay—that we were *all* okay—because that's the only thing that mattered to me now.

But until then, I hadn't noticed that he was holding a glass jar that said *Ball* on it.

"Do me a favor," Creek asked, handing me the jar. He unzipped his bloody coveralls and flinched as he slipped his arm out of his t-shirt to reveal the ghastly bullet wounds.

I threw my hand over my mouth in shock. I could see where he'd already dug out the bullets, probably with Bixby's hunting knife. Or worse, a screw driver.

"Pour the Colonel's moonshine over these, will you?"

Was he serious?

"Go on!" Creek barked. He pulled a stick out of his coveralls pocket and shoved it between his teeth. "Do me up."

Shaking a little, I tipped the jar over the worst shoulder wound and shut my eyes.

I could hear Creek hissing from the pain, cursing under his breath.

"One more shot, Robin," he insisted.

When I opened my eyes, I saw Creek's face buckled into a cringe.

"Just get it over with—quick," he urged.

I threw a splash on the last bullet wound on his bicep, and Creek gritted his teeth and shook his head.

"I can take care of the rest of that," I heard Granny Tinker call out.

When I turned, I saw her slogging through the mud, not seeming to care if her lace-up boots got all filthy.

"Hot damn! We haven't had this much water flood through Turtle Shores since the lake overflowed in nineteen sixty-nine. One of my favorite years, though, the Summer of Love—"

For once, I was overjoyed to hear her crackling voice. She carried with her a handful of herbs and a white roll of gauze bandage.

"Step aside now an' let me put a poultice on them wounds," she ordered, pulling a tiny pot from her pocket. She lifted the ceramic lid to reveal some kind of ointment.

I stared at her, wondering how on earth she knew Creek needed medical attention? But she just glared back at me as if that sort of insight ought to be obvious by now.

"Ow—shit, Granny!" Creek cried as she rubbed the herbs and ointment into his wounds and bandaged them. "That burns more than the moonshine."

Granny grabbed his chin and wiggled it.

"Don't you fuss at me, young man. I'll have you as good as new in no time," Granny scolded.

Then she put her fingers together and gave a loud whistle through her teeth.

Up popped the TNT Twins from two vats in the meadow, all covered in yellow custard and red jello.

But remarkably unharmed from the fire and flood.

"It's almost daylight," Granny warned. "Cops are gonna be sniffing around here in no time, wonderin' what all them explosions was about. I reckon I'll feed 'em a good story and send them on their way, as long as y'all are safe in the bunkers. Whoops, too late."

Red and blue lights swirled across the canopy of trees just beyond the entrance to Turtle Shores, but I didn't spot the squad car yet. Like groundhogs, the TNT Twins snapped back into their holes with a splash of water and mud, completely invisible.

"Come on!" I cried to Creek, yanking at his good arm. "Let's get into my daddy's bunker—"

I knew hiding at Turtle Shores wasn't Creek's first choice, but we didn't have time to run for a tree stand in the woods.

Creek followed me into my dad's trailer, where I threw up the sofa cushion and opened the metal panel to allow us down the stairs. Our feet drummed hard as we scampered below to my dad.

"Cops!" I cried to him, watching his left eye grow wide.

And then his right eye slowly opened wider, too.

Whoa, was my dad really starting to recover feeling on that side of his face?

Part of me didn't know whether to do a happy dance for him, or to start demanding a host of explanations.

I decided to go for the latter.

"Listen up, Daddy," I began, wondering how to dress up the fact that Creek and I had been out robbing a bank last night. But shouldn't somebody tell the truth in my family for once? Turn a new leaf?

"Me and Creek were at Cincinnati Federal a few hours ago," I declared boldly. "I think you know exactly why."

To my astonishment, my dad's eyes narrowed and he glared at Creek. He had a strangely bitter yet protective look on his face, like a . . . real father? One who actually cared where I'd run off to at night, and who I was with?

My heart warmed at the sight. But that wasn't going to stop me from pressing for more answers.

"Dad, I saw a poster at the bank for a fundraiser at *our* house. Only your partner Tweedle is supposedly the owner now. How's that possible?"

I paused for a moment, letting the information sink in for him.

"Be honest, Daddy," I insisted. "Did you embezzle that money from the law firm?"

My dad said nothing.

In fact, he wasn't even looking at me—he was looking through me, as though his mind had gone somewhere else entirely.

I heaved a sigh. What was I thinking? My dad had never fessed up to anything before, so why would he start now? His whole brain is stitched together with lies, so if he ever told the truth it would probably begin to unravel.

"Zah bawwwwk," my dad slurred, interrupting my thoughts. His focus was on the floor now, as if he could see some kind of picture there.

I rolled my eyes—a classic deflection tactic that he probably learned at law school. Act like he doesn't understand, or turn the subject onto something else so people will forget their original questions.

"Daddy," I insisted, "Answer me! Did you embezzle the money or not? How did Tweedle get our house?"

My dad's gaze was stubbornly fixed on the floor. He lifted his good hand and pointed at something I couldn't see.

"Zah . . . box!" he burst with utmost effort.

The box?

I glanced at Creek and shook my head, not following my dad's drift at all.

Creek leaned over to me. "Robin, can't you cut him some slack for once?" he whispered. "Maybe your dad didn't take all the money—maybe his gambling problem was chump change compared to what Tweedle was up to. Try showing him a little faith. You might be amazed at what happens to his speech."

My cheeks stung with heat. How dare Creek scold me. It's not like he'd lived with my dad's lies for sixteen years. But then I remembered what he'd said about forgiveness.

I folded my arms.

Could it be possible my dad wasn't to blame for everything?

It was a hard notion to entertain. I glanced at Creek—at the raw honesty that was always in his eyes, so fiercely blue and powerful it was hard to take sometimes. Drawing in a deep breath, I nodded.

Okay, I thought, maybe my dad does deserve a chance—or maybe he doesn't. So I'm doing this for Creek.

"Daddy," I said in as gentle a voice as I could muster. I stroked his shoulder and crouched beside the armchair, trying to look more softly into his eyes. "If you didn't steal all the firm's money, who did?"

My dad lifted his hand to brush a muddy lock of hair from my eyes. I'd never really noticed before, but his eyes were such a clear blue, like a country stream. And they suddenly looked fresh to me, as pure as Dooley's, but far more intense.

"Thweeeedle," he replied with startling force. His eyes met mine, and he cupped my cheek. "Buth he duzznt no about . . . zah box."

I let out a sigh, hoping he wasn't delusional. "You keep saying box, Daddy. What box are you talking about?"

My dad sucked in a deep breath, and I could've sworn I saw his eyes glisten. Just then, a tear chased down his cheek. He pulled me towards him and pressed a soft kiss on my forehead, then gazed at me as if all along we'd been speaking of his greatest treasure.

"Where . . . I . . . keeeep . . . Alessia," he said perfectly.

Chapter 19

"I keep seeing her," I confessed as I glided through the cool water of Bender Lake.

It was a scary thing to admit. Creek might think I'd gone bonkers.

We were swimming in the moonlight, after having slept on the tree stand for the rest of the day and waking up at nightfall, still grimy from all our disasters. Granny had dealt with the cops for us in her usual artful way, of course—even giving one of them an herbal tea to relieve his rheumatism before she sent him off. So our sleep had been deep and peaceful, and I'd woken up with my body entwined with Creek's, feeling genuinely connected. But now, when I turned in the darkness to try and spot Creek, I couldn't place him anymore. All I could hear was his voice across the water, as though he'd become part of the night mist that hovered delicately over the ripples.

"You've seen her. You mean, Alessia?" I heard him say. "Like where, in Granny's crystal ball?"

"Um . . . yeah," I replied hesitantly, swaying my arms to stay afloat. "And in my dreams, too. I mean, a lot lately."

I felt his body slip up against mine in the water, and it made me shiver.

"You must have the sight," he whispered in my ear. "Just like Granny. It's been running in your family for generations."

Startled by his closeness, it took me a moment to wrap my head around the idea that Granny and I might actually be related. I wasn't sure whether to be grateful, or totally spooked.

Creek wrapped his arms around me and nuzzled against my neck, sending my heart into a few aerial swoops and dives. Yet his whole body felt like a second skin now—as if he were a part of me in this watery darkness. It was as though our souls had slipped off their casings when we'd removed our clothes down to our underwear on the beach, and now we were set loose.

As free as ghosts.

But then another tremble worked its way down my spine.

Creek's grip tightened around me, as if his skin had detected it.

"Creek," I said, "do you really think my mom is still alive? Because the way my dad talked about that box, it just made me wonder if he keeps her," my voice cracked a little, "you know . . . her *ashes* in there."

Creek swiveled me around to face him.

I couldn't see him very well—it was if he'd become the darkness itself, as stealthy as the night, yet his grip and strong legs supported me in the water. But I could feel the warmth of his breath against my forehead, and it comforted me a little.

"Your dad's a hard read sometimes," Creek replied. "There's a thin line between what's truth and what's fantasy. Both are so real to him. That's why he could pass you guys off in high society. But if he kept news clippings of the de Bargona family in a secret box all these years, like he said, then we'll be able to check the dates, Robin. Maybe there'll be a more recent article about Alessia."

I nodded. It had taken us a full hour in the trailer, but we'd gotten my dad to tell us, in his slow but surprisingly smooth English this time, that his secret box was under the humidor floor in the cigar parlor of our old house. And along with articles about my mom's family, it held the numbers to my dad's Swiss bank accounts.

So maybe we weren't broke after all?

But that wasn't what shocked me the most.

What really floored me was that my dad had said there were photos—

Of my mom!

All my life, I'd never seen a single picture of her. Only in my dreams—sometimes as a nun, sometimes in a black lace shroud—which of course, I didn't know if I could trust.

Could Creek be right? Could I really have the "sight" and be sensing my mother across a distance? Or had I just been seeing a dead woman's ghost all along?

Suddenly, the lake water felt very cold, making me quiver to the bone.

Creek ran his hands along my face, cupping my cheeks. "We have to go now," he said with a kiss so tender that he made me feel as if he held my heart in his hands. "It's time to for us to find you the most beautiful dress on earth."

"What?" I shook my head, confused.

Creek's answer took the form of grasping my hand and all of a sudden towing me through the cool water with powerful kicks toward the shore. As we glided in the dark, I glanced up and saw stars twinkling above us. They seemed as far away from me as Alessia . . .

When we reached the beach, Creek grasped my elbow and helped me to my feet. And then he looked up at the stars, too.

"You deserve answers, Robin," he said. "So we're going to get that box."

I could see him better in the dark now, the moonlight reflecting off his wet hair and even creating a sparkle in his eye. To my astonishment, Creek collected my hand and did a slow, formal bow. I thought I saw him smile.

"May I request the pleasure of your company," he said, giving me a little twirl in the sand, "tomorrow evening at the ball?"

"Now sit yerself up straight so this'll turn out right, sweetie!" Brandi ordered in her good-natured way, fluffing up my hair. Her quick wrist action and finesse with a teasing comb screamed years of trailer park styling experience.

Brandi piled my hair high on top of my head. Her fingers worked nimbly with bobby pins and gel as well as several cans of aerosol spray that she had in her bunker, which was lined with every hair tool imaginable. Yet strangely enough, Brandi still wasn't wearing one of her wigs. She'd drawn little daisies and hearts on her bald head with markers instead, then added colorful body glitter.

I so wanted to reach up and caress her shaved skin—to promise her that Creek and I were doing everything in our power to get more money for her medical treatments.

But I was afraid.

Because somehow, even to speak of it felt like I might be trespassing on her fragile dignity. In spite of how drained she appeared, it was as if she'd already won some kind of duel with the Devil—stared him straight in the eye with her arms crossed and refused to surrender her courage. And I sensed that it might not be my place to barge in on her raw territory. So I just kept quiet with my hands folded in my lap and let her boss me around, hoping she might find some delight in playing with my hair. But after Brandi combed out another section of curls and added a few more bobby pins, she stopped.

She set her comb down and patted me gently on the shoulder.

"It's okay, darlin'," Brandi said softly. "You know, Dooley wanted to touch my head, too. It's only natural to be curious."

My cheeks instantly grew warm. She must've caught me staring at her, I thought, so I swiveled to face her. Brandi's green eyes looked so pure, and even though her skin was still grayish, her face appeared sweet and welcoming. She smiled and dipped her head a little.

And I couldn't believe she was generous enough to share even this with me.

So I did it—I reached out my hand and ran my fingers along her scalp. Her skin was warmer than I'd expected, and some of the glitter came off on my palm. But then I felt the slight ridge of a vein on her head, pulsing steadily. In that second, I couldn't help saying a silent prayer. *Please God*, I asked, *please keep Brandi alive until we can get her more help.*

It wasn't until Brandi lifted her head from my hand that I realized I'd closed my eyes. Her comforting grin grew wide.

"All righty!" she clapped her hands with a touch of scolding in her voice and winked at me in her sassy way. "You might be pretty as a picture now. But that won't do you a lick o' good when you get to that ball if you act like a hog." She shook her finger. "So you'd better stuff in more of Lorraine's chicken pot pie. C'mon now, a big helping!"

Obediently, I sighed and lifted a large forkful of Lorraine's comfort-food paradise to my mouth that had been sitting in a pan on a stool. The flavor explosion that hit my tongue was enough to send a girl reeling.

And I saw a glow of pride surface on Brandi's face, regardless of her ashy skin.

"Ready for yer transformation?" she said brightly. "Be prepared. Ya just might not recognize yerself!"

She spun me around on my stool to face the mirror.

Heavens, I looked just like . . . Rapunzel?

Piles of shimmering red locks were swept into a loose updo with delicate tendrils that perfectly framed my face. And the most peculiar thing of all was that those strands were mine. Brandi had convinced me that high society people could spot a wig in a heartbeat—so she used a hair rinse on me that she claimed would come out in a few washings.

But this hue was so rich and vibrant and *red* that I sincerely had my doubts.

"Lordy!" Brandi squealed. "That color really brings out the warmth of your eyes. Why, you look just like a fairy princess."

Dooley glanced up from the workbook he'd been coloring on the carpet and scampered up to the mirror, gazing at me with awe. I saw him stand on his tiptoes to try and trace his fingers through a lock of my hair, so he could touch something sparkly.

"Are these diamonds, Brandi?" he said with child-like wonder.

I studied the mirror intently, my eyes catching little reflections of light.

Oh my gosh. All over my hair were tiny, faceted crystals that Brandi had somehow brilliantly woven in.

Even I gasped now.

Brandi had performed what she called her "Makeover Magic" by applying eyeshadow and liner, mascara, rouge and lip gloss. Secretly, I feared when she was done that I might look like gussied up trailer trash. But to my disbelief, I actually appeared . . . sophisticated.

All at once, I realized that this moment was like getting ready for the prom I'd never had. And I was genuinely . . .

"Bee—oo—tee—fullll," I heard a voice say slowly behind me.

Startled, I turned around and saw my dad. I thought he'd been sleeping on the sofa. But he must've gotten up all by himself and somehow made it to the mirror.

He was panting hard, his good hand white-knuckled around a cane, and he looked completely exhausted.

"Daddy!" I yelped, getting up to bolster him before he fell over. "You should've waited for one of us to help you."

"No," he replied, shaking his head and trying to stand on his own. He closed his eyes for a second, as if he were drawing strength from deep within.

"I'mm . . . loooosing . . . my . . . girrrrrl."

For a moment, I was breathless.

"No, no you're not. It's simply a fundraiser. You've been to hundreds of them," I assured him. "Creek and I are just going to bluff our way in, since Tweedle hasn't seen me since I was little, and get that box. Then we'll split and be right back."

My dad didn't appear to register a single thing I said. Instead, he gazed at me strangely, almost like he was studying my face to remember and hide somewhere in a deep corner of his heart. Even though I kept rattling on, he cut me off.

"Yooov . . . groownnn . . . up."

"Oh Daddy," I rolled my eyes. "I don't even have my driver's license yet—"

"Buuut . . . Creeeeek . . . hazzzz . . . yerrrr . . . heart."

A lump cinched my throat. The longing in his eyes—it was just like the sad yearning he'd had all those years for Alessia. And in an unusual move for someone in my family, I found that I just couldn't bring myself to lie to him.

He'd totally nailed it. My heart *did* belong to Creek.

I gazed down at my bare feet with the pretty peach nail polish Brandi had applied, then over at the sparkly, high-heeled pumps she was loaning me for the ball.

And I cleared my throat.

"Daddy, what did Creek say to you," I asked him pointedly, "when you two talked at the hoedown behind Granny's wagon?

A stone face met mine.

A face that didn't flinch or show weakness.

A face that had won a thousand court room battles.

And a face that knew he was losing his daughter forever.

"Thaaat . . . izzz . . . betweeeeen . . . men," he replied.

Chapter 20

My sneakers pressed into the soft soil in the dark as I carefully avoided rocks and sticks while clutching Brandi's pretty shoes to my chest, afraid of getting them dirty. I was supposed to meet Creek this evening at the spot where the forest trail makes a fork. To the right is Bender Lake, and to the left is . . .

Our future?

If we succeed in stealing my dad's box tonight, with his Swiss bank account numbers inside.

A raspy screech interrupted my progress, making me jump.

Then I heard the flapping of wings.

My heart leapfrogged. After being a city girl for so many years, I still hadn't gotten used to walking in the woods alone once the sun went down.

"Creek?" I whispered, hoping he was close. "You here?"

The forest was silent.

I stepped further down the trail, pretty sure I hadn't passed the fork yet. Creek had warned me never to use a flashlight or a candle that could give my location away. There was no telling if Bob was still pissed off, and now there was Cinci Federal to think about, too. "The darkness is our great equalizer," Creek had insisted back at the tree stand. "Remember, nobody can hurt you if they can't find you."

That may be true, I thought, but couldn't we at least have arranged for a secret whistle?

I pushed aside more brush and bravely kept walking.

Only to run into a wall—

"Ugh!" I yelped, my elbows stinging. I reached out to touch what blocked my path. It felt smooth and metal with a window pane beside it, like the side of a . . . car?

But it was so dark I couldn't even see.

To my astonishment, a light flipped on in the interior.

It was Creek! And he'd just opened the door of a . . . limousine?

"Need a lift, Mademoiselle?"

"W-Where did you get this thing?" I gasped, marveling at its size. If I didn't know better, I'd have pegged it as a barge suitable for floating down Bender Lake.

"A guy up the road owed me for saving his ass in a knife fight last summer," Creek replied. "Works at a limo and shuttle service, so he loaned me this for tonight."

Creek patted the side of the massive vehicle like it was his pet elephant. "But be careful," he added, "at midnight she just might turn into a pumpkin."

"She?"

"Sure, I figure our magic coach deserves a name. So how about . . . Sadie? She's taking us to the dance, after all."

Creek's mouth slipped into a smirk, illuminated by the dome light, and I could tell the dagger scar on his cheek had crinkled into place again.

God, he was the sexiest chauffeur I'd ever seen! All cleaned up after the water tower disaster, he had on a slim-fitting black t-shirt and ripped jeans, perfectly setting off every inch of his hard, muscled physique. And his long blonde hair looked full, skimming his shoulders. Unable to resist, I lifted a finger to stroke a lock.

"You washed your hair," I exclaimed, relishing its softness. Creek shook his head.

"Naw, that was Granny. She grabbed me by the ear and shoved my head into a bucket with her homemade soap. She said if we were going to a ball tonight, it was high time I stopped looking like a lake rat."

I giggled a little, but the way Creek gazed at me in that moment stole my breath away. His eyes roamed slowly over the pretty crystals Brandi had woven through my hair, piled high on my head with tendrils dangling, and he appeared transfixed by what he saw.

"Wow," he muttered softly, "you look like someone from a . . . fairy tale. The kind my mom used tell me and Dooley before we went to bed at night. Brandi did an awesome job." He gripped my hand with resolve. "C'mon, let's see if we can return the favor. And save her life."

He opened the long side door of the limo. "Ready?"

"No way, Mister," I shook my head, fists perched to my hips. "I'm riding shotgun next to you. We've come this far side by side, and that's how it's going to stay."

"Fair enough," Creek nodded and let it swing shut. He gallantly opened the front passenger door for me, then walked around the limo to slide behind the wheel. As he started up the engine, which purred like a kitten compared to our growling motorcycle, I racked my brain for the name of the dry cleaner our maid used to go to. My stepmom always insisted that her designer outfits should only be handled by the "best." And she would know—before she lit out for monastic life in Tibet, her gowns used to run over fifty grand a pop.

"Bell . . . we need to head for a place that has the word bell in it," I mumbled, glancing over at Creek. "Bella Donna—that's it! *Perfection Is Our Poison—Never a Wrinkle or Crease Out of Place* their TV ad always used to say. It's on a corner at the edge of my old neighborhood in Indian Hill."

Our plan was to bust in and pick out a tuxedo and a gown that my dad had already paid to have cleaned, before his stroke. They were the usual frocks he and his fourth wife wore to society functions. So as Creek guided our limo over the bumpy forest road without headlights, then ambled onto a dark country lane, I tried to recall a few of my stepmom's swanky dresses that I could choose from. One was emerald green and satin with thin spaghetti straps. Another was ruby with a bazillion sparkles. Yet another was stop-in-your-tracks purple with eye-popping cut-outs in sexy places. After all, my stepmom didn't snag my dad by being a nun.

"Care for some music?" Creek asked, turning on the radio. I assumed the speakers would spill light classical notes intended to soothe discriminating limo riders. But instead they bleated a wailing country sound:

"Oh moon, oh moon just set me free,

'Cuz she's as pretty as a girl can be.

My heart done sailed to the stars tonight,

And it ain't comin' back till the mornin' light."

"Guess Roscoe likes his bluegrass," Creek laughed. "Most of his riders head for river boat casinos. Not exactly the crowd you're used to, huh?"

Just then, Creek turned on the headlights and veered onto a lonely highway. That's when I noticed the limo upholstery was a black and gold leopard pattern, and there were fuzzy pink dice hanging from the rear view mirror. In the glow of the dash, I could see half a dozen stickers with large 3s on them and the words *Dale Forever* scrawled across a bumper sticker stuck to a visor.

"NASCAR," Creek pointed out, catching my gaze. "Official Religion of the Boondocks. And speaking of faith," he slipped his hand in his pocket and pulled out a small, white feather. "Just because we ain't hitting a bank doesn't mean tonight won't be . . . dangerous."

Creek reached over and let the feather fall slowly to my lap.

And shivers scampered down my neck.

Because I knew he was right.

Charles Tweedle was a certified asshole. On steroids.

He'd always looked mean, like a hefty, trapped badger ready to bite—even in slick photos from the society pages of the *Cincinnati Enquirer,* where he always boasted about the law opponents he'd destroyed. Plus, there were persistent, shadowy rumors about witnesses who happened to just "disappear" whenever cases finally came to trial—always in Tweedle's favor, of course. Did he really have underworld ties? All I knew is that there was no telling what Tweedle would do to protect his money. *His* being a rather loose interpretation of that word.

I leaned back in my seat, trying to remember the last time Tweedle might have seen me. It had to be at that boring office Christmas party when I was about seven—heaven knows my dad didn't let family interfere with work very often. But one thing I knew for certain about Tweedle. If he was evil enough to frame my dad for sinking their law firm, and then brazenly seized ownership of our house, then he's probably the kind of bastard who'd put Bob and his bloodhounds to shame when it came to wiping out his enemies. And Creek and I definitely fell in the latter category.

"C-Creek," I muttered, my nerves getting the best of me. "What do you think Tweedle would do if he catches us stealing my dad's box?" I picked up the white feather in my lap and twirled it for a second, then tucked it into my pocket as if it might impart special powers.

"Tweedle's not going to catch us," Creek snapped. "We fight our way out tonight, no matter what. Got that? 'Cause Brandi and Turtle Shores depend on us."

He reached over and sank his fingers into my knee.

"This is a *no fail* mission," he insisted, his voice steel. "Brandi doesn't have more time. It's do or die now—we clear?"

If I could have breathed in that moment, or even remembered my name, I might actually have nodded.

But I was too busy trying to recall that whole inhale-exhale thing.

"Robin," Creek pressed, his voice softening a little, "I've got your back. Don't ever forget that. And anybody who tries to mess with you is gonna deal with a whole world of hurt."

Goose bumps paraded up and down my skin, and I punched the radio dial to make that infernal wailing go away. What did Creek mean—how far would he go? All my life I'd relied on my Geisha skills and wits to talk my way out of things. But what if they weren't enough tonight?

"Here," Creek said, removing his iron grip and softly patting his thigh. "Just lay your head down for a spell. We've got a lot of work ahead of us, and it might be a very long night."

I nodded and pushed up the arm rest. Then I curled onto his lap, closing my eyes to the boat-like sway of Sadie the Limo. I wanted to think up strategies for quick escapes routes from my old house, just in case Tweedle got vicious, but my ideas kept getting hazy. Instead, I clung to Brandi's sparkly heels while my mind drifted off to pretty images of princesses dancing at formal balls. I could hear the sweet music and see the smiles flash as the young women batted their lashes at charming suitors who asked for their hands. But before long, I found myself dreaming about a large pumpkin that sat alone in the dark, surrounded by little mice . . .

The wire hangers screeched as Creek rifled through rack after rack at the dry cleaners. When we'd found Bella Donna on a corner in Indian Hill, he'd hoisted me on his shoulders and we'd snuck into the building by wriggling through an unlocked back window that was so small it scraped against our sides. But now, we didn't dare turn on the lights and give ourselves away. So we had to go by feel.

"Here," said Creek, pulling out a dark suit from a rack. He rubbed the fabric between his fingers. "This one feels good. Is it a tux?"

I lifted off the thin plastic sheath from the garment and squinted, trying to see the brand name on the label with what little glow came from a nearby night light. I shook my head.

"I can't read anything. But I can tell the seams aren't very smooth. Keep looking."

"Why? We're already late, Robin. As long it's black and fits—"

"Listen!" I growled at Creek. "We aren't in Bender Lake anymore. This is my territory now. And the fastest way to look nouveau riche is to wear a crappy tux."

"Nouveau what?"

I sighed. "Just trust me. The whole art of how my dad passed us off in society comes down to the details. And that means the right designer labels." I brushed my hand against several suits. "Here, this one feels better."

I pulled it out, trying to read the tag from the glow of a street lamp that filtered through the window. It said Calvin Klein. But the cleaning receipt didn't have my dad's name on it. And I felt a bit spooked about wearing someone else's clothes. What if it belonged to my stepmom's pricey gigolo that she tried to pass off as her "cousin" at a few galas last winter? Single-handedly, that woman had set all of Cincinnati's rumor mills on fire.

"Creek," I blurted, "move on down to the M section for McArthur. Over there."

We stepped towards a plastic M that sat atop a rack, and I yanked out another tux.

"This is it—McArthur! My dad's been pretty skinny the last few years, ever since hitting the coke, so it ought to fit. Take off your clothes."

Creek laughed. "Excuse me?"

"You heard me—strip!"

In the spare light of the street lamp, I could see Creek pulling his t-shirt over his head, revealing that hard chest that was so beautiful, even in shadows—maybe *especially* in shadows. It was all I could do to stop myself from running my hands against his tight, muscled skin. But we had an engagement to get to, fast. When Creek turned a little, I caught a glimpse of his bicep and let out a gasp.

There it was—that ugly bullet wound on his arm where the bandage had fallen off, swollen and completely disfiguring the spot where his heart tattoo had once been. It was now a red, upraised patch of skin with dark bruises, matching the nasty wound on his shoulder.

"Clean slate," Creek remarked with a quick glance at where the heart tattoo used to be, as if it were merely an erased chalkboard now. "Guess the past is gone for good."

"Will you ever—um, I mean, you know . . . consider another tattoo?"

My cheeks swiftly prickled. Could I be more transparent? God, how I wanted to scrawl my name in hot pink across his toned chest with permanent ink, branding him to keep the other chicks at bay.

To my embarrassment, Creek smirked as if my thoughts had been broadcast across my forehead. Whatever happened to my icy Geisha routine? And before I knew it, his hands had embraced my cheeks. They were rough at the edges but warm against my skin—solid. Then his lips pressed to mine for a long, absorbing kiss. So tender yet all consuming, as though he intended to tuck my very soul inside his most secret, treasured place.

"Robin," he whispered, breaking free for a second. He ran a finger delicately down my nose, then dropped to my lips and hesitated before tracing my chin and neck to my chest. "When a girl like *you* comes along," he swiped another kiss like a thief, "and she's got the beauty and brass to write her name all over a guy's heart—well, there ain't much point in tattoos anymore."

Sparks flew wildly in my stomach. And I'm quite sure if his hand hadn't been pressed to my chest, I would have levitated right then and there.

But Creek just stared into my eyes. The raw yearning I saw there left me breathless. "Time to take off your clothes, sweetheart," he said. "We have a ball to get to."

Every cell in my body trembled at his words. I felt his warm hands clutch at my waist and slowly glide up my ribcage, pausing at the swell of my breasts. He lifted my shirt up over my head, so there was only my dorky Pinnacle bra between us now. But with a swift unclasp, even that fell to the floor, my breasts spilling to the open air.

"You said it's all about the details," Creek whispered in my ear. "You can't possibly wear that crummy old bra beneath a designer gown."

His voice was soft and smoky, pure poetry to me, and I could feel his warm breath upon my neck in the dark. Slowly, his breath descended to my collar bone, where he gave me a light kiss, soft as a whisper of air that made me shiver. Then his lips traced down to my cleavage, where my heart was pounding madly.

"You're so beautiful, Robin," he said with a depth that left me reeling. And then he whispered something more, something I ached with every fiber of my being to hear, but it was impossible! Because a loud, ringing noise shattered our darkness, as though the world had caved in on us.

Creek instinctively wrapped his arms around me like a protective shield. "Bells," he called out over the chaos of sound. "They're chiming from the church next door. We gotta count the rings—"

Holy crap, their clang was so loud I thought they'd wake up the dead. But I listened to them chime nine whole times.

"Fuck, we gotta go! The ball's already been going for two hours."

He was right, Goddamn him.

And in that moment, Creek couldn't even see the nearly naked girl in front of him—he was totally back to business again. He threw on his tux in record time and swiftly buttoned up his starched, white shirt while I helped him adjust his bow tie.

I crossed my arms to cover my chest and took a step back, utterly dazzled by what I saw.

So much for crashing the party unnoticed.

Because Creek was—without a doubt—the most handsome creature I had ever witnessed. So good looking, in fact, that I'd wager no one was going to notice the muddy shoes that peeked out from beneath his black trousers.

But what really blew me away was that he was no longer some trailer park teenager any more.

He was a *man*.

And a drop-dead gorgeous one at that.

His blonde hair and tan skin were downright God-like, set off by the crisp tailoring of the black tux. Yet that air of wildness made him irresistible.

"C'mon!" he pushed "Let's find you a dress so we can get to that ball."

But when we turned to sort through my stepmother's gowns, we discovered that they were . . . gone.

Not a single shred of women's clothing was left on the McArthur section of the rack.

"Pawn shop," Creek nodded. "Wedding rings, silverware, gold candlesticks—your stepmom probably hawked everything she could carry the very minute she ditched your dad."

"That bitch!" I howled while Creek stuffed a random gown into my hands from further down the rack. The stiff fabric billowed over my arms, and I had to lift my chin high to peek over the mound of material to meet his gaze.

"What the hell is this—a taffeta tent?" I cried.

"We don't have time to waste, Robin. It's just a dumb dress, no big deal—"

"Yes it is a big deal!" I shouted far louder and more desperately than I'd intended. And despite my truly belated effort at any Geisha girl composure at this point, hot tears welled in my eyes.

"Don't you get it, Creek?" I said, shutting my eyes for second and willing the tears to stop. "This is my one and only chance for . . . you know . . . a prom."

Creek gave me a blank stare as if I'd just spoken a foreign language.

"High school's over for me, for kids like us. We always have to be the adults for everybody at Turtle Shores. And that means no kisses stolen from the boys at Breton behind bleachers. No daydreaming about making all the guys swoon, because for once in my life I actually feel like I'm the prettiest girl in the room—even if it's not true. And certainly no becoming giddy over the prettiest dress I've ever seen. All I ever wanted was one night, Creek—just one, beautiful, hopelessly enchanted evening to turn out right for me, that couldn't be ruined by all my family's bullshit."

Creek stood in total silence.

I quickly glanced down so he wouldn't see the pain in my eyes, but it was useless. I was shaking all over.

And only then did I notice how filthy my shoes really were from tracking through the mud earlier in the woods. Cinderella from the freaking boondocks! Only there was no magic wand to be found that could cure all my stupid problems.

Just then, a blistering white light seared my vision—

Creek had turned on the shop lights. The fiercely fluorescent bulbs hummed as I squinted to try and focus again. I saw Creek walk over to a tall glass case at the side of the room that held an exquisite, vintage couture gown that was silver and dripping with what looked like little diamonds everywhere. He turned around to look at me, and then he punched his fist straight into the glass—

His hand was thoroughly bloody now, but he didn't care.

"Here," Creek said, yanking the dress with his clean hand from the hanger. He stepped towards me, holding out the most sensational gown I'd ever seen—fit for a princess. And for an instant, I saw Creek's eyes sparkle.

"C'mon, Mademoiselle," his cheek scar crinkled into that wicked dagger smile again. "Let's go knock 'em dead."

Chapter 21

My heart was in my throat as I stood at the front door of my old house.

Already it looked strangely unfamiliar to me. The new people had ripped out all the landscaping and created tiered, formal gardens lit up by floodlights so it appeared as bright as day. And the Old World-style Tudor accents to the home had been removed. The house was now painted a gleaming white with gold trim, and the walkway was lined with marble statues. Even the stoop was inlaid with gem-colored mosaic tiles that sparkled from the crystal lamp by the door.

Drawing in a deep breath, I was about to ring the doorbell when I noticed a spot of blood on my dress.

Luckily, Creek's scratches from the glass case turned out to be superficial, but still—

In a panic, I licked my fingers to try and rub it out, only to feel Creek grasp my hand.

"Believe me," he smiled as wide as Bender Lake, "ain't a soul in this whole damn world gonna notice that little stain, sweetheart." His gaze took me in as though I were a vision. "You look . . . unbelievable."

I didn't want to blush, but I couldn't stop. The admiration in Creek's eyes told me I was dazzling.

Me!

That throw-away, curly-haired chick whose parents and nannies never gave her a second thought.

"How does it feel," Creek leaned in to whisper, sneaking a kiss on my neck while he was at it, "to blossom into a swan?"

At that moment, his smile told me I was the most beautiful creature he'd ever seen. A part of me felt as if I'd sprouted wings and transformed into something elegant and ethereal. But another part of me saw the concern surface in Creek's eyes. After all, we were here to do a job—a full-blown robbery—so we could never be as carefree and giddy as the teens I used to spot each spring in poofy dresses and rented tuxedos heading to their proms in white limos. This was business, and I saw Creek steal a glance back at where he'd parked Sadie. She was nestled on a side street at the edge of the lawn because there were so many limos jammed in the driveway. I could tell he was measuring the steps from the house to our vehicle, gauging with precision our potential escape route. Then he gave my hand a squeeze.

"Okay Robin," he whispered. "Let's get to it."

I nodded and pressed the doorbell.

A melodic chime reminiscent of Bach rang in our ears. Even the sound of the bell had changed. The door slowly swung open.

A graying man with a stiff expression appeared, wearing a crisp suit that wasn't a tux—a butler for certain.

I raised my chin and gave him my haughtiest stare. If I've learned anything from growing up in Indian Hill, it's how to seize the Alpha role quickly with the staff in order to get my way.

And the first step to derailing them is always to start with a complaint.

"Must you wait for important guests to ring the doorbell like strangers off the street before you open it?" I barked in an entitled tone, yanking on Creek's hand to follow me into the foyer. "We were standing there for five whole minutes! Chloe Tweedle will *not* be pleased."

"M-My apologies!" The butler fumbled, ushering us in. "Who-Who shall I say has arrived?"

Without turning around, I waved my hand in the air to dismiss him.

"The lady of the house knows," I sniffed. "It's hardly my job to educate her staff."

I dug my heels into the plush ivory carpet beyond the marble entry way, lugging at Creek to match my marching gate as I swung a left and hastened to the ball room. Of course, I wanted to stop and ogle at all of the renovations the Tweedles had made to my house. The décor had gone from a genteel, British manor look to a gilded spectacle worthy of Versailles. But I knew even a brief pause might give us away. The best tactic for blending in is to act blasé, I thought, the way I did on my first day at high school to keep the bitches off my back. Simply behave like you've seen all of this a million times before.

"You!" I pointed to a middle-aged woman who was milling in the hall and wearing a suit that matched the butler's. "Two glasses of Dom Perignon. Now."

I gave the chick a snap to show her I meant business.

"Geez, Robin," Creek whispered. "You sure got the royal bitch act down flat."

"Hush," I replied. "You didn't exactly flinch in front of Bob and his bloodhounds. These folks are just as nasty, and they can smell fear. If you act superior, it keeps 'em guessing."

Then I stopped in my tracks in the hallway. All air evaporated from my chest—

I stared into the small room on the right that was now barely recognizable.

It used to be *my* nook.

A cozy little space that was meant to be a downstairs study at one time. My parents had finally given in and let me claim it for myself. So I'd filled it with electronics, posters, a floor-to-ceiling TV screen and an over-stuffed armchair, just like the kind you see at Starbucks. But most of all, it was my "Panic Room" as the staff had jokingly called it. A Teen Cave where I could walk in and slam the door on all of my stepmom's lovers who brazenly traipsed through the house, sometimes half-naked. Or shut out the local media who camped on our porch every time my dad's law firm won a controversial case through dubious tactics. I'd never realized it before, but it was the only spot in the whole house where I could hide my soul to try and survive my parents—the one place where not even the cleaning lady or the foo-foo interior decorators were allowed to enter.

And now, it was as if I'd been totally erased.

Ghastly hunting trophies hung on the walls with dead predators caught in angry, roaring poses, or petrified animals frozen at the very moment they'd been shot. Horns, antlers, claws and fangs were on display everywhere. It was horrible, without a single trace of me—or what I used to think was me—and it made me stop, stunned.

"My-my room?" I whimpered.

Creek wrapped me in his arms.

Granny Tinker might be the psychic one at Turtle Shores, but Creek sure had an uncanny way of knowing what to do every time something got under my skin. He hugged me tight and pressed his cheek against my hair.

"We've all lost something, baby," he whispered in comfort, rocking me a little. I could feel his strength pour into me. "That's why we stick together at Turtle Shores—no one there will ever try to replace you."

Then he cupped my cheeks in his hands and stared into my eyes. "Focus," he warned, his gaze becoming so intense it scared me a little. "Tonight, we're beautiful, and tough as nails. We're on a mission. So we're gonna get into that ballroom, and you're gonna show me how to waltz, okay? And then we're gonna fleece this asshole Tweedle for everything we can carry. Ready?"

I nodded, pumping up my courage. Throwing my shoulders back, I stood erect and raised my chin to a more regal stance. Then I clutched Creek's hand and took purposeful strides towards the double French doors at the end of the hall like a princess about to survey her kingdom. Every nuance of my Geisha training suddenly came flooding back, and my mind reeled with cold Alpha chick manifestos designed to give me an edge.

I own everything and everyone I see—

People who glance at me will be floored by my charisma and power.

Charm is a force field that silences even the harshest critics.

This night is mine. And winners take all, *no regrets*.

Okay, so maybe my Geisha mantras were a bit over the top. But as the house servant returned to hand both Creek and I glasses of champagne and then opened the French doors for us to enter the ballroom, the music stopped and a hush fell over the entire crowd.

"Smile darling," I whispered to Creek through my teeth. "You're now the son of a Russian black market billionaire who doesn't speak a word of English, and I'm your money whore. Don't worry, this crowd is so shallow, they'll drool at you muddy feet."

I glanced at Creek, but he didn't even crack a smile.

I should've known—he'd never been capable of phoniness. As long as he kept his mouth shut, everyone would be sucked in by his shocking good looks and air of mystery. And this night was in the bag.

"Sergei Azurkmonanoff from St. Petersburg and his guest," I declared to the house servant, who nodded us in.

"The distinguished Sergei Azurkmonanoff and . . . companion," the servant announced loudly over the crowd. I flashed a high-wattage smile to the sea of gray hair in the room, relieved to spy several young couples in the back who were the only ones who appeared younger than 40. Faster than I could say, "Move your ass, Creek," I tugged on his hand to make a beeline to the far end of the room, keeping up my most stellar smile.

Chamber music filled my ears as the quartet on a small platform started up their stringed instruments again. Perfect, I thought, now it will be too loud for people to ask many questions. I dared to take a sip of the Dom Perignon. It was so dry I nearly spit up. Coughing, I gazed at Creek for rescue.

"Nyet," he purred at me, shaking his head as if I were a silly child. I saw a twinkle rise in his eyes. All at once, he threw back the entire flute of champagne as though it were a shot of moonshine.

"Ah," he pounded his chest and smiled triumphantly, lifting his glass to me in a mock toast. "Ain't got nothin' on the Colonel's brew," he whispered in my ear, and we both cracked up.

In one fell swoop, he'd set me completely at ease, and we giggled as we handed our glasses to a nearby servant who passed by. Then Creek gave me a gallant little bow and grasped my hand.

"Time to dance," he whispered.

I nodded and set my hand delicately on his shoulder, trying my best to look sophisticated, when I noticed Creek's attention was glued to my breasts that bulged over the gown's plunging neckline.

"Creek, concentrate," I whispered, yanking the dress up a little over my cleavage. "We have to waltz right now to blend in."

Creek shook his head and blinked. Then he flashed me an amazing smile, the kind that lit up the whole room.

I swear, several women around us nearly fainted at his feral charisma.

"Okay," he whispered. "Follow my lead."

To my surprise, he whisked me away in a series of magical three-steps on the dance floor, smoother than any of the ballroom veterans that surrounded us. Beneath the sparkling chandeliers, I felt like we were floating. Expertly, he weaved our bodies through the crowd of black tuxes and bright, flowing gowns as though he'd done this dozens of times.

Creek caught the wonder in my eyes, and it made him laugh.

"Surprised a guy from the backwoods can sweep you off your feet?" he whispered slyly as we skirted past other couples, our moves the most graceful in the room. "When you do round dances at barns and hoedowns from the time you can walk," he said, cleverly spinning me in a twirl with mischievous grin, "you kinda get the gist of it."

The pride showed in his eyes, and in that instant I felt like we were the only two people who existed—and the music was flowing right through us and making us fly. Every note from the quartet seemed to match the sparkling feeling that alighted in my heart. I wanted to stretch out my arms, just to see if I might actually rise in the air to the rhythm of Creek's gentle swirls. But a peculiar knot began to tighten in my stomach, as though my insides were clenching like a fist.

It didn't make sense. Hours had passed since I'd eaten Lorraine's pot pie, and surely I would have digested my dinner by now?

Turning a little, I caught sight of Charles Tweedle—and the knot in my belly changed into a mean twist, like a knife. He was a short, balding man with sharp features and a strange, brooding air of darkness—the kind of guy you could feel before you set eyes on him. And if you weren't careful, something about his dark energy could make your throat tighten up and squeeze.

Tweedle's badger eyes locked onto mine, and I saw him smile. Not just any smile, but the grin of a pirate. We were making his ballroom look good, and he knew it—and he would probably parlay the success of this event into climbing several rungs up the social ladder. As Creek kept maneuvering our bodies into smooth waltzing steps, Tweedle glared at me and gave me a nod. Shivers skimmed down my back. His eyes appeared like they already *owned* me, and the "taking" was merely a matter of logistics. He broke away from the men he'd been chatting with at the edge of the dance floor and walked straight towards us.

"Dance?" he commanded in a husky tone, ignoring Creek.

Creek stiffened, offering no response. But he refused to let go of my hand.

I gave Tweedle a sweet smile. "He doesn't understand English," I apologized. "Do you Sergei?"

"Well I insist," Tweedle said, and before I knew it, he'd shoved himself between me and Creek.

And I got scared. Really scared.

Not because Tweedle's thick hand gripped mine until it hurt while his other hand thrust into the small of my back as if he were ready to throw me down and have sex right then and there. But because the ferocious look that took over Creek's gaze made me fear he was about to tear him apart.

Creek's angry eyes searched mine.

Go—I can handle this, I lip-synched silently to Creek as Tweedle pushed me away from him far too hard, forcing my body into jerking, three-step strides. He was so short I could feel his hot breath upon my cleavage, but it wasn't until his foot crunched mine that I nearly lost it. Stifling a yelp, I held my ground as he shoved me round and round in disorganized circles. By the greedy look in his eyes, it quickly became apparent why he'd picked me.

He thought I was the prettiest woman in the room.

He probably had no idea I was only sixteen—or maybe he just didn't care.

And when I glanced to the side of the dance floor at his skinny, helmet-haired wife Chloe, who was laughing with some of her society friends, it was obvious to me that she didn't give a damn either. I knew her type. As long as Tweedle kept the big bucks rolling in, she was happy to amuse herself at the country club or with her own string of secret lovers.

"I didn't catch your name," Tweedle interrupted my thoughts. His words sounded a bit winded by his own aggressive dance pace.

I offered him another smile. "R-Regina," I lied. Thinking fast, I decided to make this dance from hell count big time. "You know, my poor friend Sergei doesn't know a speck of English." I clutched Tweedle's shoulder and forced his body into a hard left to make him see Creek standing alone by the wall. "He can't entertain much small talk with your guests. Believe me, Sergei's not good for anyone when he's unhappy. Do you happen to have a Smoking Room somewhere that we could enjoy? So he might want to bring me *back again* to see you some time?"

I knew damn well where the Cigar Room was in the house, but I wanted Tweedle to feel like it was his idea.

Then I shocked myself by seductively tracing a finger along Tweedle's sweaty temple and dragging it down his cheek to his lip. Moving in on him, I invitingly edged my mouth within a hair's breadth of his. Tweedle reciprocated by nibbling a little on my fingertip, his mouth slipping into a smile.

"Sure," he said. I could feel his hot breath on my finger. "The Smoking Room's upstairs. Very secluded—perfect for intimate entertainment, if you know what I mean."

Ew—ew—ew!!

I wanted to yank back my finger and then crawl underneath the dance floor and die.

And I spotted Creek to the right of me by the wall, his hands balled into fists.

Swiftly, I shook my head at Creek, but his rage didn't decrease a bit, despite the gaggle of women who'd begun to flutter around him, laughing and trying to grab his attention.

What bothered me most wasn't even my finger on Tweedle's icky lips, but his *smell*. The guy reeked of something oily and musky and overbearing—maybe his amped up testosterone. But I was on a mission, and I knew failure was not an option right now.

Tantalizingly, I traced my finger all the way around Tweedle's mouth. "Well, why don't you let me show your Smoking Room to Sergei, and then, who knows? While he finishes a cigar, you might just have to give me a tour of the rest of your house? I especially love little, out of the way rooms."

Tweedle nodded with a gleam in his eye, which I took as my cue to break away. Keeping my hand on his shoulder, I ran it teasingly all the way down his arm before I let him go.

"Thirty minutes?" I said. "And then I'll come back down to the ballroom, and you can give me a *private* tour?"

Tweedle nodded without looking me in the eye. His attention was too firmly focused on my breasts.

So I turned and scurried towards Creek with a secretive thumbs up sign. He nodded at me, appearing relieved.

"The stairs," I whispered as soon as we were face to face. I shot a glance at another set of French doors at the back of the ballroom. "As soon as we exit, they're to the left, and they go directly to the Cigar Room."

Creek grasped me by the elbow and we tried to leave the ballroom as nonchalantly as possible, even though I could feel Tweedle's possessive gaze zeroing in on my back the entire way.

"Dirty old man," I sputtered the minute we busted past the doors and let them fall shut. By this time, Creek had clutched my hand and was leading me in a race up the stairs.

I nearly fell off Brandi's shoes. I'd never been allowed to wear high heels at Pinnacle or anywhere else before, but luckily, Creek's grip was sure and steady.

"Hold on, baby," he said as we scaled the steps, focusing on a door we could see above us on the left. As soon as we reached the top, we darted inside and flipped on the light.

Nothing was the same here, either. Instead of the dark, cherry wood paneling and the pool table that used to sit in the middle, the Cigar Room was now was filled with airy frescos painted on pale, stucco walls and what looked like Louis XIV-style chairs. Some decorator must've made a killing on the original artwork.

But fortunately, the old humidor was in the exact same spot. Creek and I dashed to the glass door and stepped inside the slightly warmer and humid space that had shelf upon shelf of expensive cigars—with a few bags of coke sandwiched in between.

"Guess Tweedle aims to please," I nodded at Creek with a shrug.

We both stared at the parquet floor. It had little zig-zags of dark and light hardwood planks spread across the bottom of the humidor. My heart was racing out of control. I tried hard to remember what my dad had said about the location of his secret box.

"Third ebony plank to the right, just underneath the section for illegal Cuban cigars," I said aloud, squinting at the floor, then up at the shelves.

But the Cuban cigars weren't there any more.

I gasped, running my hand up the boxes. They were all from Brazil, Camaroon, the Dominican Republic . . . alongside bag after bag of white powder, and a few grayish rocks I didn't recognize.

"Oh my God, where is it?" I cried, stomping my foot on the floor to see which piece of wood might fidget a little. "How can we possibly find the loose plank?"

Creek got on his knees and began banging the planks with his fist. "None of them move, Robin. I don't think it's actually the same floor."

Horrified, I kneeled down beside Creek in shock. He was right—upon closer inspection, I could tell this wasn't the same floor at all. My dad's parquet floor had been fashioned from rare woods. When I pressed my hand against the surface, I realized it was cold and made of *stone*.

Panicked, I felt my own body heat rise to my forehead, and my pulse throbbed in my ears.

"Creek, what are we going to do?" I howled. "We only have a few more minutes!"

Creek grabbed me by the shoulders.

"You *saw* her. You told me you did. You have the gift, and you can find her now—"

"What?" I shook my head. "What the hell are you talking about?"

"The feather!" Creek's gaze met mine with a laser-like focus that rocked me to my bones. He pulled one of Brandi's high heels off my foot and held it up. "Before you put on your shoes at the dry cleaners, I slipped a feather inside here, in case we needed it."

"Those feathers aren't magic, Creek!" I said, flabbergasted. "We're not in the boondocks right now. Granny's voodoo doesn't work here."

Creek glared at me, his stare so cold I felt like he'd frozen my heart into place.

"Maybe the magic *does* work here," he challenged, "If we let it. There doesn't have to be a difference between the deep woods and this humidor. What matters is what we feel in our hearts. We don't have anything left to lose, Robin—except for Brandi's life."

Leave it to Creek to say the one, piercing thing that could totally knock the wind out of me.

He was right.

"Okay-okay," I folded my arms in a huff and closed my eyes. I felt incredibly silly in a sparkling ball gown like some over-the-top New Age chick hoping to channel a spirit, but it's not like we had a whole lot of options left. I cracked one eye open just long enough to yank the feather from Creek's hand, and then I waved it in the air and tried to focus.

"M-Mom," I said haltingly—I'd never called anyone that out loud before. "I need your help right now. I don't know if you're alive or dead. But I need your spirit to show me how to find Dad's box."

I felt Creek's warm hands cover mine, but other than that, nothing came.

No images of Alessia's beautiful face. No hearing her penetrating words in a dream-like moment. My mind was a total blank.

"M-Mommy," I whispered. My teeth clenched together as I allowed myself to go deep inside, to that tiny but very golden place where I dared to believe—in spite of all of the odds—that there might actually be a mother who existed for me somewhere. One who really cared. And it left me feeling totally vulnerable and exposed. I licked a tear that had slipped onto my lips and pressed on. "We don't want to lose Brandi," I blurted in a pleading tone. "All it takes is money. Stupid money! Please, Mom, *please* help us—"

And that's when I noticed it. Not all at once, but gradually, as though embracing me like a mysterious hug. A fragrance began to envelop us, similar to lavender, with a touch of wild grasses from warm, sunny fields. The smell started to permeate the humidor, dominating the husky, leathery scent of cigars. And then I heard a thump that scared the freaking daylights out of me—

A plain wooden box had fallen to the floor, jolting my eyes open.

Creek and I stared at each other, spooked. We glanced down, noticing that cigars had spilled from inside the box, along with a small feather.

And two cards.

La Fortuna and *Amore* —

The Wheel of Fortune and The Lovers.

I began trembling.

"It-it's a sign," I stuttered, my fingers quivering as I picked up the cards.

Creek gently lifted up the box and ran his hand along the bottom of the inside, giving it a hard knock. Sure enough, it sounded hollow. Before I knew it, he'd smashed the box against the stone floor.

There they were—a sheet with the Swiss bank account numbers typed on it and old newspaper clippings. I seized them, my whole body shaking now. On a yellowed article stared back at me, in faded black and white, the most beautiful face I'd ever seen. And I recognized her—she was the same woman from my dreams. The caption below the photo read: *Alessia de Bargona, the most striking young woman to grace the Cincinnati social register in decades.*

"It's her, Creek!" I gasped. "The contractors must've found this box when they replaced the floor and put it on the shelf. Her picture's so beautiful. This must be what my dad meant when he said he keeps Alessia here."

"No it's not," Creek replied.

He held out his hand and opened his palm. In it was an enormous ruby, the size of a golf ball, cut and faceted to resemble the shape of an exquisite heart.

"*This* is Alessia."

I sat utterly stunned. The ruby was spectacular—a deep, vibrant red that seemed to radiate all the way through with crimson light. Creek picked up another old article that had been lying inside the box.

"The priceless de Bargona ruby has been in this aristrocratic Italian family for generations, but recently was reported missing by the Count before he departed from Cincinnati."

Creek pointed to the date on the article. It was written sixteen years ago.

"Did my dad steal it?" I shuddered.

Creek shook his head.

"No, Alessia gave it to him before her father shipped her back to Italy. I heard rumors about it in Turtle Shores, but no one ever saw the ruby, so I thought it was a tall tale. Lorraine claimed Alessia's dad made her walk up to Doyle on the day she was scheduled to leave and declare that she never loved him. But when she did, she slipped this heart-shaped ruby into his hand."

"So he'd know she was lying," I breathed. "And she'd love him forever and ever—"

"You got it," Creek smiled a little. "This *is* Alessia. To Doyle, anyway. It's her heart."

I scrambled to my feet. "Okay, we gotta get out of here." I picked up the pieces of the box and shoved them to the back of a shelf. "Put those tarot cards in your pocket," I said, grabbing the Swiss bank account sheet from the floor and the ruby in his hand. "And those news clippings of Alessia."

Creek stuffed them into his tux. I folded the account page and slipped it inside the bust of my dress and gripped the ruby firmly in my hand. But when we opened the door to walk out the humidor, our eyes met a very disapproving figure.

Not Tweedle, which was no surprise since we'd hadn't been there for half an hour yet. It was a tall, older woman with gray hair pulled back into a severe bun and wearing a matronly, white gown that stretched awkwardly over her thick middle, making her look like an upright refrigerator. She had a long forehead and a hooked nose, and she held a gnarled, mahogany cane in her hand. As soon as her raven-black eyes rested upon mine, I knew . . .

"M-Mother Superior?" I faltered.

She smiled in that chilling way she always had that could stop even the liveliest girl's heart.

"Robin," She trilled. "I thought I spotted you on the dance floor tonight. You look ravishing, my dear. Especially with that new red hair. Now surely you intend to pay your debts, am I correct?"

"What?"

"Your tuition. The thirty thousand dollars your father still owes Pinnacle." She pointed her gnarled cane at me. "You *do* realize that's the reason for the fundraiser this evening. Your old Alma Mater?"

I gasped like a fish.

I had no idea Mother Superior ever stepped out of her nun's habit, let alone for a benefit. And it wasn't like I had the chance to read the fine print on that poster at that bank.

"Certainly," I piped up, trying to buy time and choking down the urge to take a swing at her. But I knew the woman outweighed me, so I scanned for a way to make a run for the door.

"Then hand over that lovely gem in your palm," she insisted.

I stole a glance at Creek. For the first time ever, I saw him look at me in total shock.

How did Mother Superior know about the ruby?

At that moment, Tweedle appeared at the door.

Mother Superior simply gazed at me and smiled.

"Never mind him. I want that stone." The grin on her lips faded to a thin, tight line. "All of Cincinnati knows about the de Bargona ruby that went missing years ago. And obviously, you've found it. Give it to me—"

"What? You *knew* Alessia de Bargona was my mother all along?" My cheeks flushed with rage.

"Let's just say, I suspected as much. Little details—the birth certificate and social security number that didn't quite match. And your olive complexion and curly hair do make you look just like her, you know. Alessia was the talk of society once. Her father even enrolled her at Pinnacle. He never dreamed she'd be a little whore on her home visits and get pregnant with that white trash boy. Fortunately, at Pinnacle we're paid to keep these kinds of secrets. But that doesn't mean there isn't a day of reckoning."

She gripped her mahogany cane in both hands and gave me a fierce whack upside the head, then reached out for my hand. The woman was built like a Sumo wrestler, so I didn't have a chance—

Except for the fact that Creek made a dive and knocked her over like the tower of Pisa, throwing aside her cane. In an instant, Tweedle was on top of him, drilling him with punches.

Creek gave him a hard left hook, sending him sprawling across the Cigar Room floor.

He bolted to his feet and grabbed my hand, yanking me upright.

I was still holding my head, which throbbed like a jackhammer had been cracking at it.

"Do you trust me?" Creek cried.

I shook my head, confused. "What? Why would I be here if I didn't—"

Tweedle moaned and began to stir.

Creek gripped my shoulders and shook me so hard it hurt.

"Do you really, *really* trust me?" The urgency in his eyes made me shiver.

I saw Mother Superior stumble to her feet along with Tweedle. They both blocked the door of the Cigar Room, so it looked like we were goners.

"Then hold on, no matter what," Creek said. "Hear me, Robin? Just hold on!"

With that, he jerked at my hand and we made a mad dash for the windows that faced the front lawn—

A huge crash echoed in my ears.

For a brief moment in time, we were weightless . . . floating . . .

And I saw little specks of glass sparkle all around us like gems as we fell—fell—fell into the beams of the floodlights below.

Chapter 22

I still had a white-knuckled grip on the ruby as Creek raced down a country road at over a hundred miles an hour, taxing poor Sadie's engine to the max.

But near as I could tell, we'd gotten away scott free!

As long as I didn't count my royal headache and the smeared blood that had ruined my beautiful gown. The shards of window glass we'd broken through had cut us both all to hell. Even my forehead was dripping, and I could taste the weird iron flavor of blood that trickled down to my lips. After falling from the window, we'd landed in a thick hedge that Creek had been smart enough to notice surrounded the entire house, just in case we needed an emergency escape.

I didn't even want to know how often he'd used *that* exit strategy.

I just felt lucky we were alive—and safe. Bleeding and scratched up like nobody's business, maybe, but nothing Granny's bandages couldn't fix.

Swiveling around in my seat, I peered through the limo's rear window. No headlights followed us, and we were almost home.

A part of me couldn't believe I'd just thought of it that way.

Home used to be my term for the mansion we'd left. Now, it was a humble tree stand in the middle of fricking nowhere.

But the difference was that Turtle Shores was filled with people who truly cared about me, and Indian Hill wasn't.

"Creek," I said, fretting about Brandi now that we'd had a chance to catch our breaths. "How long do you think it will take us to get money out of the Swiss bank accounts?"

Creek glanced over at me. He hadn't dared to turn on the headlights, so I could only see his face in the silvery moonlight that filtered through the windshield. His forehead was streaked with blood.

"Hard to say for sure—maybe a week or two." He wiped some blood off with his tuxedo sleeve. "Nick of time for Brandi, I reckon. As long as we provide proof that we can pay, the chemo center won't expect the balance for another month." He nodded. "I think everything's gonna be okay."

I heaved the deepest sigh of relief I'd felt in ages.

Leaning my head back, I rubbed the smooth, ruby heart between my fingers.

"I have no idea how much is in those accounts," I said. "But it might change our lives."

"Not for a *long* time, baby," Creek replied mysteriously.

I could feel Sadie slowing way down on the gravel road as Creek braked to make a turn into a really black stand of woods.

"We barely made it out of there tonight. We're just lucky Tweedle and Co. don't know where we live," Creek said. "But let me tell you something. Smart crooks don't make hasty changes—that's how idiots get caught. So as far as we're concerned, we pay for Brandi's health care, and that's it. No frills."

I bit my lip and nodded.

It would be so nice to move my dad into a more comfortable apartment with better amenities, but I could see Creek's point. It wasn't worth coming out of hiding and getting us all arrested.

The limo dipped and swayed over the forest road until Creek brought it to a stop.

"C'mon," he cut the engine. "Let's head for our tree stand and sleep for, I dunno, maybe three days."

I laughed a little. Sounded perfect to me.

When Creek opened his door, no dome light stung my eyes. He'd turned it off in case anyone was on the prowl. But still being gallant, he walked around the front of Sadie to open my door. I sank my bare feet into the cool dirt and stood up—Brandi's pretty high heels had been casualties of our crazy sprint across the lawn to escape the house.

"Mademoiselle," Creek said, taking my hand.

He stared at my bare feet in the moonlight, and I could almost hear him smile.

"I have to say, this has been one of the most amazing nights of my whole life. And a hell of a thrill ride."

Creek's lips pressed against mine in the dark.

A soft—exhausted—and totally enchanting kiss.

I wanted to fold into his arms right there and fall to the soft forest floor, then sleep for perhaps a thousand years.

But there was something still nagging at me, something I couldn't shake.

And I was unable to pretend it didn't matter any more.

"Creek," I asked as his lips pulled from mine. He gave me one last kiss on the forehead and tugged on my hand to lead us away from the limo, deeper into the woods. "We've been through so much together," I continued, walking alongside him. "I mean, we could've failed tonight and gotten caught, and never seen each other again. So I want to know, I mean, I think I deserve to know—"

Creek stopped and turned to face me.

He was stunning even at night, with the way the moonlight highlighted his features and made strands of his blonde hair look pale as an angel's.

"Say it, Robin," he sighed. "You can be straight with me. What do you want to know?"

"What did you say to my dad? Behind the gypsy wagon at the hoedown? Neither one of you will tell me, and you both dodge it every time I ask."

"Shhh," Creek gently put a finger to my mouth. Before I knew it, his lips met mine again.

Only this time, it was the kind of kiss that made me feel as if he were pouring his soul into mine, tinged with blood, sweat, and even a few slivers of glass.

His arms enveloped me in the moonlight and he held me close. When he finally lifted his lips, he edged them to my ear.

"I told him . . . I love you," he whispered.

I know he said it in his very softest voice, but his words resounded in my heart like a kettle drum.

"And I asked him," Creek paused, "if some day he'd let me have your hand. I wanted an answer while he was still well enough to speak."

White-hot tingles coursed up and down my body and fanned out to my limbs, making me feel like I glowed from within. I opened my mouth to let out squeal, but Creek slipped his palm over my lips.

"Robin," he said quietly, "your dad bowed his head and cried. He knows I've made you a criminal."

I wriggled fiercely from his grip until I'd broken free.

"But we don't have to stay that way," I countered. "I love you, too! What if we pay back Cinci Federal from the Swiss bank accounts? We don't know how much is in there—it could be millions. And we didn't take anything from Bob or Tweedle that didn't really belong to other people. Think about it, Creek. We don't have to let any of this define us. There's still a chance we can start over—"

An eerie, white light suddenly flooded the woods.

I half-thought it was my own euphoria from Creek admitting he loved me. But the light was so bright it cast black tree shadows all around us and made our eyes burn.

We turned to what looked like the source and heard heavy engines roar. Two huge Hummers plowed through the woods with enormous light racks mounted on their roofs. They were headed straight for Turtle Shores.

Creek clutched my hand and dived behind some brush. He grabbed my shoulders in a panic.

"Tweedle's got henchmen?" he cried. "Robin, why didn't you tell me—I never would have come back here!"

"I—I thought everybody knew!" I said, spitting leaves. "I mean, they were always just rumors in Cincinnati, but—"

"God dammit! Don't you know rumors mean facts in the underworld? No, no," he hugged me close, "of course you don't. You weren't raised on the wrong side of the tracks. Listen," he pointed to the Turtle Shores compound. "If Tweedle's men have come here, then that means he knows all about your dad's roots, including where the trailer park is.

Maybe that Mother Superior chick filled him in. We have to be crafty as foxes to get him out of there."

"Who?"

"Your dad! Don't you get it? They'll use him to make you fork over the ruby and anything else they think you've got. Whatever's important to you they'll take for ransom. Just keep hold of my hand, and don't make any noise. I know a back way they won't suspect."

Creek began to crawl on his knees and I followed suit, hating myself for mourning the total destruction of my dress. Surely it wasn't as important as my dad! Yet with each rip and tear, I had to shake my head. My one beautiful moment in life was over. We were back to reality now, and the rocks on the ground cut and bruised my knees. After a few minutes of sneaking through shadows, beneath the scope of the Hummer headlights, Creek stood and tugged on my hand until I stumbled to my feet.

He hugged me so tight that we blended in with the long, tall shadow of a tree. We could still hear vehicles crashing through the woods and voices hollering, but we couldn't make out their words over the racket. Creek grasped my hand and splayed my fingers to feel something against the tree trunk—a wooden plank. Then he patted my shoulder and I could feel his body brush against mine as he ascended up the tree. Must be a ladder, I realized. I tucked the ruby into my cleavage and hoisted up the hem of my tattered gown to follow him.

When I reached the top, I felt for a tree branch but instead touched a wide board. Creek snatched my arm and lifted me to stand on a plank that I assumed must connect between trees.

I'd never dared to walk on one of them before like Dooley, let alone in a ball gown—

"Go, Robin!" Creek whispered. I could see his dark figure moving across the plank, and I tested it with my bare foot, feeling like I was about to step on a highwire. But the problem was I'm not an acrobat! Carefully, I padded across the wood, holding out my arms for balance, until I got so scared that I just scampered to the other end, breathless.

"Good job," Creek whispered, giving me a high-five. "Now only fifteen more."

"What?" I gasped.

"You heard me," he stepped out on the next plank. "Let's get a move on!"

My heart beat as fast as a hummingbird's as we criss-crossed from tree to tree. Thank God the planks were stable. And the fact that I was barefoot helped me grip the wood with my toes and steady myself each time my balance wavered. I carefully inched over each one, watching Creek's silhouette in the moonlight trot easily across the boards. In his dashing tux, he looked like a character from a fairy tale who could magically skip between trees. That thought made me giggle for a second, and I lost my footing and found my body pitching into the night air . . .

There's nothing like falling under a canopy of stars in a sparkly ball gown to make your life seem completely surreal.

The ground met my back with a cruel thud. Reality check—

"Robin, you okay?" Creek dropped from the tree and was instantly at my side.

Roaring engines sounded perilously close, and we could see the bright lights of the trucks closing in. Creek quickly laid on top of me, covering my iridescent dress with his black suit.

"Ow," I whispered. "You're really heavy."

My complaints were interrupted by an awful silence.

Creek and I both held our breaths.

We could hear the Hummer doors slam shut, then the sickening crunch of boots through brush.

"They gotta be here somewhere. We saw their car."

"You know these backwoods types. They can vanish like groundhogs."

I elbowed Creek. "That's Tweedle's voice," I panicked. "He came with them."

"Shit, these woods go on for miles. They could be anywhere."

"Then shoot."

"What?"

"You heard me," Tweedle ordered. "Open fire and flush 'em out."

"What if we hit one of 'em?"

"What do you care? You get five grand a piece no matter what. You can bury them out here and nobody'll know."

I swallowed hard.

Oh my God, five grand is all we were worth? Before the ball, the very dress I was wearing could've commanded five figures—maybe six! We should've just sold it to pay for Brandi's treatments. But then we would never have found my mother's heart—

I wriggled my hand over the bust line of my dress, relieved to find the ruby was still there.

Creek gripped my fingers with a painful urgency, as though it might be the last thing he ever did.

"I love you, baby," he whispered, before he buried his face against mine.

Shots rang out through the darkness.

A million times a minute, I could hear the horrible sound of machine gun bullets pummeling the trees—

Creek covered my mouth to stifle my scream.

All around us, birds, deer, rabbits, everything dashed for safety.

But Creek held me stone still.

"Ain't here, boss."

"Then hit the damn Trailer Park."

"There could be a lot of people in there."

"Ten grand a piece. Fucking hear me? I want that ruby and that little bitch! Pull her dad out by his hair if you have to and shoot 'em all."

My cheeks writhed in a grimace. I was so scared. We were out-manned, out-gunned, out-everythinged! How could we possibly defeat these people?

Creek clamped his body down on me harder to keep the crystal facets on my dress from giving us away.

Then I heard a soft, tinkling sound in the distance.

Like the ringing of little bells.

Choking down my fear, I inhaled a shallow breath of relief. The bells! The folks at Turtle Shores had rung the alarm bells, so they'd be in the bunkers by the time Tweedle's gang got there—

We could hear the men walking through the brush back to their vehicles. Slowly, the bright lights faded as the roar of the

Hummers became more distant. When all was completely quiet, Creek got up and pulled me to my feet.

"Watch out!" he whispered, holding on to my waist.

Beside us was a black lump that looked like a boulder in the dark. I reached out briefly to touch it. It felt soft and warm.

I yanked back my hand in shock.

It was a dead deer.

Shaking my head, I felt the hot vomit rise to my throat. I swallowed as hard as I could to try and keep it down.

Creek grasped my shoulders, his face inches from mine.

"Robin, this is it. Worst case scenario. Hear me? You've gotta be tough. Tougher and meaner than they are—got that? Tell me you can do it!"

I nodded my head, gritting my teeth.

"I don't know how this is gonna end, but we *fight* for our people at Turtle Shores. Never give in! Now listen—"

Creek brushed back the hair from my forehead.

"These guys are smart. They might've guessed there are bunkers. Chances are they're searching the trailers right now. C'mon, we gotta flush 'em out before they get to your dad. He's got no defenses, sweetheart."

I nodded again, biting the inside of my cheeks to keep my eyes from tearing up over fear for my dad.

"So we're gonna enter the compound from the back way. Hold my hand, baby. Let's go!"

We ran as though all hell broke loose through the woods. My feet were scratched and bruised beyond belief, but I couldn't even feel it anymore with the mad adrenaline shooting through my veins. My lungs burned as I tried with all my might to keep up with Creek, weaving past trees and bushes and leaping over logs. Just as I thought my chest was about to burst, Creek slowed to a stop.

Heaving, I leaned my hands on my knees to catch my breath.

"Do you hear that?" Creek whispered.

Over my gulping sounds, I could hear doors slamming—

Creek grasped my hand again and we edged toward the clearing, staying in shadows.

It was as bright as daytime from the Hummer lights, but not a soul was to be found except for Tweedle's henchmen. One guy was waist high in one of the TNT Twins' holes, covered in red goop, while the rest had guns in their hands and were going from trailer to trailer.

"We can kill 'em. Easy," a strange voice whispered beside me.

I nearly leaped to the stars!

It was Bixby. He stood next to us with his foot-long hunting knife raised and glinting from the Hummer lights.

Creek shot me a glance. I could tell from the look in his eyes that he was weighing the homicide option.

"It would make things quicker," Creek admitted, pulling something from inside his tuxedo pocket. A knife suddenly flashed into view—a switchblade. "But then it won't end tonight. It won't *never* end. We'll be dealing with Tweedle's gang forever, and they ain't worth it."

"Then we'll scare 'em so bad they'll be begging for death."

The Colonel had come up from behind us with a machete, and the TNT Twins were beside him in their boulder costumes, waving swords. "Men," the Colonel ordered, "man the stations. We do Attack Plan Five."

"Five?" I asked.

Bixby nodded. "That's when intruders have guns." He yanked on what looked like a vine hanging from a tree. "Ready?"

"Wait, what do I do?"

"You git on a helmet, honey!" crackled a voice in the darkness. Granny Tinker appeared next to us with a pot on her head. She shoved one onto mine. "This here's WAR."

All at once, they scattered like ants. Except for Creek.

"There's a tree stand right there," he pointed to a large oak on the perimeter. "I want you to go up and be safe, where Tweedle's men won't spot you. No matter how bad it gets, baby, don't come down for nothin'. Hear?"

"No, I want to be with you—"

"You can't, Robin! There's gotta be somebody left to take care of Dooley."

Creek's words hit me like a blow to the gut.

He meant, if nobody else from Turtle Shores *survives*.

I paused for a second, trying to grasp the enormity of his words.

Oh God—of course I'd take care of that little boy! I'd do anything for my . . . family.

"I love you!" I cried, stealing a kiss. "You come back, Creek. 'Cause we've just barely gotten started—"

Creek brushed aside my hair and stared into my eyes. With one, last sweet kiss, he nodded and darted into the darkness.

And I was left in the shadows.

Totally alone.

Chapter 23

I'd expected explosions.

Full-on assaults.

Attack Geese charging from every direction.

Maybe even a snake pit or two—

But what I hadn't anticipated was the silence.

As Tweedle's men went from trailer to trailer, Creek and the Colonel and the rest of them had disappeared into the night like Ninjas. What they were up to, I had no idea.

And the waiting was pure agony.

I sat on the tree stand watching it all with a stupid stick in my hand, as if that were enough to defend me or anyone else.

My pulse throbbed against my skull, so I took off my make-shift metal helmet. I knew if they'd found my dad, they would've hauled him out by now—maybe even shot him. So he must be safe, right?

Tweedle's men stepped out of another trailer that they'd searched in vain. Cursing, they stood in front of it and opened fire.

Their guns were so loud they overwhelmed my screams.

Gasping, I hoped they hadn't hit anyone, since they were just aiming at an empty metal shell—

I trembled and pulled out my mother's ruby from my dress for comfort. Cupping it in my hands, I prayed from the bottom of my heart for everyone in Turtle Shores to be safe.

Then something else happened that I didn't expect.

While my eyes were closed, I saw her again.

Beautiful Alessia . . .

Her dark hair spilled over her shoulders, and she was wearing a thin, yellow sundress. To my surprise, she ripped open the fabric over her chest, revealing a gleaming red heart.

Just like the jewel in my hands.

And I swear to God, the ruby in my palms grew so warm that I could hardly hold on to it any more.

"Can our love triumph?" she whispered, her eyes searching mine. She looked so sad, yet caring, and she stretched out her hand—reaching—reaching—as if both our lives depended on it. "*Cara mia.* Believe—"

I felt her warm fingers brush against my cheek, soft as a feather.

Then a loud crash made me open my eyes with a start.

Across the meadow, a trailer had turned over. The door was blocked against the ground now, and the TNT Twins, the Colonel and Granny were alongside it with ropes that they'd latched onto the roof by metal hooks. Tweedle's men were trapped inside!

Before any of them could break out a window, Creek and Bixby swung from high vines and landed onto the overturned trailer with short, two by fours tucked under their arms. They proceeded to slide the boards into metal brackets that had been bolted on each side of the windows. Then they leaped from the trailer and lay flat on the ground while everyone else hit the dirt.

Gunfire sprayed from inside, piercing the metal and glass.

I sucked air in horror, when I heard the Colonel speak through his megaphone.

"Y'all wanna LIVE?" he called out, his words booming over the compound like the voice of God. "'Cause my boys got grenades ready to drop in there right now if you don't surrender them guns. You jest push 'em on out those broken windows like you're told. Ya hear?"

Creek and Bixby stood up on either side of the trailer and dangled their grenades in front of the windows with their fingers on the pins.

For a moment, nothing happened. All remained quiet.

Then I saw the gun barrels slowly poke out.

Creek and Bixby grabbed them faster than frogs snatch flies.

They slipped the guns under their arms and dropped hoses with running water into the trailer windows, flooding it.

"Just to keep you boys honest," the Colonel called out. "Hope you can swim! We'll leave you a little room for air, if you're good."

"Good won't make a bit of difference for Royle." I heard a coarse laugh underneath my tree stand. "Or shall I say Doyle? Which name do you go by in the boondocks?"

It was Tweedle! Oh my God, had he really found my dad?

"Amazing how far an asshole can get with a cane, huh? Guess he figured out we'd discovered some of your bunkers, so he limped into the woods and dragged this tyke with him."

Slapping my own cheeks, I tried as hard as possible to stop hyperventilating and kneeled to peer over the edge of the tree stand.

There was Tweedle with my dad in his grip—and a pistol to his head. Little Dooley was clutching my father's hand.

"Grandpa?" Dooley yanked on my dad. "Are the bad guys winning?"

It pierced my heart to hear him call my dad that.

I saw my father straighten his back, as much as he could with the support of his cane, despite the hold Tweedle had on him.

"Nooo," he shook his head at Dooley. He turned and glared at Tweedle. "Leth himmm gooo."

"What's that?" Tweedle laughed. "What's that you say old buddy—speak English!"

My father hauled off and decked him.

To my total shock, Tweedle was splayed on the ground.

"Runnn!" My dad barked at Dooley, giving him a push.

The child sprinted for his life, but not before Tweedle had scrambled to his feet and shoved his gun back into my dad's temple in seconds flat. Panting, he'd been too quick for Creek and Bixby to nail him with their machine guns.

"Got your licks in, eh Royle?" Tweedle taunted, flashing a mean smile. "Try this on for size—"

He shot my dad in the leg.

If I'd had any air left in my lungs, I might have let out a blood-curdling scream—but I was too astounded to make a sound. My father's moans made my stomach twist until I thought I was going to hurl.

I looked across the compound. To my astonishment, I saw Brandi standing on the grass, guarding Dooley behind her legs like a human shield. She must've crawled out from the bunker after they'd tipped over the trailer. And even in her weakness, she'd put Dooley first. Creek stared at me, stone still. Oh, how I wished he could tell me what to do . . .

"Give me the ruby!" Tweedle demanded, shaking my dad by the shoulder. He kicked the bullet wound on his calf and watched my father grimace in pain. "You got ten seconds for that little bitch daughter of yours to come out of hiding and hand it over, or you're a dead man. Got that? Ten . . . nine . . ."

"Shoot us!" My father cried with perfect clarity at Creek and Bixby. "Shoot us now!"

My hands clamped over my mouth as I saw Creek actually consider it, taking a step forward with his gun raised.

It made perfect sense. If Creek shot them both, then we would've gotten away with the ruby and the Swiss bank accounts. Brandi would be taken care of and we'd all be set for life. But I wouldn't have my dad—and we were *finally*—God bless him—a family!

I stood on the tree stand, certain now what to do.

They were directly beneath the edge of the wood. If I hit them right, I could knock Tweedle down, maybe even get that gun from his hand.

Creek's alarmed eyes met mine, and I could tell he'd sensed my plan. He knew I was gutsy, ball gown or no ball gown. I saw him cleverly slip his fingers into his tuxedo pocket where Tweedle couldn't see and pull out a small feather. Closing his eyes for just a second, he released it to the wind and gave me a nod.

I tucked the ruby back into the bust of my gown and hitched up my hem.

Holy Toledo, this is it. All for one and one for all—

I leaped from the stand like a flying squirrel, aiming for Tweedle's head. All the while, I prayed to God—to Alessia—and to several saints at once for love to be *real* and worth fighting for.

My body hit Tweedle's like a pile of bricks, and I heard his gun fire.

Fortunately, his chubby physique had broken my fall. I scrambled for his pistol on the ground, barely skimming its metal with my fingers when his hand clamped down on mine. He viciously ripped the gun away and poised it at my head.

"The ruby," he hissed. "Hand it over!"

He started patting my dress, detecting the lump in my cleavage. Humiliated, I felt him brazenly sink his fingers into my breasts—but I'd had enough.

"No!" I cried, backing away from him. I didn't care any more if he shot me. I'd led a totally loveless life up to this point, all for money, and I wasn't going to back down. I saw where it had gotten my dad. "This is my mom's, it was her only treasure, and you can't have it! It's going to pay for my friend's health care. I think my mom would be proud of that."

I clutched my hands to my chest, the ruby digging into my skin.

And I felt as though something broke open in me. The stone was so warm—radiating heat—that I felt incapable of spouting my worn-out Geisha lines any more. Every word that spilled from my lips was the truth.

"Take this!" I whipped out the folded piece of paper from inside my dress. "They're my dad's Swiss bank accounts. Take all this filthy money that's been nothing but a curse and be gone."

I waved the paper in the air and watched Tweedle's eyes light up like a kid at a candy store. But his pistol was still aimed squarely at my forehead.

"If you grab this now," I challenged, "we'll let you head out into the woods. There's a limo there. You can beat it back to Cincinnati on one condition—you never bother any of us again. Think about it. No dead bodies to bury, no police, and even better, no trailer park militia who'll hunt you down until the day you die. You be gone and you stay gone!"

Out of the corner of my eye, I saw Creek subtly motion for me to move over.

I'd completely forgotten—there was probably a hole near me, one of the TNT Twin's vats—and Tweedle might fall into it if I could just edge him towards it a little more. Scanning the ground, I spied a patch where the grass was a little brown, but it looked like more of a rectangle? Either way, it was a good plan.

My father eyed me and the dry spot on the grass, and he nodded. All at once, he gripped his leg and howled so loudly that it distracted Tweedle for a nano-second, but that was all I needed to shift a little. The rectangle was in front of me now, so I went for it.

"Here!" I chirped, holding out the paper right over the discolored grass like a carrot. "Take the Swiss bank accounts, before I change my mind."

Tweedle grinned and took a step forward. I saw Creek run like a madman across the perimeter, behind Tweedle's view. He dove for a dry spot on the grass, and just before Tweedle could grab the paper from my hand, his body vaulted in air . . .

Disappearing like a rocket into the starry night sky.

"Lordy, would ya look at that!" I heard Granny's voice holler. "Who knew a fat little bugger could reach so darn high?"

My mouth dropped as the wooden arm of the huge trebuchet returned to the ground with a crash, bouncing a few times on the grass.

And Creek was at my side in a shot, his arms engulfing me.

"You did it!" He cried, laughing and swinging me around. "Tweedle's somewhere in the middle of Bender Lake right now!"

The TNT Twins were jumping up and down in their boulder costumes while Bixby and the Colonel let out whoops and Granny Tinker threw her pot helmet in the air. But it was the sight of Brandi and Dooley rushing over to check on my dad that finally made me break down. Tearing up, I grabbed Creek by the hand and dashed over to his side.

"Daddy!" I cried, reaching down to rip open his orange polyester pants leg with blood stains all over it.

His wound appeared ghastly, but it wasn't bleeding as much as I thought. I wanted to tell him that I would personally carry him through the woods to an emergency room tonight if I had to. And by God, we were going to get Brandi her treatments first thing tomorrow. With the Swiss bank accounts in hand, we would pay any price for both of them to get better.

But the words didn't come out.

Because I was too busy cradling his head in my lap and tenderly giving him a squeeze.

"Everything's going to be okay now, Daddy," I finally assured him, kissing his forehead. "We're gonna get you all taken care of."

I glanced up at Creek and Brandi and the rest of the motley folks at Turtle Shores who'd surrounded us in a circle, like a *real* family. They might have pots on their heads or camouflaged boulder outfits, but they were loyal to the bone, and their concerned eyes said they loved me. Reaching up, I tousled Dooley's hair.

"This time, sweetie, the good guys really did win."

Chapter 24

My dad leaned back on his flamingo-shaped chaise lounge on the grass at Turtle Shores and licked his fingers from Lorraine's fried chicken like the happiest guy on earth. When we'd brought him home all bandaged up from the hospital, Lorraine had cooked enough food for an army—including her amazing sweet potato pie. But this time, Creek didn't have to steal sacks of flour or bags of sweet potatoes. We'd humbly paid for them at a local farmer's market with cash.

And subtracted that amount from the four million dollars in the Swiss bank account that had been secretly registered in my name.

My *real* name—Rubina de Bargona.

I was rich again.

Or I guess I should say, I'd been rich all along.

Only now, it scared the hell out of me.

Because during my journey through total brokedom to the trailer park, I'd actually found more love in my life than I'd ever known. Now I had people who genuinely cared about me and who didn't bolt the minute their paychecks dried up. I didn't want to jinx that—I wanted love to stay.

I thought about what my mother had said in my vision: *Can our love triumph?*

Well, the only person I knew for certain who might have a clue about my future was Granny Tinker.

She sat on a chipped white rocker next to my dad with one of her old quilts stretched out on the grass. On it was a faded lawn chair that held her crystal ball, sparkling in the afternoon sun. She'd told me the outdoors was good for the crystal, "Lets in fresh air and cleans them vibes."

I had my doubts.

It was hard to imagine the vibes getting any purer with Bixby and the TNT Twins exploding things all over the place. Just beyond the compound, I heard another boom! and saw a purplish plume rise in air. The three of them did awkward cartwheels and jumped up and down in victory. The smoke and gases they'd released made me cough.

"JUSTIN! JASPER!" Brandi swung open her trailer door and marched with her yellow platform sneakers onto the grass, waving her fist. "Cut that out! You're making too much racket for Dooley to finish his homework." She had on a blonde Afro wig today with a colorful striped jumpsuit that made her look like a soul superstar. On anyone else, the outfit would have been ridiculous, but for those of us who knew Brandi, it brought nothing but joy. Her crazy get-ups were a sign that she'd gotten her mojo back, and she was determined now to beat cancer.

The doctors had said her prognosis was good, provided she kept up her treatments.

And Granny promised me it wasn't her "time". She'd been seeing bluebirds land on Brandi's trailer all week. Omens, she insisted, hinting at a happy future. "Besides," Granny had said, "Dooley needs Brandi—we all do—and we ain't about to surrender our earth angel to the hereafter without a fight."

Granny pitched back and forth on her rocker and watched Brandi return to her trailer. Her mouth broadened into a smile, allowing the sunlight to glint off her gold front tooth.

"Reckon everything's back to the way it's supposed to be," she remarked, glancing at me. "But yer worried about true love, ain't ya?"

Goose bumps prickled my skin. I folded my arms to distract myself, but Granny caught the uncertain look in my eye.

"Then what you doin' here, darlin'?" she prodded. "Git on out to the lake."

"What? Why?"

"'Cause that's where yer gonna find Creek." She leaned back on her rocker and laughed. "He's workin' on yer answer right now."

"My ans—"

I paused before making a fool of myself. Of course Granny knew I was worried about love—she always picked up on my emotions. And what had been eating at me for the past two weeks was that Creek had only ever said he loved me when I was poor. While my dad was in the hospital and Brandi was getting her chemo treatments, we'd barely had a chance to say two words to each other. Now that the dust had settled, Creek had disappeared for days, not even showing up for Lorraine's fried chicken. Did he think I'd become just another rich bitch, like that awful chick whose name he'd scratched off his arm? Could he find it in his heart to love a loaded Robin—a.k.a. Rubina—with a hoity-toity last name like de Bargona?

Nervous, I shot a glance at Granny's crystal ball. Oddly enough, it began to mist over with a purplish smoke. Then I thought I saw an image of Creek. He was sitting by the lake, and he appeared to be arranging something on the sand.

Another boom startled me, and the picture was gone—

Granny let out a loud cackle.

"I keep tellin' ya. Your *soul's* marked," she said. "You couldn't run from love if you wanted to, not with an expert tracker like Creek on yer trail. So I suggest you git on down to that water now. 'Cause everything you've ever wanted is waiting for you at Bender Lake."

I stared at her, bewildered.

"Have a nice trip, sweetheart," she said mysteriously.

I swear, it felt as though her words clung to my skin, yet echoed across the compound at the same time.

Shaking my head, I took a deep breath, feeling butterflies swell in my stomach as I began to walk across the meadow—towards whatever fate held for me—and maneuvered around the TNT Twin's holes. Nearing the edge of the compound, I saw the spot where Tweedle had been launched into the air by a camouflaged trebuchet. Turned out he'd suffered a bad concussion and couldn't remember his name, let alone anything that had happened that night. When the Colonel and Bixby caught up with him on the shores of Bender Lake, lost and dripping wet, they'd resisted the urge to tar and feather him and throw him back in. Instead, they'd called a cab to take him to the address listed on his driver's license.

Which meant that Tweedle had probably returned to *my* old house.

And I bet he was living it up on the money he'd embezzled. But odds were that he couldn't remember me or my dad—perhaps ever again.

Given my latest turn of fortune, I decided to call our Karma even. It was more than a fair trade to leave Tweedle and his kind far, far behind.

As I followed the overgrown dirt trail into the woods beyond the compound, I inhaled the sweet aroma of honeysuckle with just a hint of pine and damp wood that filled the air. Only a couple of months ago, I would have scoffed at such a scent because it hadn't come from a designer label. But now the smell seemed fresh and earthy, complex, and it reminded me of Creek . . .

Creek, who'd single-handedly taught me how to value simple things.

And most of all, who'd showed me that true wealth was found in people's hearts, not in their pocketbooks.

But did that mean he still loved me? Now that I'd become Miss Moneybags?

I pushed aside some raspberry canes and brush until I came to the clearing at Bender Lake.

There was Creek, sitting quietly on the sand beside a rowboat.

Just like I'd seen in Granny's crystal ball.

In front of him was a pillar candle with two tarot cards on either side. And my mother's ruby heart—

I gasped and patted my jeans pocket. Empty! I dashed over to him on the beach.

"You thief! What are you doing with my mom's ruby?"

I tried to snatch it up, but Creek grabbed my arm so fast it made me wince. He pulled me down to the sand.

"She's been telling us where she is, Robin. All along, in the box—it held the clues."

His icy blue eyes met mine and gave me chills. I could see in their cool intensity that he was back to business again.

"When you first came to Turtle Shores, Granny pulled me aside one night and told me history repeats itself. Loves comes back around for those who are brave enough to grab it. But I didn't know what she meant."

Creek grasped the two cards on the sand and held them up to me. On their backs, surrounded by little white stars, was the word *Venezia*. Then he set them down and pulled out a yellowed newspaper clipping from his jeans pocket and unfolded it, revealing my mother's photo. Her astonishing beauty always made my breath catch. He underlined the words beneath the picture with his finger: *Associated Press/Venice*.

Creek handed me the ruby heart. It still felt warm from his hands.

"Do you want to find her?"

My eyes welled up.

Of course I did! I wanted to run up and hug her and hold her in my arms. And then tell her how much Daddy loved her—that he'd never forgotten her all these years.

And neither had I.

All my life, there'd always been a hole in my heart that nothing seemed to fill, no matter how much I went shopping. And the only time I even came close to feeling full inside was when I was with Creek, or when I shared a bear hug with my dad, or held this ruby in my hands.

Creek stared into my eyes.

"Robin, I want *all* of you." He took my hands in his, our palms cupping the gem stone. "And that can't happen till you patch those cracks in your heart. You've made a lot of inroads with your dad. But you need to find your mom. To be whole."

I shuddered. Was I that obvious? Or had Creek become as psychic as Granny? A tear trickled down my cheek, and I dropped my gaze to the ruby in our hands. It sparkled like a crimson fire in the sunlight.

"I took back the money," Creek confessed, rubbing his hands over mine. "I used the passcode from your account to withdraw two hundred thousand dollars, and I put it in a sack and left it in the Cinci Federal vault. So it looked like it had been . . . misplaced." He paused. "Let's just say I gave the security guard a little incentive to do things my way—and to keep quiet."

He gave me that sinister, dagger half-smile that I absolutely loved.

"That's why I split for a while. I wanted us to be free and clear, like you said. But I'll never touch your money again."

"*Our* money," I countered. "Without you, I never would've found my dad's box—"

Creek shook his head. "We're partners of the heart, Robin. That's all."

"What do you mean?"

Creek gazed at the candle on the sand. He was silent for a moment.

"It means I love you. And I want us to have a future that can't be killed by dollar signs."

A lightning bolt shook me inside so hard I wondered if I appeared incandescent. He does still love me! But I couldn't escape the fact that there was a giant wall of cash between us now.

"I love you too, Creek. You gave me a whole world—and a family—that doesn't change with every shift of the stock market. So how do we keep this money from being a curse?" I asked, gazing down at the ruby. "The kind that destroyed my parents?"

"It didn't destroy them—that's the key," Creek replied. "They loved each other all along, we know that now. They were just too afraid to admit it. But I'm *not*, Robin."

Creek leaned in to kiss me. An intense kiss of promise, scented by the sunshine on the sand, the rich honeysuckle, the clear water of Bender Lake, and a whole life together that felt eternal in that very moment.

But when his lips gently slid from mine, he reached into his pocket for a knife and clicked it so that the blade flashed in the sunlight.

"Write it," Creek said.

"What?"

"You know."

He rolled up his t-shirt sleeve on the same arm as the snake tattoo that held nothing over his bicep. His skin stared back at me like a blank page.

Creek handed me the knife.

"You gotta be kidding!" I protested. "You want me to carve my name in your arm?"

"No, I want you to hold this feather first."

He handed me the small feather.

"Ask for our love to last forever. Then let it go and hold this knife over the candle. Start cutting."

I shook my head, floored—

"Robin, if you don't do this," Creek gently grasped my cheeks, "then you'll never know if I love you, or if I was just after your money. That will eat you alive, trust me. So I want you to dig this blade in as hard and deep as you can."

My fingers began to tremble.

"Okay, hold up your feather and release it."

Closing my eyes, I said a quick blessing for our love. To who, I wasn't quite sure—I just imagined my mother and father together again, full of love, and everyone at Turtle Shores smiling at us like saints. Then I tossed the feather into a breeze and opened my eyes, watching it swirl over Bender Lake.

Swallowing hard, I raised the knife and poised it over Creek's bicep. I couldn't believe I was about to even consider something like this.

And God almighty, which name should I carve? Robin or Rubina?

Creek grabbed a stick from the sand and shoved it between his teeth.

"Partners," he nodded before shutting his eyes tight. "With a big ol' heart around it."

I laughed for a second, certain he was joking.

But he wasn't.

He sat very still with his eyes closed, waiting.

When I thought about it, I realized that was the one name that would never change, regardless of which birth certificate or social security card had been faked, or whose last name I took next—McArthur, McCracken, or de Bargona.

Summoning all my courage, I gritted my teeth and ran the knife through the candle flame, flipping it over several times, then sank it into his arm.

The blade was so sharp it sliced through his flesh like butter.

Creek winced, but made no sound.

Hyperventilating, my hand shook as I carved a big cursive P and an A, watching his blood trickle down his forearm and drop to stain the sand. I could hear his breathing halt as I removed the knife and sunk it in again, moving on to a flowing R and T. If this scar was going to last forever, then I decided I wanted it to be beautiful. After fashioning the rest of the letters, I held up the knife and dug it in one last time to swoop a giant heart around the entire word.

When I finished, I realized that my hands were dripping in blood.

"Okay," I said, pulling the t-shirt sleeve over Creek's arm and letting it saturate a deep red. "It's done."

Creek nodded, opening his eyes and pulling the stick from his teeth. He blew out the candle, and I noticed his gaze appeared totally focused. "Come on," he said, "we have to get to Cincinnati by four o'clock."

He stood up and held out his bloody hand for me to step into the rowboat. There, I saw a bottle of alcohol and some bandages in the center, along with a flannel shirt and a couple of backpacks.

"Why would we go back to Cinci?" I asked.

Creek took the knife from my hand and threw it with all of his might into the middle of Bender Lake.

"Because, Partner," he gave me a wry smile and dug into his pockets. Then he held up what looked like two passports. "We gotta plane to catch. We're going to Italy."

Chapter 25

So here I am now, on a 747 flight over the Atlantic Ocean with Creek by my side, heading to Venice. All we have to our names are two backpacks, a couple of fake passports, and one hell of a fat bank account.

As well as an old picture of Alessia in my pocket and the most beautiful heart-shaped ruby ever created.

What am I hoping to find on this journey?

Myself.

That's what Creek says.

Because only a couple of months ago I was somebody else: An angry boarding school chick with a big axe to grind against her dad.

Well, I ditched that school and that axe—for good.

And I found my *real* dad, who turned out to be someone who loved me far more than I could ever know.

In doing so, I got a huge part of myself back. Like the tin man, I guess you could say I grew a heart, leaving my flinty modern Geisha ways behind.

Now, Creek says I have to do the same thing by finding my mother. Not just for the sake of reuniting with her, but to uncover a big part of me as well. Regardless of how everything turns out, he told me, the journey will bring closure. Whether that means a new beginning with my mom or an ending is anybody's guess. But at least the road will be taken, and I'll never be left to wonder again.

So will Alessia be in Venice, in a nun's habit in a convent somewhere, the way I keep imagining in my visions? Is she even still alive?

Oh, how I wish Granny Tinker was on this plane so I could ask.

All I know is that I found a lovely bird whittled from wood and painted blue in the front pocket of my backpack a few minutes ago. One of Granny Tinker's strange talismans, I suppose. I hope it will bring us luck.

I leaned back in my airplane seat and glanced at Creek, who'd fallen asleep. His messy blonde hair against his tan skin made him look like a rugged angel, and his expression was more peaceful than I'd seen in ages. But the bandage that bulged beneath his t-shirt sleeve was a cold reminder to me that he was still one incredibly tough Partner.

Reaching out, I swept my fingers tenderly along his cheek, relishing the warmth of this guy that I love. Then I took a deep breath and pulled my mother's ruby out of my pocket, staring at it for a moment before I gazed at the blue ocean below that filled the entire horizon.

"Alessia," I whispered softy so no one else could hear, "may this beautiful, crimson heart bring us safely home to you."

I tucked the ruby into the front pocket of my backpack and closed my eyes.

"And to me."

Acknowledgements

I would like to thank the following individuals for giving me courage and inspiration throughout the writing of this book:
Suzi Reed, DJ Reed, Sheila Townsend,
Jen Sokoloski, Marcia Porcelli,
Lindsay Horlander, Christine Hardin,
and Erin McGraw.

Cover Design by Najla Qamber
at Najla Qamber Designs,
www.najlaqamberdesigns.com

About the Author

Diane J. Reed has a Ph.D. in English and writes novels that are infused with enchantment, where characters dare to break through boundaries and believe in true love. She has a soft spot for artisans and outlaws of the heart, those of us who burn brightly to live each day as a gift—because it is! Along with her passion for literature, she enjoys hiking, painting, chocolate, and spending time with her husband and two children in the Rocky Mountains.

Diane J. Reed loves to hear from readers, so feel free to visit her at www.banditsranch.com to sign up for her newsletter and to share the whispers of your spirit.

If you enjoyed this novel, please consider writing a review at Amazon.com and Goodreads.com.

Thank you, and have a magical day.

CPSIA information can be obtained
at www.ICGtesting.com
Printed in the USA
FFOW02n1731270514
5554FF

9 780984 912933